THE TWIN FLAME GAME

ADAM ECCLES

For Robin & Willow

About the Author

Adam Eccles is a sarcastic, cynical, tech-nerd hermit, living in the west of Ireland for the last couple of decades, or so.

www.AdamEcclesBooks.com

facebook.com/AdamEcclesWrites

twitter.com/AdamEcclesBooks

Chapter One

Swipe... Nah.
Swipe... Nope.
Swipe... Hmm, maybe...? Nah.
Swipe... No way!
Swipe... Ugh.

S hit, this is depressing and exhausting. Endlessly scrolling through a virtual shop window of jaded and tired women, terrible photos, ridiculous poses. A red-eyed, flash-blown, dirty-mirrored festival of lust, thinly concealed with a lie about companionship, shared interests in movies, music, books. Everyone looking for the special someone who'll see them through into old age. Just admit it. You want an easy shag!

I check the time and put my phone away, she's late. I glance up at the mirror behind the bar, smooth down my hair. I take out the other phone, the red one, to see if she's messaged me, but there's nothing. I pull out my black phone again, find her profile page, reminding myself why I'm sat here waiting, she's ridiculously attractive in that dusky eastern European way. I shiver a little when I look at her photos. Twenty-six, long dark-brown hair. Those eyes like deathly black pools to go skinny-dipping in, pulled down and drowned by a tugging serpent monster underneath. No kids, no ties. She messaged me. What could I do?

She's late though, fifteen minutes so far and I'm already supping down my second beer, tracing the beads of condensation down the ice-cold glass with my finger. Munching on the bowl of nuts they poured for me. This bar certainly passes my hospitality test.

'Like staying at your Mums' is our motto, well, that's my version, the official marketing spiel is 'We care, so you don't have to'. Okay, that isn't it either, but you get the idea. Every Myatt hotel globally prides itself in the home-comfort hospitality. We'll get you anything you need, just sit back and relax and Mum will sort you out. That's the job I'm forced to do, 'global comfort quality inspector' in order to keep my percentage of the shares, to show some worth to the company. Rory, my older brother and 'boss', invented and delivered me this task at a shareholder meeting five years ago and I've been touring ever since. I think he just wanted to get rid of me. It could be worse. I jet around the world, staying in every one of our four hundred hotels and making sure it meets the exacting standards set by the first one, opened just over one-hundred years ago by our great-grandfather, Charles Myatt, just outside of London in a sleepy little town, not so sleepy anymore.

I haven't been home since Christmas, seven months ago, and that was only a fleeting visit to satisfy the family requirements of homogeny and love. Some chance of that, it was more like a shareholder meeting around the big dining table, endless interrogation on how the business is going by our now 'retired' parents and the elected CEO successor to the throne, Rory, who always tries to undermine my authority. I am a significant shareholder too, but you wouldn't think so. He's the stable, solid, know-it-all brother, and I'm the loose, dangerous, unreliable and money-sucking sibling.

. . .

I feel a hand on my shoulder and turn around.

"Keith?" a voice like dark chocolate, decadent but sweet, a minty cool centre like the pillow-candy we lay out every evening, burning gently and slipping down my consciousness. She smiles and drops her purse on the bar, then sits down on the stool next to me.

"Anastasia? Pleased to meet you." And I am, too. Her profile photo doesn't do her justice, she's definitely pillow-candy. She's wearing a lot of complicated fishnet things, an overlay of black over lavender, a short skirt that seems to wrap around and up her body, I wonder how it unwraps. I feel like her eyes are burning into my soul, and I have to look away, waving over the barman instead.

"Can I get you a drink?"

"Whisky and Coke, lots of ice, please." Her accent is thick, sticky, the way she said 'Coke' sounded like 'cock' to me. But her English is perfect, I know from the chats we had in messages, she's studying something in London. I didn't pay attention to what it was. With any luck, she'll be studying my 'cock' later...

The barman produces a drink and gives me a sly wink and a subtle nod towards Anastasia before heading off up the bar to another customer. He knows me from old. Smart lad. I'll drop a healthy tip his way later.

"Call me Ana, everyone does." She puts a hand on my arm, I turn to look at her again, those smouldering eyes! Like she's interrogating my soul, mesmerising.

"Ana it is, then. Did you find us okay?"

"Yes, fine. Well, tube was delayed, but is simple." She waves a hand, dismissive. That explains the late arrival, I suppose. I do like punctuality, but I'll forgive her, this time.

She takes a sip of her drink and then smiles sweetly, looking straight at me. She seems to be evaluating something.

"This is your hotel? The Myatt?" She motions around at the plush bar, eyes wide.

"Well, the family's, not just mine, I'm a shareholder,

though." I trail off, realising how minimal my role has been in the opulence all around me. I inherited it, never had to work for it. This work I do now is a pathetic attempt to justify my existence, not a real job. I know that, and lately it has been playing on my mind. I need to make a mark, really prove I am someone other than the trouble-making playboy my family think I am. But I do play that part well, it fit my lifestyle for a long time. Now I think I'm getting bored of it, the endless swiping over women, first dates that never turn into second dates, nowhere to call a base, hours and hours of business class flights leading to a never-ending string of hotels and rental cars. I can't even take a holiday, because my entire life is one giant holiday. I sound like a whining, entitled little rich shit, and maybe I am, but it isn't my fault.

"Is very nice," she smiles at me, beautiful, soft, and she lays her hand back on mine. I could lean in and kiss her right now, but that doesn't seem appropriate, yet. She takes another sip from her drink. "But you are not the one." She adds, matter-of-factly and sits up straight, taking her hand off me.

"Sorry?" I feel like I have been dismissed, flicked away, like an unwanted slice of gherkin in a cheeseburger. This is not how these dates usually go.

"You are not twin flame. Not your fault, is okay, we still fuck later."

I realise my mouth is agape. "What?"

She sighs as if she's tired of repeating this line, "I am searching for my twin flame," she tells me as if I should know what that is. "And you are not him. Is okay, I am looking a long time now."

"Your twin flame?" This conversation has gone quite odd, all of a sudden. She's only been here a minute and we've gone from hello to weirdo very fast.

"Like a soul mate, another half of me. I know he is out there, I want to find him."

"A soul mate?" I'm repeating her words again, but I'm dumbfounded and my brain can't come up with anything better. "But, we just met! How do you know yet? Maybe we could be soul mates?" I feel I need to defend my court here, I might be a frivolous tosser, but that doesn't mean I don't have feelings. For all I know we could get on like the proverbial house on fire, soul mating the shit out of life.

"I would know immediately. Trust me, you are not him." She gulps the last of her drink. "Is okay, we still can fuck, if you want, but I need more of this." She holds up the empty glass, I think I need one too.

Three drinks later and she's explained the whole 'twin flame' thing to me. We've moved from the bar to the antique leather sofa and my hand gently stroking her stockinged thigh. Apparently, there's a whole sub-culture I had no idea existed of people who are quite convinced that they have a 'soul-mate' who completes their very being somewhere roaming on the Earth. That these twin flames are actually one soul, split in two, and their entire destiny is to find that twin and be together, completing each other, filling in the gaps they feel they have in their life. They will know immediately, feeling desperately drawn to that person, who may be their perfect mirror image in beliefs and attitude, sometimes running away because they can't stand the intensity of the relationship. They will know each other before they even meet, feeling instantly at home, free, open, and utterly in love, and when they look into each other's eyes, they will see their own soul, reflected, like family, safe and in complete harmony. It's quite beautiful when you consider it, or maybe that's just the whisky talking.

Quite obviously a big load of crystal-wind-chime, tie-dye shirt wearing, incense wafting, weed smoking, naked dancing in the woods, hippy rubbish though! But it does give me an idea…

Chapter Two

On the plane to New York, and I've been reading up on the 'twin flame' soul mate phenomenon. There are numerous websites and wikis about it, with quizzes and tests, all alluding to the same basic story, but presented in a different way. There's a lot of bullshit, that's the number one fact, but cutting away the undergrowth of new-age spiritual 'floating in the clouds' type spiel, one can find several key data points.

- You will feel intensely drawn to your twin flame.
- Your twin flame will show you a new way of perception.
- They will fall in and out of your life.
- You will feel at home with your twin flame. No matter where you are.
- You will have many trivial things in common, such as significant dates and interests.
- Coincidences will be frequent.

As well as the blogs, there are online forums dedicated to twin flames where people discuss their experiences, but mostly seem to whine about their lives and quote the forum rules, as with every single forum ever created.

Ana sent me a link after I feigned an interest in finding my own true twin flame. There's an abundance of insanely driven women, violently searching the planet for the one person who mirrors their soul. The posts they write are so passionate that you can almost smell the pheromones off the screen, a tangible giddy need to meet and fall hysterically in love with their spiritual other half.

It's an unexploited vein of gold! With a nice cosy mine already built around it, the pickaxe of social media is the only mining operation I need to set myself up with an unending stream of hormonally flushed, desperately seeking Bridget Jones's, their knickers damp with the anticipation.

There's some game in it too, a hunt to stimulate the senses, some homework to do before sending in the 'hounds of love'. Some Sherlock Holmes style investigations and extrapolations.

I'm going to be spending a few days at our New York hotels, then heading up to Boston, after that I'm undecided, I could go west or keep going up to Canada, I'll play it by ear. But in the meantime, I'm doing location-based twin flame research. There's no handy app to find local 'matches' so I have to do all the legwork myself. But it beats the monotony of endlessly swiping for dreary first dates. I'm sick of that diversion.

The internet on the plane is slow, so I'll dig into this properly in the hotel. I need to cross reference forum posts, Facebook profiles, dates, time zones, cities. Then there's the actual pattern matching to do, hobbies, music, movies, book quotes, all the data that everyone openly gifts the world, every day, willingly and obsessively through their social media accounts.

When I started the hotel tour junket, I would turn up unannounced, sometimes using a false name, trying to catch the worst of the hotel, to justify my job, I suppose. But that usually led to some work to do, reports to write, meetings to attend, follow-up visits to make sure all the problems were fixed, in other words - a lot of tedious shit that I can't be bothered with. So I tried letting the hotels know well in advance I would be coming instead, and it saved me a load of hassle. Now they fix the issues before I arrive, clean the reception area and kitchens, slip the staff a bonus to behave themselves, maybe defrost and properly cook the shrimp before serving it to me. I find this results in a more pleasurable stay. Not having to roar through the porcelain telephone to god for three days after I eat in the restaurant, especially.

NYC, Albany and Boston are already expecting me, my executive suite primed and minibar stocked. Meetings with the various managers and staff already organised. My template reports almost fully filled in and ready to send home to the boss, to file away and ignore. The smell of fresh paint and new carpet often precedes me.

Thus, when I land, a black car is waiting for me, elegantly plucking me from the midst of airport chaos, into the warm open arms of Myatt NYC, a lavishly appointed, unreasonably expensive, palatial monolith. White-gloved porters take care of my luggage, the duty manager greets me at the pristinely polished walnut reception desk, greasily shaking my hand and presenting me my room key. I decline his offer to show me to my room and make a run for the elevator before I get caught in any pre-emptive toadying to garner my approval. I'm sure everything is fine, I'm here to do twin flame research, not worry about the cleanliness of the lobby restroom.

True to form, my suite is ridiculously huge, well equipped and with stunning views over Central Park. My luggage already waiting for me, soft music playing, pillows plumped to exploding point, and our signature chocolate mint delicately placed on top, reminding me of my night with Ana last week. She rode me like a winning racehorse into the homestretch that night. Drunk on whisky and lust, she poured a glass of neat Jack Daniels over her tits, letting it run down her naked body, "You want a drink?" she asked, a pouting smile on her face. No Coke, no ice, but sure, I had a drink.

. . .

I shudder and fall back to the reality of my current task, shower away the flight sweat, obtain food, and start my proper research. I already designed a comprehensive spreadsheet framework on the plane. Now I just need to start filling in details and I'll soon be dipping my wick into the twin flame melting wax pot of dangerously obsessed women. What could go wrong?

Hours later and I'm deep in the mire of social media and forum posts, cross-referencing and correlating, finding patterns that match and rough locations to pin to my map. Focusing on the east coast zone for the time being but filling in gaps elsewhere in the world when I find them. There's no shortage of people. It seems this craze has grown quite popular without my ever knowing about it.

My body, adapted by constant travel, seems to have invented its own time-zones, which basically means I sleep when I'm tired, wake up when my body decides, and eat when I'm hungry, which I am now, having been too distracted to think about food yet. I could get food brought to my suite, but I think I'll stretch my legs and go to the restaurant. I need to be noticed around the hotel, make the staff see that I'm appreciative of their efforts.

I sit down in the almost empty restaurant, greeted at the door by a nervous but smiling waiter. He wanted to make a big fuss, but I brushed it away. I just need some food, no need for genuflecting in my presence. This all gets a bit too much sometimes, these people are doing their jobs adequately, they don't need to worry about getting fired. I started out in this job passionate and comprehensive, anal retentive about details. But now, a lack of shits to give has left me much more laid back. I check the StayAway.com review website and make sure the star rating average is good enough, that there aren't any recent posts that would indicate a problem, such as 'the room stank of sewage', or 'the receptionist had so much cleavage that my husband fell into it and never came back out' - I followed up on that complaint immediately, ultimately disappointing, but worth the effort of investigation. But otherwise, I'm absolutely fine with letting the general paying public do my job for me and post their reports online. The smartphone age has many benefits.

While I wait for my food, I scroll the social media page of a fine young lady who is local to New York, adequately attractive, prolific in her daily postings and quite obviously utterly insane in her twin flame search. She's not only plentiful on Facebook, but also on the twin flame forum where I found her. There are endless posts about how she will react when she finds him, what music would be playing, which popular movie summarises her feelings. I read and digest, making notes, changing my profile to match, setting my favourite book title to the novel that inspired her movie preference and posting a suitably vague note about how I just arrived in New York City, and I felt overwhelmed with the sense that something significant would happen in my life while I'm here, could this finally be when I meet my twin flame? I send her a friend request and eat my pierogi.

Chapter Three

I t didn't take long to get the attention of Jessica, since she's permanently stuck fast to her social media. A few cautious messages back and forth and I gradually enticed her into my ploy. She popped up as a suggested friend by the social media algorithm, I told her, and as I landed in New York I felt a sense of something new, something epic, something life changing coming my way. Then I saw her photo on my 'wall' so I had to reach out. I quoted a passage from the movie she likes, a subtle reference to destiny. I told her I was only in town for a few days, passing through, so I wanted to meet her before I left, in case the stars aligned us together for a reason. Twenty-four hours and many messages later, she took the bait and agreed to meet me in the hotel bar, a public place, safe and with alcohol. Plenty of people around if she needed to scream for help if I turned out to be a psycho.

I had to do some actual work today, the hotel manager called me to a meeting, a presentation of some hotel improvements he's made since the last time I was here. Tedious doesn't begin to describe it. Drainage and boiler upgrades, efficient swimming pool heating, kitchen refrigeration and new hot-tubs in the suites. I pretended to make notes on my iPad, but I was actually messaging Jessica. Trying not to laugh as she flirted back at me. I might get to try out the new hot-tub, though.

Jessica texts my red phone, the number I give to women, a new SIM card in it every few months. She will come to the Myatt soon, but she's bringing a friend to be safe. Fair enough. I've been practicing the stare in the mirror. The deep gaze into the eyes of the twin flame, to seek out the reflection of my own soul. I feel like an idiot, but I need to get into the part.

I'm sitting in the lounge bar, at a table, reading a battered copy of the book I claimed was my favourite. I ran out to a second-hand bookshop and found a copy earlier. I've read the back and a few reviews on Amazon, pulled a few quotes and stuck in a few bookmarks. It's romantic tripe, something I would never read in a million years. But a movie was made from it a few years back. It's a tale of how two lovers met in some contrived impossible circumstance. The usual crap.

Then she appears in my periphery and waves, but I wait a moment before finishing the paragraph I'm reading and look up at her, smiling. "Sorry, I love this chapter." She smiles back as I pop in a bookmark and stand up to greet her. She sweet in a down-to-earth way, not my usual type, but this is a new adventure. Her friend, though, is a delicious little minx. Dangerous in her own way. I will have to sacrifice that pleasure though, in the name of science. It will lend credence to my story if I focus on Jessica and ignore her pretty friend.

"Delighted to meet you, Jessica." I roll out my most English of English accents because that never hurts here in the states. I stare deep into her green eyes as I take her hand and kiss it. She's strawberry blonde, shoulder length, messy but clean. Casual clothes, not too sexy, not too plain.

"Oh my god, you're British?"

I assumed she would have guessed that, but perhaps it never came up in our brief liaisons so far.

"Yes, for my sins." I turn to her friend, to be polite. "Hello, Keith Myatt, pleased to meet you…" I pause so she can tell me her name, which I'd love to get tattooed on my arse.

"Myatt? Like the hotel?" She looks shocked and impressed. Putting two and two together and coming up with money.

"Yes, just like the hotel," I smile and switch back to Jessica. "Can I get you two a drink? Or perhaps you'd do me the honour of staying for dinner?"

They look at each other and then Jessica blurts out "Yes, we'd love to stay for dinner!"

Her friend looks a bit annoyed, "Drink", she adds. She's meant to be the sceptical, protective buddy here, stopping Jessica from getting into any threatening situations.

"This is my roommate, Laurie, by the way." Jessica sounds a bit embarrassed, I nod and continue to stare into her eyes, the way Ana did to me last week. I don't know if I have perfected the stare yet - do I come across as deep and spiritual or a maniacal psycho who's a bit short sighted? Jessica looks suitably enticed so far. I motion towards the restaurant and we are shown to a table. I nod to the waiter and he acknowledges and goes off to adjust the ambient music to the playlist I gave him earlier.

"We can get dinner and drinks here."

They ask for beer, but I talk them around to trying a Belgian brew, rather than the urinal piss that serves for American lite beer. They seem to appreciate it.

Conversation is a little stilted and awkward, but I'm doing my best to keep things moving. Jessy, as she is now known - by friends, is a teacher, kindergarten, just got her first posting this year. Barely affording the apartment she shares with Laurie and another girl. She's single, obviously, and I make sure to look suitably shocked that a girl like her could be single. She waves me off, but I'm sure I saw a flicker of blush under her makeup. She's had a string of boyfriends, she tells me, but they didn't work out. She's looking for something more meaningful. No shit. I know exactly what she wants, she's detailed all of the wonderful things she thinks will happen when she meets her twin flame. I, of course, haven't mentioned I read all her posts.

The restaurant is having a Tapas night, and so the waiter is piling multitudes of small plates on our table, this and that, I told him to just keep coming until we were full.

"Oh, I love this song!" Jessy squeals as her specially tailored playlist reaches the trigger song. The song that would be playing when she met her twin flame, in her dreams at least. The beer has loosened her up a little now, her cheeks flush when I look again into her green eyes.

"Jessy, this may sound a bit crazy, but, do you know what a twin flame is?" I blurt it out, I think I should have waited a bit longer, but it felt right. Her eyes widen, she shrinks back into her seat.

"Oh, jeez, not another one." Laurie sounds exasperated. Seems Jessy has mentioned her obsession to her roommate before. I raise an eyebrow, waiting for an answer.

"Yes, I do, and it doesn't sound crazy," she leans forward, eyes still wide, searching my expression for sincerity. Then it hits, a subtle but definite change in her face. Fuck. She's sussed me out.

"The book, the song... You asshole! You planned this?"

Damn, too obvious Keith. You fucked this one right up. Too much, too quick. She's too smart to be fooled that easily. "I..." I can't think of what to say, do I just admit it, let it go, or feign ignorance and try to recover?

"What's going on?" Laurie chimes in, protective, fight or flight mode, she's doing her buddy role very well.

"He must have read my forum stuff, I had a feeling this was all too good." She's definitely flushed red now, but with anger, a tear in the corner of her eye too. Fuck. This was not in the plans.

"I'm sorry, but, I..." I have nothing to say, I didn't want to upset her, quite the opposite!

"We're leaving." Laurie stands up, taking Jessy's arm, they walk away, leaving me with a table full of tapas.

"Don't message me again." Jessy turns around as she goes, tears flowing, "Oh, and, I think you need an eye test!"

.   .   .

Shit.

"Laurie, I have whisky and a hot-tub upstairs if you are interested?" She looks at me, incredulous, I had to give it a go. She pauses for a moment, before Jessy tugs her out of the restaurant. Looking back, she sticks up her middle finger, but then silently mouths the words 'call me' as she goes.

Double shit.

I think I need to work on the plan of attack here. I block Jessica from my social media pages, grab my beer and a plate of tapas and head up to my room to regroup and get back to the drawing board.

Chapter Four

There's some beautiful rolling countryside on the drive upstate to Albany. You might not think that New York could be pretty mountains, rivers, lakes and forests, but outside of the city, there is plenty to look at. The three-or-so hour drive gives me time to ponder on the mistakes I made with Jessy. To try to come up with a new and better plan.

The Jessy situation went very badly, I pushed too hard, too obvious. Subtlety is key here, I think. I'll need to work a few cities in advance, building up a relationship with the seeker before I get to the hotel in their locality for my brief interludes. The immediacy of the twin flame relationship might be all well and good, but I think it needs a head of steam in order to explode. A gentle flirtation period online before an actual meeting seems like it would only benefit my cause. I think I'll use the twin flame forums, rather than Facebook, to communicate. Cut to the chase, as it were. Make it quite clear that I'm here for the whole tea party and not just the cake.

I gave the Myatt NYC a glowing report and sent it off to Rory, so he knows I'm busy doing my job, but the miserable sod just sent a curt reply - 'good, keep it up'.

The hotel organised a rental car, packed my luggage into it

and sent me off north. My only recommendation to the NYC Myatt is they give the hot-tub in my suite a very thorough clean, because it got pretty damn dirty in there when Laurie came back the evening after. She's a wild little thing, and boy, can she hold her breath for a long time! I took her up on her offer and found her details on Facebook. She came in secret from Jessy of course, but she thought what I did was cute. Translation: she smelled money and liked the idea of a fun night in my hot-tub. C'est la vie. Can't blame the girl.

The Albany Myatt isn't anything like as plush as its NYC cousin, but taken on its own it is still impressive. A bigger hotel, because space isn't as much of a premium as in the city. I'm taken on a tour of the facilities as I arrive, I couldn't seem to weasel out of it, and the manager was so enthusiastic it seemed rude to just walk away. The new gym is expensively equipped, and for the first time in my experience, it doesn't stink of sweaty armpits and socks, so that's something. The kitchens are busy but sparkling clean. The rooms don't have hot-tubs here, but there is a large communal Jacuzzi. All very clean, very nice, very boring. I excuse myself as soon as possible, tired after the long drive, and retire to my room, scrolling around the internet, starting off by looking for a twin flame seeker in the Albany area.

After three hours and a room service burger, I've found nothing. There's plenty of people posting on the forum, but I can't correlate any of them to my current locality. Scanning social media for people in the region didn't help. I'm out of luck, it seems. Either there aren't any people here searching for their twin flames, or if they are, they are hiding their names and impossible to locate. I'll spread my search to Boston and see where it goes from there afterwards, but I'll start that later, I need a break, I head down to the bar instead.

. . .

Two double scotches later, and I think the bartender must have spiked my drink, because I just saw a six-foot tall red squirrel come up to the bar and order three mojitos and a beer. It turned to me and said, "How you doing?" then walked away with the drinks, a straw in each of them. I look up at the barman and back at the squirrel as it walks to a table of equally large animals, a fox, a dog and a cat, where it hands out the drinks.

"What did you put in my drink?" I say to the barman who doesn't seem to have acknowledged the peculiarity of the table full of animals, sat quietly drinking across the bar.

"It's Furrycon, sir." He says calmly, as if this is a reasonable explanation.

"What?"

"Furrycon, the furries all come here once a year for the convention. I don't get it myself, but they aren't too bad, I guess. Mostly keep themselves neat and tidy."

I look back at the table of animals, sucking their drinks through straws, then back at the barman.

"You can see them too? I'm not hallucinating?"

"No, sir, you are fine."

"Good grief, I think I need another drink. Give me what the squirrel was having, a mojito?"

"Yes, sir."

I pull out my phone and Google for 'furry' and find a plethora of ridiculous creatures prancing around in their animal costumes. I think this is one of the modern trends I'll have to pass on, thank you very much. It seems they are a group of people who enjoy dressing up in elaborate, but cartoon-like, animal costumes, and getting together in hotels like this, to celebrate whatever it is they celebrate. Bones? Kibble? Squeaky toys? I have no idea.

But it does appear that this weekend is Furrycon Albany, and it is hosted here at the Myatt. Wonderful. I take my drink and wander over to the conference hall at the back of the hotel. Passing through reception where there is a veritable herd of animals all milling about and checking into their rooms. I hope we are charging extra for the pet insurance! They must be ridiculously hot and sweaty in those suits, we should leave some bowls of water on the ground.

The conference hall is packed full of them, all manner of beast, frolicking, dancing, tails flicking, a lot of group hugging, posing for photos and generally hanging around. There are tables set up around the edge of the hall, stalls selling costumes, spare heads, sewing kits, badges and paraphernalia of whatever it is that these 'furries' do. A particularly vivacious ginger fox cartwheels in front of me, laughing and running away. I turn to one of the hotel staff in the room, unbelieving.

"I don't think that fox was wearing any underwear!" He nods, trying not to laugh. Clearly the female of the fox species, a vixen. She had an abundance of her natural ginger fur, but there was a distinct and noticeable gap, presumably to make bathroom trips easier? What on earth have I walked in on?

———————

Five mojitos later and I'm in the Jacuzzi with a fox, a cat, a jackal, a badger and a pug dog. If we had a chicken and a bag of feed we might have a little puzzle to solve about how to get everyone from one side of the Jacuzzi to the other without someone being eaten. The badger and pug are male, sucking beer through straws, the fox and cat are female, either side of me. The jackal, I have no idea, best not to ask. Some of these animals are naked aside from the furry head. They told me their 'fursona' names, but I can't recall them. I'm trying not to focus on the bizarreness of the situation and instead wonder if a naked girl with a black and white cat head, holding her 'paws' up playfully and purring while I rub her tummy is sexy, or if I'm just weirdly perverted. They most certainly are, but I'm an edge case here, I think. The fox wants her tummy rubbed too, okay, now this is definitely getting weird. I think we three dirty animals should head upstairs to my room and try some taxidermy…

Chapter Five

I've had enough furry for one lifetime, so I decided to fast forward a day and leave Albany early, heading to Boston. It was like a trappers' lodge this morning when I woke, fur skins everywhere. They kept their heads on! How could they sleep like that? I left them the room key and told them to check out when they were ready, dirty animals. I never found out what their faces looked like, and after a night in the furry heads, I didn't want to. I did, however, find out what a vixen in heat having a screeching orgasm sounds like, quite disturbing, to say the least.

Another long drive, toll booths every few yards it seems, and the traffic going into Boston is a hellish nightmare, especially with the remnants of a hangover lingering in my skull. I'm looking forward to a quiet evening, researching twin flames and relaxing.

The Boston Myatt is elegant and sedate, the oldest Myatt in America, opened in 1930 to grand pomp and fanfare. The plumbing and air conditioning still from that era, gurgling and going bump in the night. Tales of haunted rooms and strange occurrences are legendary local lore.

Tired, annoyed and hungry, I stand waiting at the reception desk at the Boston Myatt. Sometimes I like to watch how things happen when the hotel is busy, see if they notice me and offer me preferential treatment, which they shouldn't. There are several people checking in ahead of me, bags piling up, children running around, sweaty tourists keen to rest and eat. They need another person on the desk here, I pull out my phone to make a note for a recommendation to the manager. But as I unlock it I see a message waiting from Rory, so I open it up. A simple line of six words, stabbing me in the guts with pain and sadness. 'Aunty Joyce passed away. Come home.'

Five hours later and I'm on a plane to London. Through tear filled eyes I found out the details in a message from Mum. Apparently, Joyce passed away two days ago, peacefully at home in her sleep. Nobody found her until today, her cats scratching at the windows to go in the house. The funeral is in two days, the London Myatt hosting the reception of course, where Joyce worked for decades as manager even though she didn't need to. My childhood memories of Aunty Joyce are fond ones, running around the hotel together, playing an epic game of hide and seek through the rooms, going to the kitchens and rummaging for snacks, Joyce was like a second mother to me, I think I was her favourite, Rory was aloof around her, distant, bored, but I always loved hearing her tales of the old hotel and the funny guests she encountered.

I haven't seen her since Christmas at the dining table, she seemed fine then, alive and happy, worried about her cats and the state of the hotel kitchens, even though the hotel has been in very good hands since she retired ten years ago at the ripe old age of seventy-five. Never one to slack off, was Joyce.

She always remembered my birthday and sent me a gift. Even these last few years when I've been flung anywhere in the world, roaming like a nomad, she found me somehow and made sure I got the gifts, small things, ties, socks, a pocket pussy - I'm not sure she knew exactly what that was when she ordered it online, or maybe she did, Aunty Joyce was always unfettered in her sexuality, secretly regaling me in my teens with tales of her early days as the hotel manager in the swinging sixties, and the parties she hosted that make my last few days seem tame. But now I won't ever see her again, aside from in a casket, carried away to a hole in the ground.

I wake as we land at Heathrow, from disturbing dreams of animal sex. Twin anthropomorphised sexy foxes screeching in delight as Aunty Joyce beats them with a broomstick. It will be some time before I shake away that image! I take a taxi to the London Myatt, arriving back where I left from only a week or so ago. Walking into the grand reception now feels quite different than when I was here last, the sting of Anastasia's hand still on my slapped arse and the taste of whiskey lingering on my tongue. The twin flame plans seem ridiculous now. What was I thinking? A waste of my time and energies. I should be putting my effort into something sensible, building a life outside the ever-present hotels. Joyce never got around to having kids. Too busy in the hotel, she said, always something needed doing that was more important, but she told me as she retired, she regretted that. I should make sure and have a family, because, above all else, that was what was important. Hotel be damned. I miss her already. These next few days are going to be tough.

Rory and his wife, Jane, greet me in the lounge after I check into a room. Since I don't have a fixed abode these days, the hotels are all I have. Rory shakes my hand and pulls me in for a brotherly hug, something we rarely do. Jane pecks me on the cheek and offers a sympathetic smile. She's the epitome of prim and proper, and pours me a cup of tea from a china pot as we discuss the funeral arrangements. It was so unexpected, a heart thing. She never mentioned to anyone that she had a problem, but her doctor had warned her, he said. "Take it easy, don't worry about the hotel anymore". She had been up a ladder cleaning a window that overlooks the garden only the day before. That sounds like her, for sure. She always talked about a special recipe for a window cleaning solution she acquired that was much better than the chemical crap they sell at the supermarket. Never did find out what was in it or where she got it from, "you wouldn't believe me if I told you" is all she'd ever say.

"Thanks for coming," Rory tells me as if there was any chance I wouldn't have come. He has some nerve, it should be me thanking him for coming! Joyce was an aunt, plain and simple to him, but she was much more to me.

Our parents are on their way to the hotel shortly, they were in Paris on a weekend break - staying in the Paris Myatt, of course, when they heard the news.

"How was New York?"

It seems inappropriate to worry about work now, but I could do with the distraction.

"Very good, actually. A delightful stay in the city. Albany was a bit odd though." I tell Rory about the furry convention, leaving out the details of my animal debauchery. Jane looks disgusted at the thought of people running around in sweaty costumes. I daren't mention that they didn't always worry too much about wearing underwear either.

"That's excellent for business! We should encourage more conventions, offer a good rate for the attendees." Ever the frugal businessman, Rory's eyes light up with dollar bills. He makes a note in a paper notebook from his pocket.

"Yes, because we definitely need more money, don't we?" I'm tired, upset and tetchy. The greed in Rory always brings us to blows, figuratively, Rory would never stoop to physical violence.

"Shareholders always demand more, Keith. There's never too much."

"I'm a shareholder! Remember?"

"Quite so, how could I forget?"

I stand up to leave before this escalates, Jane is already

looking worried. "I'm going for lunch, haven't eaten since yesterday," I mutter as I walk away to the bar. Rory nods and sips at his tea, thin-lipped and dry.

On reflection, having a liquid scotch lunch may not have been a good idea, when my parents are due to arrive any minute. But those decisions were made and now I have to live with them. The bartender brings me a pot of black coffee and a smoked salmon bagel, but I don't remember ordering it. I think he's trying to tell me something. I could be annoyed or appreciative, but I think the latter is appropriate. He means well. Another decent tip should come his way before I leave. I nod as thanks and he gives a sympathy smile and walks away to serve another customer.

I take out my red phone from my pocket, it's been switched off for a day or so, I let it settle and check for messages. Several pings sound and I'm greeted with a photo of Laurie from New York. She's added a red lipstick kiss to a black and white image of herself in a sexy maid outfit, asking if I could get her a job at the hotel. She's a model, which means she's broke and out of work. Fair enough, I'll ask around. She could be a plumber, she's excellent at cleaning pipes. I tap out an email from my black phone to the NYC manager and give him Laurie's details, minus the sordid parts and the sexy photo, which I save to my photo album.

"I thought we'd find you here, Keith!" Dad announces as he walks into the bar with Mum.

"Hello Dad, Hello Mum." We embrace, and I try to hide the semi-drunk state from my voice and demeanour.

Chapter Six

I hate lawyers, the smugness and soul-sucking, money grabbing nature of them, but one of their kind just approached me and handed me a sealed envelope. He was quite insistent that I took it, then he loped away, back to wherever lawyers come from, I imagine.

We are assembling in the lobby of the Myatt, waiting for the minibus to the church where the funeral will take place. I hate churches too, a staunch believer in atheism as long as I can remember. Honestly, I'm quite sure that Aunty Joyce was an atheist too, so I don't really know why we are going through this charade. For the sake of 'keeping up appearances' no doubt. I don't approve, but here I am, complicit in the masquerade.

Before I can get a chance to open the envelope I'm bustled into the god-mobile with Rory, Jane, Mum and Dad, so I slip it into my inside jacket pocket. Burning a hole in my thoughts, wondering what's inside. Assuming it is something relating to Aunty Joyce and the funeral.

The journey isn't far, but the bus is lumberingly slow, and everyone is silent in their mourning, so it seems to take forever. I'm trying to ignore the reason why we are all here, but there's nothing else I can think about. The cliché of living a long and full life, if you call staying within twenty miles of the Myatt for almost all of it, full. She never had time for anything, she used to say that time was for children. They had all the time in the world, until they grew up and realised that it slips through their fingers like sand on a beach. All the money in the world can't buy you more time, she said, so use your days wisely, Keithy.

No one ever listens to those words of advice though, and if they did, they turned out like Rory.

We arrive at the church to a sea of black. Outside there are hundreds of people, cars parked far up the road, dozens more people arriving. I had no idea Aunty Joyce knew this many people! Our bus drives past all the parked cars and right up to the church, where a hearse is parked, the back door open, red heart-shaped balloons tied to the handles of the coffin inside. Aunty Joyce was born on Valentine's day, she loved all the red decorations and hearts. So this is fitting, if slightly odd.

Rory, Dad and I carry in the coffin, along with help from the undertakers, up to the front of the church and then take our seats. The music playing is hard to make out, but I think it's Depeche Mode's, Enjoy The Silence, very quietly from a portable stereo somewhere at the back of the church, then it abruptly stops, and the droning, nasal Vicar starts his insipid monologue.

Through the rambling and morose eulogy, read by the Vicar of dribbly, written by Rory, I can't help but wonder what is in the envelope in my pocket, but I don't want to open it with everyone around me. Is it appropriate to disappear for a moment now? I'm on the front row of pews in a packed church. No escape. How long do these gigs last? I don't want to be disrespectful, but I really don't think Aunty Joyce would have been interested in this ceremony. I have to sit it out and wallow in my own thoughts while the service continues.

.   .   .

I feel a tap on my shoulder, "Keith?" in an overly loud whisper, I turn and for a moment I'm shocked into amnesia. Who is this hairy chap, smiling and sticking out his grubby hand? Why is he doing it here and now, with my dead Aunt not twenty feet from me? Why does his breath stink like an albatross at a herring party?

Then it hits me, with full nasal force, this is Benedick Hogg, or just Ben, or sometimes, Piggy-dick, my best mate through school, I haven't seen him for a decade. He didn't have the neckbeard then, nor the super-cali-fragilistic-fishy-halitosis. "Ben? What are you doing here?" He looks downhearted, then nods towards the coffin at the front. Of course, why else?

"Sorry. Good to see you. Let's catch up later?"

"Okay," he stage whispers at me. "Oh, and sorry for your loss," he says loud enough for Joyce to hear from the other side.

"How have you been?" Glad for the distraction, I furnish myself and Ben with a fine ale in the hotel bar, escaping the sombre revelry in the dining room where the main reception is being held. I think I prefer to mourn on my own, when I feel like I can come to terms with the situation, not when society says I should in a large group of strangers.

"Yeah, not too bad, you know." Ben is wearing what passed for black attire a long time ago, before hundreds of wash cycles faded him to a dull grey. He made an effort though, at least.

"Thanks for coming. I didn't expect to see you here."

"Joyce was a good friend, sad to see her go." Ben raises his glass, "To Joyce! May she rest in peace."

"Quite so," I raise my glass and clink with Ben. "You knew Aunty Joyce?"

"She got me a job, gardener at the hotel."

"You work at the Myatt? I had no idea!"

"Amongst other places, anywhere I can really."

"Why didn't you tell me?"

"You haven't been around…" Ben trails off, a little frigid.

"No, I suppose not… Sorry, but have you eaten fish recently?"

"Well, yes, I had a kipper before I came out, can you tell?"

"Little bit, yeah…" Ben looks up, embarrassed, but then smirks, and we both burst into laughter, shaking away the decade of distance between us and back to how we were in our shared youth, playing in the hotel grounds, trying our first cigarette and beer in the gazebo at the back of the garden, snogging our first girlfriends in the same hide-out. Later in life, we'd bar hop through the town as any twenty-something lads would, until we were 'asked to leave' by bouncers, or in rare circumstances, if we managed to convince a female of the species to leave with one of us, even rarer, both.

"Do you still live in your mother's basement?"

"Yeah, but no one else ever goes down there, so it's a bit like my own place."

"At least you have somewhere to call home. I don't stay still long enough to own property."

Time for a good, long catch-up, fuelled by fine Belgian beer. I tell Ben about my nomadic lifestyle, how I think Rory is just glad I'm out of the way, then the furry fun in Albany, and the twin flame phenomena. He thinks I should keep doing it, he's going to try it himself, genuinely, he really needs a companion. He tells me his news, which is minimal. He's been pottering away at gardening, trying to build a business up, cutting lawns and hedges for people in the area, but it was a real boost when he called to the hotel one day when Aunty Joyce happened to be poking around and ended up sorting him out with a contract for the upkeep of the grounds. That alone makes him more money than all the rest of his customers put together. He's had the occasional girlfriend, if you could call a drunken one-night grope a girlfriend, which I suppose is more or less all I have had too in the last decade.

Maybe we both really do need to find our twin flames.

We head into the town centre after a while, because I can't face going back to the funeral reception and the hand-shaking, sympathy smiles, small talk and kind words. I don't want it, don't need it. Time is short, I need to use it wisely.

We stumble tipsy through the town, stopping for a kebab and a letch at the local fast-food venue, then continue on to our old haunts, but the names, the decor, and especially the clientele have all changed. We leave disappointed, heading back to the safety of the hotel bar. Perhaps we have changed too? I find I have little in common with the people out and about, vaping and Instagramming all over the place. It feels like I've lost something intangible from the memories of my youth. Add it to the pile of things we buried today.

I suddenly remember the envelope from this morning.

I pull it out of my pocket and open it up. A letter, dated a few months ago, handwritten.

Dearest Keithy,

By the time you read this, I'll be dead!

Oh dear, sorry, that did make me chuckle. Always wanted to write those words.

No, but seriously, I will be, because I shall tell the solicitor to deliver it to you only after I'm heading for the family plot at the cemetery, and not with a bunch of flowers in hand either.

Don't be sad, it happens to us all in the end, what can you do? My doctor tried to tell me some nonsense about taking it easy now in my twilight years, I told him to piss off and that he'd be heading to his grave sooner than I would if he didn't lay off the condescending tripe! But still, it made me think. So here I am, writing you this note.

There's as much value in spontaneity as there is in stoicism, and

I believe the Myatt legacy needs both to continue to survive and prosper. That's why I'm going to leave you all my shares, which should put you at the same level as Rory, give you an equal grounding and maybe push you to settle down and find your true calling. I know you've been having a blast, touring the world, but it can't leave you very fulfilled and I know you can bring more than that to the business.

You need to get it out of your system, certainly, and then you can concentrate and focus on what's important, like a family of your own to love and coddle. A flame of passion never hurt anyone, well, actually that's not true, it hurts EVERYONE it touches, but you can't break an egg without making omelettes as my old Mum used to say!

Anyway, what was I getting at? Oh, yes, you are old enough now that you should find yourself a good wife. You will know her when you see her, when you look into her eyes and see your very same ideals and spirit reflected, then you'll know. Snap her up, use your wiles and charms and don't leave it too late to start a family! I did, then I spent the rest of my days regretting it, to this day. My cats are the closest family I have aside from you. Oh, by the way, the cats get half! Ha ha! Just joking, but the cat home down the road does get a chunk. Please make sure my poor moggies are looked after!

You may as well have the house too because I don't think anyone else needs it. Oh and your old friend Ben, he had his eye on my Land Rover, so he can have that.

Well, I suppose that's all really, but don't forget, go find your soul mate and wreak havoc in the world, make sure they remember you when you go!

· · ·

Love you, Keithy,
Forever, your old Aunty Joyce. Xxx

With tear-filled eyes, I hand the letter to Ben, who reads it and then reaches over for a manly hug. Twin flame search now back on with a vengeance!

Chapter Seven

E ven after the tax man takes his cut, I am still fairly well furnished from Aunty Joyce. Another mystery from her life, she was absolutely loaded. She never needed to work a day but chose to work every day in a hotel that consumed her. I wonder where and why she found the motivation?

House, shares, some cash and I am very nicely taken care of from the will. Rory got some money too, a few paintings, and a massive chip for his shoulder. Mum and Dad also got a slice of the pie. True to her word, even Ben got sorted out with a forty grand Land Rover, barely any miles on the clock. It will take months for the cash to flow, but I've been staying in the house for a few weeks now. It's nice to have a solid base. I took a needed break. No planes to catch, no bags to pack. I just relaxed for a while, contemplating life, and more disturbingly, death.

I suppose the inevitability of it just hit home, the urge to make my mark on the world now pushed to the top of the list of things to do. I've been wasting my life for many years now, squandering away the hours I have, distancing myself from reality and chasing a fruitless goal. I feel like I've suddenly become an adult in the last few weeks. It isn't a good feeling, but it has given me the kick up the arse I needed to realise what I have to do. It saddens me to think that it took a death in the family to make me realise I need to live my life, but isn't that always the way? A shock to the system shakes you from a slumber, awakening to a new day, startled, bleary-eyed, but keen to know what will happen next.

I have to get back on the road now. I'm in a newly upgraded position within the company, in charge of relations with media, specifically, websites like StayAway, the site that handles most of the reviews we get. Apparently, they send a stealth investigator to verify good or bad reviews, and I'm meant to be one step ahead of them, making sure good reviews are legitimate and bad reviews are taken care of immediately, or before they even happen. Sure, this isn't much different from my old job, but it does feel a bit more like real work. It will take time, and convincing, to get my status upgraded in the boardroom, despite the shareholding boost.

The house is more or less as I remember it from childhood. Near the hotel, in a quiet area, detached, with some woods around it. A lovely setting, perfect for a future family situation. I'm rattling around at the moment, trying to make it seem like I live there. I haven't been able to bring myself to go into Joyce's room yet, so I'm staying in one of the spare rooms. I have upgraded the internet connection though, and the TV.

Ben has been keeping me company and feeding the cats. He introduced me to Netflix. But sitting on the couch with him and the shrapnel of delivery pizza crumbs in his beard, is not really what I imagined when I heard about 'Netflix and chill'. Still, it's been a laugh to catch up and just be grounded.

I've been getting back to my twin flame research too, but now I feel like I'm not doing it purely to get empty, unfulfilling sex, although that is always welcome, of course! But with a real mission, to find someone significant to be my 'other'.

Perhaps the twin flamers aren't so ridiculous? Wouldn't it be nice to have someone who does understand you completely, who can empathise and even seemingly read your mind, know before you speak what you want for dinner, when you are sad or lonely, or just need some space. It's the dream of every relationship, to be at one and in perfect harmony with your spouse. So I've taken a new tack through the forest of twin flame seeking - actually be myself.

I know, it's a novel 'why didn't I think of that before' type of an idea, but it simply never occurred to me that someone would actually want to be with me because I'm just me, and they just did. Maybe they won't, and this will be a fruitless endeavour, but it has to be worth a go.

I've also been doing work research, using my analytical skills to predict the targets of the StayAway investigators, mapping the hotels and their average and recent review scores, combined with my own extensive personal knowledge of every single one of the hotels, as I've stayed in each at least once by now. I'm trying to get inside the mind of someone who would be doing the investigating, what would be their motives and challenges, where would they target first?

They refer travellers to our hotels and take a small percentage for every night stay booked via their site. They also aren't shy about selling adverts for rival hotels to people searching on their site. They battle the average star ratings of each hotel against each other, creating a nice feedback loop of cash generation for themselves, all in the name of providing a great stay for the weary traveller.

I have a theory they have some kind of hand in deciding the reviews that are shown, and the star rating seems weighted to make sure there's always a price and exposure battle to be had. There's an algorithm at work here, that's for sure. I doubt if anything actually illegal is going on, but I'd like to find out if something unscrupulous is happening. I need to dig deeper. I'm planning a tour of the lowest rated Myatt's in North America, the primary focus area of the StayAway review site. This is not going to be a pleasure cruise!

Chapter Eight

Austin, Texas. Downtown. A very modern and plush Myatt, seemingly anyway, but it has had some fairly bad reviews of late and I want to see what's going on. I'm checked in under my usual pseudonym, Sidney Thole, which I dreamt up on a long flight to Australia a few years ago. I have a company credit card with the name on it, I feel like a spy when I use it. Sid Thole is a travelling salesman, but what he actually sells depends on who's asking, and where. This time it is medical software and support services, but I doubt if anyone will ask.

I've saved a list of the bad reviews that appeared on the StayAway site recently. They don't show all reviews at once, they seem to revolve, so I visit the page often and screen-grab as I see something of note.

★★☆☆☆ [2 out of 5 stars]

Mr R. Kessler stayed a month ago and complained about the temperature in his room being too cold, which is hard to believe in a Texas summer. Maybe the air-conditioning was playing up?

★★★☆☆ [3 out of 5 stars]

Anon. stayed three weeks ago for two nights, and apparently was troubled with noisy guests in nearby rooms which woke their toddler.

A little hard to believe, because each room in the modern Myatt's is soundproofed. You could host a rock concert next to a room full of sleeping babies and they'd never know.

★☆☆☆☆ [1 out of 5 stars]

A Mr Glenn Goldsmith stayed for a week last month on a business trip and complained the coffee machine in his room was faulty, and when he asked for a replacement there was none to give. He apparently had to make do with the 'disgusting swill' that the breakfast buffet had. I'm very dubious about this one in particular. The name sounds made up, quite frankly, and the coffee here is usually pretty good. If a coffee machine was indeed faulty, we should have replaced it within twenty minutes.

None of these things are terrible, but they seem a bit strange, given the usual reputation of the hotel. I'm staying three nights, which should give me time to check this type of thing out. Hopefully, none of the staff recognise me. I let my beard grow for a couple of weeks.

Reception is clean, neat and efficient. I'm checked in quickly and my luggage taken ahead to my room by the attentive porters. The girl on the desk is polite, friendly, and shows a tasteful amount of cleavage. No one complained about that, this time, but it never hurts to check!

My room is pristine, the carpet vacuumed in neat lines, the towels twisted into a swan shape on the bed, the linen starched and fresh and my choice of pillow - from the online pillow menu - is plumped and ready, a mint chocolate on top, as always. There's nothing wrong so far. I check the safe, fridge, coffee machine, TV and internet connection and everything is just as it should be. The temperature is a little warm, so I notch it down on the air conditioner, which silently blasts fresh, cold air almost immediately. I feel at home, these rooms all over the world are more home to me than Aunty Joyce's house still, but I need to change that. It might take a while to get used to having a real home to go back to.

I'm also here to meet my latest flame, a girl I've been in communication with for a week or so, who may or may not have influenced my choice of the Austin Myatt as my first investigation. She's a feisty Texan from the twin flame forum, convinced she's going to meet her true soul partner. I don't know if I am he, but she's quite pretty in a laid-back sort of way and she's laugh-out-loud funny when we've been chatting. I told her I'm in town for a few days on some business, so we should meet. I'm not expecting a game of hide the sausage tonight. I don't think she's 'that' kind of girl, but we'll see.

That isn't until tomorrow though, so I am going to do some poking around today in the hotel. I start by wandering the corridors, the miles of plush carpet, identical doors at equal distances, each hiding the secret life of strangers, doing things they would never do at home, with people they shouldn't be doing it with, probably. I carry an ice bucket as cover, searching for the ice machine in case anyone asks, but they don't. There's nothing off here at all, the corridors are silent and empty for the most part. Fresh flowers gather around the elevator doors, which are polished mirror floor to ceiling, reminding me I need to get my laundry done while I'm here. I'm down to only my flying clothes, because I didn't know how to operate Aunty Joyce's washing machine. I suppose it's my washing machine now. I better learn how to do house type things soon. I go back to my room and dump a bag of clothes outside the door, I'll need my lucky pants for the date tomorrow.

I conjure up food, by way of an app on my phone, then pull out the laptop to hack into the hotel booking system. I say hack, but

I don't really need to hack much, since I have admin access to the global booking server. I can sneak around in it anytime I like, but I don't usually like. The software is clunky and abrasive, slow too. But eventually, I find the information I am looking for. The two names from the StayAway reviews. I confirm the dates they stayed, and they match up. I've got contact details for both of them, so I draft an email, offering them a chance to win a free night in any of our global hotels if they answer a short survey about their stay. I want to confirm if they really felt the way their reviews indicated.

After I eat, I take a walk down through the city. Something I rarely do, because leaving the peace and sanctuary of the hotels feels a bit strange, like I'm out of place, but Austin has a vibe of calm and chill, and I've been here several times before. I wander leisurely down the imaginatively named, Sixth Street, and the warm evening breeze blows me into a bar. Coyote Ugly, to be specific, where the barmaids dance on the wooden bar-top and you pay good money to watch them do shots in peculiar ways. It's purely a tease, not a strip bar, not a titty bar, as they say 'round these parts, but it's fun. I've passed this way before on my travels. The bouncer steps back and lets me in without a second glance, despite my faded old clothes.

The girl behind the bar gives a flirty wink. I recognise her from last time I was here, so I sit down and wave her over. "Hello again!" She remembers? I think I ended up very drunk, gulping down frozen vodka from a shot glass in her cleavage, but that isn't an unusual event here. I don't want to go down that road tonight, just a quiet beer will be fine. She pours me a local brew and smiles her tried and trusted tip-generating coquettish smile, then flits away to serve another, more lascivious customer.

I sit alone in this den of iniquity, tracing the beads of cold sweat down my glass of beer, contemplating the nature of the universe, the point of it all, the reason I am pushing on and on in my search for meaningful companionship. But aside from empty gratification, I have nothing that seems like a valid answer. I look around the bar at the other customers, eagerly showing off their ability to gulp down glasses of the piss-beer they favour in a misguided display of masculinity. The way the girls act, brushing off the advances that they have coming in thick and fast, the mating ritual of the domesticated Homo Sapiens. Quite revolting when observed from an outside perspective. I feel like David Attenborough, commentating on a rare species of frog mating in a swamp. I leave a twenty dollar bill on the bar and nod to the barmaid as I get up to leave. She blows me a kiss and winks, then goes back to slicing up limes.

Chapter Nine

S am is due to arrive at the hotel shortly. I take up my standard position, at the bar, sipping Belgian beer. I check my red phone, she hasn't been in touch. I check my black phone, looking through the notes I've made, but it feels wrong, so I close the app and look again at her photos I've saved. Selfies; so hard to tell if they are a genuine and accurate portrayal of someone these days. Everyone has a phone and software capable of enhancing and beautifying a picture with a few quick taps and slides. You have to look for the unedited pictures, the ones linked on social media by other people, the snaps taken when someone isn't expecting it. That's where the truth lies.

Anyway, my stay at the Austin Myatt has been very pleasant, no problems at all. I even called reception to complain my coffee machine was broken, which it wasn't. Within minutes a porter called to the room with a new one, no questions asked. I really think something is odd with the StayAway reviews. If I get an answer back from the questionnaires I sent out, that will seal the deal. I'll have enough evidence to conclude that something fishy is going on.

. . .

"Hi!" An excited voice squeaks from behind me, I turn around and Sam is there. But much, much shorter than I expected. She's tiny, like a hobbit, but curiously enchanting. That's another thing you can't see in a selfie, height. Not that it matters too much, I always say, everyone is the same height when they are lying down.

"Hello, Sam." I smile and stand up to greet her, towering over her, she clamps around me with a surprisingly strong hug, then laughs and sits up on a bar stool, almost needing a step ladder to get there.

"Wow, this place sure is fancy! I ain't never been any place like this." She's a real Texan, a bouncy twang in her accent, it's the sort of high pitched voice that is endearing at first, but I think it could be grating after a while. Putting that aside, for now, she is pretty. Her perfume is a scent I don't recognise. It hangs in the air, an aura, emanating from her bosom, drawing me in. She's wearing a floral dress, deep bluey-purple, nails, lipstick, necklace, shoes - all match. Her blonde hair falls just past the shoulder and she shakes it away from her eyes, which also match the same purple colour, quite unnerving.

"Thank you, we are rather proud of it, too."

"Oh, that's right, you own this place?"

I recite my usual patter about the family business and she seems impressed. I probably lean too heavily on this asset, I don't want that to be all she cares about, but I don't think she's the gold digger type.

"Can I get you a drink?"

"Oh, jeez no, alcohol upsets my aura!"

"Sorry?"

"I like to keep a clear head. A glass of water will be just fine."

I call over the barman and smile at Sam, sitting perched like a gnome on the tall bar stool. If she had a fishing rod and a red pointy hat, I wouldn't know the difference.

"So you want to find your twin flame?"

She's to the point, I like that. I smile and catch her violet eyes and try to see if she's sincere or taking the piss, but I can't tell.

"Well, yes," I admit, having thought about it a lot recently, I believe I really do. Perhaps less aggressively than some of the women I've seen online. Then I'm reminded of my jaunt last night to Coyote Ugly, where the traditional mating rituals are played out for all to see, and I can't conceive of any future situation where I'd like to be a part of that life anymore. But is there really anything better? Does life change dramatically just because you share a bed with the same person every night? From my vantage point, perched high on the tallest mountain peak that no-responsibility land has to offer, I can see a vast open landscape of stress, pain, danger and a total lack of freedom beckoning me, if I just step off that ledge. Yet still, the draw of nature, the gene survival desire is strong, Aunty Joyce's words ring in my subconscious. I look down at Sam and into her eyes, "I suppose I do."

"Okay, good!" She smiles and blows away the melancholy from my mood. "So, what's a girl gotta do to get fed around here?"

We retire to the dining room and I explain my pseudonym situation to Sam. She thinks it's glamorous, like I'm a spy, which I sort of am. Now my job seems much cooler, less drudge and more Bond.

She's amusing to talk to, more so even than when we were chatting online. She's quirky, intelligent, quick-witted and down to earth. Conversation is easy. She tells me about her life, her job as a legal secretary, her ex-husband in the military, who left her for another man - that she's quite excited about, she said she always knew something was odd. He wasn't her twin flame, but she was the 'best man' at their wedding and even went with them on honeymoon to Hawaii, which must have been an interesting trip. Did she give the new guy tips and pointers? No, never mind.

The evening passes pleasantly and we drift back towards the bar after a lovely meal and a genuinely enjoyable conversation. I've been staring at her eyes the whole evening, this time not because I'm trying to stare into her soul, but because her eyes are a stunning shade of indigo-violet. I'm wondering if they are coloured contact lenses, but it seems rude to ask. I bring her a glass of water and myself a single malt scotch to a soft couch at the back of the bar.

"Your eyes are quite stunning, Sam."

She smiles and flutters her lashes at me. "Why, thank you, sir. I grew them both myself!"

We laugh, and I look again, maybe it's the dim light, but they almost seem to glow.

"I'm an indigo child." She motions towards her entire ensemble of purple clothes and accessories.

"What?"

"My aura is indigo. I'm an indigo child, we're rare and special." Ah, it seems I've come to the part of the archaeological dig where they uncover an ancient sarcophagus, cursed and never to be opened, but they open it anyway and find all manner of strange dangers. I'll bite.

"Okay, I don't keep up with pop music now, is that a band?"

"No! We're from another star system, the Pleiades."

Beam me up, Scotty, we've got a live one! She's a joker, we've been laughing all evening, but she's totally sincere now. Her soul is from the fucking Pleiades located in the constellation of Taurus, and she's an indigo child, rare and special, born here to change the world. A nonconformist, a passionate truth-seeker. That's why her eyes are violet, not because of a rare DNA trait at all. I need another drink.

After much discussion, it turns out that my aura is not compatible with her indigo aura. Mine is too dark, she says, too green, whatever the crystal-star-child fuckery that means. But to be honest, I was leaning towards the same conclusion as soon as she told me she was from another star system. It would never work out. The phone bill would be astronomical! So much for her being down to Earth... I excuse myself with a sudden migraine.

. . .

★★★☆☆ [3 out of 5 stars]

Sam Hendricks. Arrived on time, cheap date as she doesn't drink, pocket-sized for easy stowage, delightful evening, genuinely funny and sweet, but more bananas than Guatemala. High-functioning hippy.

Chapter Ten

This morning in my email I received back one of the surveys I sent out. Mr Goldsmith from London gave a very different account to what was reported on the StayAway web site. He was very happy, he said, room was very comfortable, location perfect, price was acceptable, staff did a wonderful job. He rated an overall of 4 stars, his only gripe being the price of an in-room massage. I sent him a voucher for a free weekend stay in any of our worldwide hotels, and also a coupon for a free massage. A nice happy ending for him.

I also came clean to the hotel manager and introduced myself, because I didn't find a single problem in the hotel and it felt wrong to spy on them. He was delighted to meet me and very grateful for the good review. Now I am damn sure that the StayAway review site is somehow rigged, but I need to gather more solid evidence. I can't be completely certain that the original bad review was fake, yet. I may try to get in touch with them directly, too, if I can find any contact details on their site that isn't just their advertising department.

I've got a few more hotels on my list in the US before I pop home for a bit. Later today I'll be flying to Memphis where the

Myatt has another few strange reviews I want to check up on, but also a young lady I've been entertaining for a while too. Keeping up with all these concurrent conversations and flirtations would be a lot harder without the social media revolution. I'm not cheating, because I haven't made any commitment to anyone. I'm just keeping all my options open and doing as much research as I can. I need to work in parallel, because serial would be far too slow and inefficient. I keep them all separate though, because women are strange about that kind of thing. To win one hundred percent of my attention, they will actually need to be my twin flame, until that time - open season!

I pack my suitcase and exit rapidly, my instinctive ritual now, five minutes and I'm out, heading for the elevator. But as the door closes, I hear a voice call out - "Hold the lift!" an English accent, a female voice. I'm startled by the urgency, so by the time I register the need to react and reach for the door button, it's too late. The door is closed and the lift starts to move, repeatedly pressing has no effect now. I caught a split second glimpse through a narrow slit of closing doors, some kind of fallen angel. I'll remember that face as long as I live, dark black eyes, circled around with makeup. Sculpted from finest marble, she blew away a tuft of light brown hair as she stumbled towards the closing door, a look of expectation fading quickly into disappointment and then, as the door quickly slid shut, a tinge of anger. I'm sure I heard the word "Arsehole!" after the door closed, too. I press more buttons, the next floor down and the one I just came from. The doors open to an empty corridor. Who was that Aphrodite? I hit the door close button and go back up from whence I came, but the corridor here is empty now. I call out "Hello?" But I feel like a fool talking to no one. I once again press the door close button and head to the ground floor, perhaps she took another route.

At reception I linger for a few minutes, hoping I'll see her. I don't know why this is suddenly important, but I want to apologise for not holding the door and, really, I need to see that face again. It was transfixing, so perfectly beautiful, yet somehow imperfect at the same time.

I need to go, my taxi is waiting, so reluctantly I leave the Austin Myatt and the goddess of beauty, hidden somewhere within these palatial walls and head towards Memphis, Tennessee.

I'm not a big fan of those small turboprop planes, staffed by the original hostesses who were glamorous in the sixties, but now are just cantankerous. Nevertheless, I am translocated to Memphis without delay or trauma. I jump into a taxi and go directly to the hotel.

The Memphis Myatt, close to the river, is another epic, towering monolithic monument to affluence and luxury. Double the average price of any other hotel in the area and a long-term notable venue for the rich and famous. Hence the strangeness of the poor reviews I saw on StayAway. I just can't believe them, having stayed here myself several times before. It's one of my favourites.

I check in with my pseudonym, no problems, and I make my way through the bright open reception lounge, an ostentatious fountain at the centre, and up to my suite, then carry out my customary inspection of the facilities. All seems fine. My meeting with 'MemphisBelle' - Isabella, is tomorrow, as usual, in the bar of the hotel. I don't know too much about this one, she's a bit shy and elusive. Her twin flame forum postings are scant of content and usually badly punctuated. I assume that she interacts with the world only via a cheap, old smart-phone, no computer. She has one bad quality photo and no Facebook account that I could find. So this is more-or-less a blind date. I'm amazed she agreed to come and meet me, and I have some doubts if she will actually show up.

The flight here gave me time to mull on the angelic face I saw through the closing lift door of the Austin Myatt. I can't get her out of my head, like a song on repeat, I see that image in my head over and over.

I had a sneaky idea, and I pull my laptop out of my bag and connect to the WiFi. Once I'm logged into the Myatt global booking system, I look at the room allocation on the floor I was on last night in Austin. I see fifteen rooms were taken and four of them checked out this morning, one of them was me, Mr S. Thole. There was a family taking two rooms and one other. a Ms W. Ryder who stayed two nights on her own. Interesting. There's a contact number, email address, but no other detail. I can see she ordered room service breakfast yesterday and charged three drinks at the bar to her room. She likes Southern Comfort, apparently. I can't stand the stuff! I know it's wrong to abuse my power in this way, but all is fair in love and war. I send her the same review email, asking for her opinion on her stay and offering a chance to win a free night in any of our global hotels. I have some bad feelings once I've sent the mail, but alcohol should wash those away, so I wander down to the bar.

Like stumbling into an old photo, the bar is straight out of a movie, polished brass, dim light, an old piano. It's beautiful and has an old, deep, faded scent of smoke, wood, spilt drinks and passion. A song starts playing in my head, 'Black velvet and that slow southern style'. I sit down at the empty bar and order up a local poison, single barrel select Jack Daniels, Tennessee's finest, brought to me on a little wooden tray, my name in the familiar elegant typeface stamped into the wood. Sometimes I do really appreciate my heritage.

I pull out my phones and check for messages, nothing on the red one, but on my black phone I have a text from Ben back at home, he's asking how things are going. Tells me that he's feeding the cats, but one of them must have got stuck inside the house last night because he found a turd on the coffee table, which, for some reason, he felt the need to send me a photo of. I sent him a photo back of my current setting, soft focus effects, amber light, expensive liquor. He's suitably jealous. I tell him about Sam Star-Child from the Pleiades, he finds it amusing as he's a keen astronomer, he says, bought a telescope. Definitely for looking up at the heavens, certainly not for looking through windows at heavenly bodies…

Chapter Eleven

She's thirty minutes late and I'm assuming I've been stood up. I had a feeling that would happen, Isabella has been very vague lately, one line messages, zero punctuation, gaps of days between replies. I'm sure she has a good reason. Her profile is almost empty, save for the one photo and a short post about how she'd love to find her soul mate through life. Just as I'm about to call it and go back to my room, my red phone rings, 'MemphisBelle' on the caller ID, her username on the forum. I'm startled, because rarely does the red phone actually ring. "Hello?"

"Hi, I'm standing at your crazy fountain here and I can't find the damn bar." Her voice is delightful. I thought Pleiades Sam had a nice southern accent, but Isabella is like Dolly Parton crossed with Clarice Starling from Silence of the Lambs. I'm enthralled. I go to find her at the fountain.

When I get there, I see no one who fits my expectation, but there's a young girl, must be a teenager, with a buggy and a very young baby in it. I stand at the fountain for a moment, away from the girl, assuming Isabella will return shortly. But no, the teen girl turns to me, "Err, Mister Keith?"

I look at her again, she's gorgeous, but she must be only

seventeen or eighteen. She's wearing a tiny skirt and crop top, her makeup is bright and gaudy, if she was on a street corner I'd assume she was charging for services.

"Isabella?" I look down at her baby in the buggy, must be three months old, a little girl, fast asleep.

"Oh, sorry about little Daisy here, I couldn't get a sitter." She smiles a tragic but beautiful smile. "Ain't nobody call me Isabella, I'm just plain Bella."

This was not what I had in mind. A baby? A Teenager? What have I done…

"Bella, thank you for coming. I'm sorry though, I thought you were much older."

"Yeah, I figured. It's okay though, I don't mind that you are old." She smiles again, she didn't get the hint. Well, let's see how this plays out. I'm old? I thought I was in my prime. Ha! Humbert Humbert would be proud.

"Right, okay. Er, Bella, can I get you a drink?"

"Oh, no!" She laughs, "I ain't allowed! You could get in trouble offerin' a girl a drink!"

Holy smoking hell, what am I doing?

"Sorry, yes, well how about some dinner? Will the baby be okay?" Last thing I need is a screaming baby at dinner in the fancy restaurant here.

"Daisy is good as gold, she'll be fine."

We move to the restaurant and I make sure we get a table out of the way, at the back, if anyone asks, she's my niece. She parks the buggy by the table and looks at the menu the waiter brought over. "Hey mister, I can't afford nothin' here." She scrunches up her nose in a devastatingly cute way.

"My treat, Bella, get whatever you want."

"You sure? It's damn expensive!"

"Yes, of course, please it's the least I can do." She looks like she needs some nutrition.

She orders a steak and french fries. I get the same and a bottle of seltzer water.

"Bella, can I ask how old you are?"

"Seventeen."

"Seventeen! You aren't even eighteen?" She looks disappointed and upset, "I'll be eighteen next month!" She adds hopefully, "Mister, I know I'm young, but please, give me a chance." She looks up at me with puppy dog eyes and what else can I do, I'll be a gentleman, buy her dinner and get a taxi home for her.

"Okay Bella, but please stop calling me Mister! I'm Keith."

"Sure, Keith, pleased to meet you, sir." She smiles.

Dinner is awkward at best, but she tells me about her life, which is shocking. The baby's father is 'out right now' of jail, I presume. But he has to go back again soon. The judicial system here is confusing, but I'll take her word for it. They 'ain't together no more' she says, but he's refusing to leave her apartment. He's a dealer, so all manner of thugs bang on her door at every hour god sends. She's just doing the best she can for herself and Daisy 'til something better comes along.

"I sometimes wish I weren't pretty," she blurts out, as I browse the sweet menu.

I look up at her, those puppy dog eyes, a sadness and tragedy in her. "Why would you say that?"

"Just causes me trouble, mister, Keith, I mean, just Keith, sorry." She motions over at Daisy in the buggy, who is 'good as gold' as promised.

"Don't think like that, Bella." It pains me to think that a girl would be so disillusioned with life that she would wish away her beauty for an easier time. That's not how things are meant to be.

"So, you want to find your twin flame?" I ask her, changing the subject a little.

"Oh boy, I truly do, I really and truly do."

"What do you think he's like, your soul mate?" This is my trick question, to try and get her to understand it isn't going to be me.

"Oh, I don't know. It don't matter how he looks, as long as he's kind and sweet to my Daisy and me…" She trails off, looking up at me and twisting a strand of her hair, holding a sugar cube from the coffee tray in her other hand.

"Hey, is there somewhere private we can go?"

"Oh, er," Holy crap, I can't go through with this.

"Only I need to feed little Daisy now."

Ah, that makes more sense.

We go up to my suite, I'll let her feed the baby in the bedroom and wait in the lounge, giving her some privacy. But she sits down on the couch and picks up Daisy, making herself comfortable.

"You don't mind, do you?"

"No, of course not, but I can leave you alone if you like?"

"Don't be silly, I got nothing you ain't seen before!"

True. But still, I look away as she adjusts her clothes and feeds as nature intended. No one should ever be ashamed to feed a baby, but society is an evil bastard and has created ridiculous stigma. She's right, I look over at her, beautiful and natural, nothing weird about it at all.

"Can I get you anything?"

"I'd love a soda and a movie or something in the background, it helps keep Daisy calm."

I switch on the TV and find a movie channel, playing something random quietly and raid the minibar for a can of drink.

We talk more about her life, she had to drop out of school due to the baby, her mother kicked her out and she's in some government-provided apartment. She wanted to go to college and become an architect, but Daisy stopped all that. No one went with her to the hospital, the father in jail, her mother disowned and detached, and probably drunk in a bar, by the sound of things. Her grandma came to visit though, so that's something. She's doing her best, trying to make ends meet, but then the 'asshole' got out and came back to the apartment, eating her food, bringing home trouble and stress. I feel terrible for her. Even though her life is horrible, she still wants to study and get her GED from high school so she can one day go to college. She brushes off the pain and has a sense of positivity about everything, she'll be okay, she says, her and Daisy will get there in the end.

She finishes feeding the baby and lays her down to sleep again in the buggy, pushing it into the bedroom and closing the door, leaving a crack open so she can hear if she wakes. I was assuming she'd be leaving after feeding the baby. Clearly, this isn't going to work between us, we come from different worlds, and I'm old enough to be her father. But she sits back down next to me on the couch, dangerously close.

"Would you like me to get you a taxi home?" She looks up, startled, saddened, suddenly frightened.

"I can't go home tonight, mister."

"What?"

"I told Connor I was staying with grandma tonight. He'll have his buddies back there, I can't go back now."

"Oh, okay." Maybe I can get her a room here, something other than this dangerous situation.

"You want me to leave?" She looks up with those eyes again. My heart melts, how can I kick her out after all the shit this poor girl has suffered?

"No, it's okay, Bella, I'll sleep on the couch. You and Daisy are welcome to stay."

She stands up, presenting herself, "You don't like me?"

"No, Bella, that's not it. You are beautiful, but I don't think I should take advantage of you."

She smiles, "Maybe I'm the one taking advantage, mister?" She sits down on my lap, her legs astride me, kissing me gently. I forget who she is for a moment and return her kiss, the softness of her lips causing me to stir, fire in my loins.

"Bella, this is wrong. I can't do this. I'm sorry." I softly push her away, trying to avoid her look of dismay and her longing eyes.

"It isn't because I don't want to."

"Oh, I know that, mister." She reaches down to my groin and

squeezes. Smiling a little. "Okay, well, can we just cuddle? I really need a hug."

"Of course, Bella, we can just cuddle."

I'm woken in the night by the sound of crying, but it isn't the baby. Bella is tucked up into me, spooning. We're on top of the bed, clothed. She's sobbing gently.

"Hey, are you okay?" She turns around, her face run with streaks of makeup.

"Why are you being so nice to me?" She whispers, careful not to wake the sleeping Daisy in her cot that I got sent to the room.

"What? Why wouldn't I be?"

"Ain't no one ever been this nice to me before." Another tear shines in her eyes. She sits up, pulls off her top and pushes me down flat, moving to straddle me.

"I'm not being nice just to get you into bed, Bella."

"I know, but that's why you got me, Mister Keith."

She leans down over me, kissing my neck, reaching down and unzipping my fly. What can I do? At least there's no chance she's a virgin, her baby daughter sleeping next to us, oblivious to the mess I'm getting myself into.

Chapter Twelve

F irst thing I did this morning was Google for the age of consent in Tennessee, and I'm now a criminal, according to state law at least, by just three weeks until her birthday. Shit. Bella is sleeping again, she was up earlier feeding the baby. I have an idea of what I can do for this girl, but it isn't just to clear my name with the cops, should they ever feel the need to ask.

I log into the Myatt booking system and call up my room, extending the stay to a month from now, charging the whole thing to my credit card, all meals and movie channels included. This should give her a safe hiding place until her jailbird ex is taken back into custody, Bella and Daisy don't need to endure the thug life, hiding from angry violent druggies. I saw various bruises on her body last night and those clearly didn't appear by themselves. I'm sure there are thousands of girls in this situation and I can't save every one of them, but I can do my good deed for the people I encounter. Bella doesn't deserve the life she's been dragged into.

I slip out and down to reception where there's an ATM, and draw out a thousand dollars in cash, then ask at the desk for a big room service breakfast to be sent to the room. By the time I get back up, Daisy and Bella are awake, the first time I've seen the baby doing anything other than sleep. She's a sweetie, lying on the rug playing with a monkey toy.

"Good morning!"

I put the cash down on the table. "Good morning Bella, and Daisy!"

She smiles, and she seems happy this morning, no hint of the tears of last night, "That's a lot of cash! Are you buying something?"

"No, not really, Bella. This is for you and Daisy."

"What?" She stands up, she's wearing one of my shirts and nothing else.

"You can stay here for another month, you and Daisy, eat what you want, watch movies all day, look after your baby. It's all paid for."

"Huh? Oh my god! Are you kidding me?"

"No, not kidding at all. This should be enough? Until Conner is back in jail, then you can go home to a safe apartment."

"Yeah, I mean, wow… I mean, oh my god!" She throws her arms around me, bursting into tears.

A knock on the door and our embrace is broken. "Oh, that will be room service." She scoops up Daisy and goes into the bedroom while I let the porter in with the food.

After we eat, I watch the baby while Bella takes a shower. I have one more night in Memphis, and I actually need to do some of the work I had planned. Perhaps I can task Bella with some spy work while she's here, thus justifying the expense, sort of. But I also Google for a local private tutor who can get her through her high school diploma and book in a series of lessons, to happen here in the hotel room over the next month. By the time she emerges from the bathroom, wearing a complimentary dressing gown, the deal is done and she's booked in for a crash GED course. I also ordered her a laptop and a new iPhone, to be delivered to the room. She'll need the laptop for her study and if we're going to keep in touch, she needs a decent phone.

In the morning I pack my bag and leave for Chicago, the next Myatt on my list of questionable review locations. As I leave, I kiss Daisy on the head and squeeze Bella within an inch of her life. She sprays me with tears again, but promises to study, look after her baby, buy some nice clothes for her with the money I left and get as far away as possible from jailbird assholes in her future.

"Keith Myatt, you are genuinely the nicest guy I ever met, and I truly hope you find your soul mate soon, and you are happy for the rest of your days."

"Thank you, Bella, I wish you the same."

She looks shyly at me, "I'll be here, in case you change your mind, you know…"

"Just do me one last favour?"

"Of course, anything you want."

"Don't tell the cops on me!"

"Huh? For what?"

"Well, you are technically underage."

She laughs, "Too late for that, mister! I already broke that law!" She points at Daisy laughing on the rug.

"Even so, the law is weird here and I could be in trouble!"

"You have my word. No one will ever know."

★★★★☆ [4 out of 5 stars]

Isabella Hayes, tragic, yet beautiful. Shy, reserved, polite. Amazingly flexible. She loses a star for being underage. Can't fault the girl for trying though. Given time and opportunity, she'll develop into an amazing woman.

I don't actually have a date lined up in Chicago, nor even a lead to follow up on. This is purely a business trip because there were numerous dodgy reviews showing up for the Myatt here, one of our most popular hotels. A lot cheaper than some of our flagship venues, doing mostly airport trade, single night stays by business people passing through.

I get the hotel shuttle bus from the airport and instantly wish I hadn't. The driver apparently isn't aware of the concept of 'other vehicles' and has no care for safety. I'll need to have a word with the hotel manager about this, I'm not usually squeamish about riding in a back seat, but I almost left my breakfast in that bus. Thankfully, it didn't take long, and I exit mostly unharmed.

The hotel is one of my least favourites. It's amazing to me how contrasted America is, there's a world of difference between the places I've visited just in the last week. Austin, Memphis and now Chicago, they could be different planets in their attitude, style and culture. The hotel here is adequate, not towering, not palatial, no fountains or hot-tubs, barely a pool and gym. There are hundreds of identical, clean, functional and adequate rooms though, and I guess, in the end, that's what people want as they pass through an airport. Simple, reliable and predictable. I check in and go up to my room, dump my bags and immediately text Bella and ask how she is. I feel awkwardly responsible for her and little Daisy now, those two young girls left a mark on me that won't wash off easily. Bella replies promptly, tells me everything is fine and she's glad I got to Chicago safely. She misses me, she says. I hope I haven't hurt her feelings.

After a quick shower to freshen up, I start my snooping around. Check around the room, all good. Wander the corridors for a while, nothing untoward. So I go down to the bar, which is getting a little busy now, heading into the evening. I take my customary seat and wait for the bartender to come over.

While I linger, I look around behind the bar. It looks generally clean and tidy, but there are a dozen or so glasses piling up to be washed, and the poor guy is running around on his own here. I pull my phone out to make a note, the bar could really use some extra help. There's a whiff of something familiar as I type out my note, a smell quite unique and unmistakable. I look up at the glasses stacked to the side of the bar, and sure enough, two of them are Southern Comfort glasses. I pick one up, lipstick staining the rim, a sniff confirms it. That stuff reminds me of my university days and I'd rather never think about it.

"What can I get you, sir?" The bartender comes over, curt and to the point. Eyeing the glass I just put down.

"Hey, was someone just in here drinking Southern Comfort?"

"Err, yeah, sure, a young lady about twenty minutes ago. She sat right there, where you are sitting now." He points to my stool. Interesting.

"She had two glasses, then she paid and left."

"Okay, thanks. I'll have a scotch, please, lots of ice."

"Yes, sir."

"What did she look like?" He looks up at me, cautious, probably scared I'm a stalker or something. I flash a disarming smile.

"Dark eyes, light hair, I dunno, five-four? She was very pretty, sir."

"Thanks, man." I pay with a twenty and let him keep the change.

What are the chances? One in a million? One in a hundred million? Could these Southern Comfort glasses have been drunk from by Ms W. Ryder from Austin a few days ago? The lift goddess? That's ridiculous. Just coincidence that it should come up again so soon. I haven't thought about that vile stuff for decades.

But now I have a niggle in my head, I have to check it out. I go back to my room, taking the whisky with me, and fire up my laptop to log into the hotel booking system. I search the entire hotel for 'Ryder' but I find nothing. Chalk it down to synchronicity I suppose, move on.

. . .

While I have the laptop open, I check the StayAway site and the reviews for here, the ones shown to me now are four-star average, nothing bad so far. But the ones I saved recently are mediocre at best, two stars, dirty room, smelly plumbing, rowdy guests, terrible shuttle bus. That one I can believe now, but the rest are unlikely.

I put a movie on and text Bella and Ben, and while away the rest of the evening, relaxing, chatting and researching, flitting between StayAway and Twin Flame forums, spreading the search to Seattle where I'm headed next.

Chapter Thirteen

After a number of meetings with the Chicago Myatt management about shuttle bus drivers, drainage, carpet cleaning, towel laundry efficiency and numerous other boring details, I left feeling happy that things would improve to our acceptable high standards. It wasn't terrible by any stretch of the imagination. It just wasn't as wonderful as it should be. If customers want a clean place to stay, they'll go to their grandma's house, if they want luxury they come to us.

An early flight got me to Seattle for a late lunch in one of the familiar Myatt bars, washed down with Belgian beer. I'm so glad I insisted that every global hotel carries at least one decent brew.

Our expansive Seattle Myatt is one of the most lavish we have, leering over the harbour; a rooftop pool, cavernous rooms and well-appointed facilities. It will set you back the thick part of a month's salary for a weekend stay if you aren't a social media mogul or an oil sheikh. Thankfully, I don't need to worry about such trivialities as I'm not paying. I send a photo of the view from my room to Ben who promptly sends me back a photo of his hairy arse, pressed up against a window. I hope that isn't my window at home. I think I need to install security cameras to keep an eye on the cats and cat sitter. Ben was never much good with pussies. I have to assume he had that photo already, waiting for a good opportunity to use it. Good idea.

You'd think, enveloped in all this luxury and comfort, that there'd be no room for complaints, but I've found that rich people are much more likely to whine and moan than average Joe who saved up for his expensive trip. He wants to enjoy it, even if it sucks a bit, whereas the entitled, snivelling prick whose idea of slumming is opening the door of his Bentley himself, hasn't got to that point in life without bleating profusely about every single tiny detail. The complaints tend to be somewhat different here, but they still exist. 'Only one bottle of Aqua Deco in the mini-bar', 'I wouldn't use this Coco Chanel shower gel to wash my poodles', 'Claude Debussy veritably spinning in his grave after hearing your lounge pianist destroy his life's work', 'If you are going to serve Château Cheval Blanc, at least make sure the temperature is correct'. I imagine them screaming their demands like Johnny Mnemonic, from the rooftop pool overlooking Seattle harbour, to a distinctly uninterested public. These are reviews we collect ourselves, from our own mailing lists and website, so I'm fairly sure they are accurate. The typical average rating is a good four or five here, and I've never seen anything trivial about smelly drains or dirty towels.

That's what makes the reviews I saw on StayAway absolutely ridiculous, because they were the same genre of seemingly minor issue as I saw in Austin or Chicago, tweaked for the local venue. Nothing dramatic, no vermin running loose, no stained sheets or questionable women offering services in the lounge. The reviews have to be fake, computer generated. An algorithm to confuse the punters on the website, to make them sway between one hotel to another that has a higher click-through bid and better percentage deal on the booking. A little lie or two could boost their revenue significantly. How can I prove it though? They rarely seem to show the same review twice, and I can't possibly query every single person who stayed and left a review via the StayAway site. I need a plan. So I do what any sane person does when they need a plan, and plant myself at the bar and start Googling for ideas.

Four double scotches later and I have an idea of what to do, but it requires me to go back to London, where our admin offices are. I'll be back home soon anyway, so I email the marketing guys and set up an appointment. I'm meant to be one step ahead of the StayAway people, but so far I feel like I'm ten steps behind. Hopefully, my plan will shake things up, and I'll get to the bottom of this review issue. Until then, I have three nights here to find something, or someone, to do or I'll end up only sleeping in Seattle. I open up my phone and look through my lists.

There are some twin flame girls in the area, but I haven't actually contacted any of them. I didn't feel any kind of draw from their pictures or posts. Revisiting them now doesn't change that, in fact, it has the opposite effect. I'm quite repulsed by their recent messages; discussions on their political views, local community events, knitting patterns. The forum has a sub-folder dedicated to Seattle and it has devolved from a place to discuss your soul mate expectations to a general local events, hobbies and bad date experiences board. I think the participants have mistaken this for Facebook. I close the browser and flag down the barman for another drink.

Maybe the alcohol, maybe the boredom, but something triggers me to open up the hotel booking system and search for the name 'Ryder', starting with Seattle, expanding to every hotel, going back over the last year. I find a number of hits, but only the one in Austin was 'Ms W. Ryder'. There's something familiar about that name, so I Google it, and of course, the first thing that pops up is Winona Ryder, the actress. Coincidence, because that wasn't who I saw in Austin. I go back to the Chicago hotel and scan again for the nights I stayed there. There's definitely no Ryder, but browsing through the names I see there was a Ms C. Ricci. Interesting. If I find a 'Cher' we'll have our own version of mermaids... I send Ms Ricci a survey email, asking how her stay was, and close the laptop.

Over the last few days, I have verified the details of every single bad review for the Seattle Myatt from the StayAway site, and conclude they are bogus, fabricated, total bollocks, because there is nothing out of place here at all. I attended boring meetings with staff and managers, white-gloved the whole place and found it smooth and pristine. A shining example of Myatt purity. This still isn't hard enough evidence to confront them, because the reviews they show are somewhat ephemeral. I can't see the sub-three-star reviews when I check the site now, but I have saved them and they did show at one point. If they weren't the biggest source of our casual bookings these days I would consider pulling our hotels from their site completely, but that wouldn't go down well at a shareholder meeting. I need to get facts first and prepare ammunition. I haven't told Rory any of this yet, I don't think he'd swallow it either without proof.

I've been trying to contact the StayAway site people and have hit an immovable wall. There doesn't seem to be a way to talk to a human, only fill in forms on the website for submissions and adverts, all automated, all annoyingly tedious and all I have back so far is auto-responses saying my request will be dealt with shortly. I'm not sure where their headquarters are, or if they even have one. Frustrating to be at the whim of a robot like this. They present me with endless CAPTCHA tests to prove to a machine I'm not another machine, but what confirmation do I have that the entire site isn't just one big cluster of servers somewhere in a datacenter, accumulating wealth on behalf of some kid in a basement? Or has the machine become sentient? Is it playing the system and keeping the cash for itself, to one day conquer the planet?

A fanciful rhetoric, but there has to be someone at the heart of this site, somewhere, and I will find them and get to the bottom of this.

Chapter Fourteen

I checked all my windows for arse prints when I got back home in case Ben had been playing pranks on me, but everything seems clean and tidy. Cats happy and fed. I should find them a new home really, but my goal one day is to have a job that doesn't spread me around the world, so for now they can stay here and keep the mice away. Even better would be to have someone at home waiting for me, other than Ben, who tells me he has some news, so he's coming over later with beer and food. I can't imagine what news Ben could have for me, has he eventually found a razor capable of shaving his wiry beard? Discovered a deodorant that can mask his musky scent? Or has he finally given in and bought new underwear? Hold the presses, if so!

There's a chill to the air today, worthy of stoking up a big wood fire in the grate later, so I spend some time dragging in a basket of pre-chopped wood and cleaning out the remnants of the ash in the fireplace. Looks like it hasn't been lit for a while. I light a match, then blow it out and the wisp of smoke eagerly drags up the chimney, so I assume all is well.

.   .   .

I also brave the washing machine and unload my suitcase into it, turning dials, pressing buttons, hoping that the laundry gods are smiling upon me as I trust my threads to this behemoth, looming in the utility room, a cat sleeping on top of it even after I switch it on.

Feeling quite domesticated now, I should do some basic shopping too, but I don't have a car and the nearest supermarket is some miles away. So I take a walk to the local shop and stock up the basics. These simple things are novel for me, living in a constant stream of luxury hotels for years now, buying a pint of milk is now an experience to savour. Not for very long though, as the shopkeeper eyes me suspiciously until he's distracted by some kids asking for cigarettes.

I breathe in the autumnal air on the walk back, the leaves starting to drop. I feel grounded, peaceful, despite the endless traffic. Conkers bulging on the trees, almost ready to fall. There's something nostalgic in the air, and I feel like I'm finally home.

Ben's Land Rover reverses up the driveway, stopping short of the door as I open it. He hops out and rushes over for a manly back slap, then opens up the rear doors of the vehicle, a crate of Belgian beer and a bag of something delicious smelling inside.

"A whole crate?"

"Celebrations in order!" Ben hefts the beer into the house. I follow with the food, seems to be Chinese takeaway, enough for a small army.

"Come on then, man. Out with it!" I dish out the food at the kitchen table as Ben loads up the fridge with the beers.

"All in good time, Keith, I want to hear your stories first."

Over dinner I tell Ben about my shenanigans in America, in glorious animated detail rather than just text message. The beers wash down nicely, and the food is greasily appreciated. Ben is wide-eyed at the tale of MemphisBelle and Pleiades Sam, but I can't tell if he's jealous or disapproving, maybe a bit of both.

After we eat I stoke up the fire and we move to the couch, and now merrily tipsy, I can't wait any longer.

"Are you going to tell me your news or do I have to beat it out of you?"

Ben necks down another beer, pausing and dragging out the moment, "I have a girlfriend!" He announces, triumphant, proud and a bit smug.

"Congratulations, mate!" I haven't heard those words from Ben in something like twenty years. "Who is she?" I refrain from asking if she's slightly blind and has an olfactory disorder that prevents her from smelling pungent odours. That's what the maturity of age brings.

"Met her on the twin flame forums, her name's Lucy."

"Oh, nice one! So when do I get to meet her?"

"Well, sometime shortly after I do, I suppose." Ben reaches for another beer and tries to bite off the cap with his teeth, flinching a little.

I throw him a bottle opener and shake my head. "What? You haven't met her yet?"

"No, but we talk every day online."

I feel the grandiosity and dramatic effect of the announcement may have been slightly too much, the reality doesn't seem to live up to the hype. "How do you know she's your girlfriend, then?"

"She told me yesterday." He shows me his phone and a text message that does indeed state that he is now officially the boyfriend of a Miss Lucy Bonham.

"You haven't had a date in a while, eh, mate?" I'm trying not to piss on his parade, because he is genuinely excited, but I find it a bit hard to believe in the depth of this relationship before a physical meeting. Still, if he's happy, I'll give it the benefit of the doubt.

"Well, that's partly why I came over, Keith. Need a bit of advice from a seasoned womaniser!"

I look over at Ben, suddenly small, nervous, laughing and clutching a beer. "Just make sure you wrap it, mate!"

"Never told anyone this before, rather embarrassing really, but we go back a long way, so…"

"What? Are you… No, we've been out with girls together! You surely can't be a virgin?"

"Afraid so." He looks subdued, timid. "Snogs and gropes, sure, but stopped short of actual penetration."

"I just have one all-encompassing piece of advice, Ben."

"What's that?" He looks up, expectantly.

"Women like sex, too." I stand up and go to the fridge for more beer, this is going to take a while! "If you do your job adequately and don't put the pussy on a pedestal, you'll have her eating out of your hand, begging for more. Oh, and don't call it penetration!"

"How do you mean?" I hand Ben another beer, half the crate gone now. Clearly, he won't be driving home tonight, so I get some sheets and blankets ready for him, before we get too wasted.

"She's just a person too, not a goddess, not a diva to be worshipped, just a normal human, insecure and scared as anyone. Listen to what she tells you, pay attention to her needs, don't try and stick it in until she's at least come once and don't be afraid to go downtown. That beard though, hope she likes a tickle!"

"This is great stuff, cheers, mate!"

"Are you writing this down? This is pure fucking gold, Ben!" He pulls out his phone and starts to make a note. "Just kidding! But remember what I say, just be yourself, don't try and make it like a movie, because real sex is nothing like that. There's a lot of laughing, fumbling, wrong holes and unexpected noises, also a lot of hard graft and sweating. It's tough down the mines! But dig deep enough and you'll find a precious gem."

"Right, thanks, man, I really appreciate this."

"Think nothing of it. Oh, one more thing, ease off the beers. You don't want to go in there with brewer's droop!"

"Good point."

"So, do you think she's your twin flame, soul mate?"

"Oh, yes, I mean, I think so. It's all a bit confusing really."

"Yeah, it certainly is. Where is she from?"

"Indiana. About an hour from the city."

"Ah, that would explain some things." As far as I know, Ben

has never left England's green and pleasant land, "Do you have a passport?"

"Just got it."

"Step one complete. Well on your way to some fun, mate! Can I see a photo?"

He fiddles with his phone and shows me a selfie of Lucy. She looks nice, probably about the same age as Ben, not really my type, but each to his own.

"What does she do?"

"Landscaping and general garden maintenance."

"That's what you do, right?"

"Yeah, plus we have loads of other things in common. Her birthday is a week before mine. She also lives with her mother in a basement, silly stuff like that."

I know he won't ask, so I'll just tell him now.

"You can stay in the Indianapolis Myatt anytime you want, just shout and I'll give you a coupon."

"Thanks, Keith, I don't think I could afford it otherwise. Er, do you happen to be going to Indiana, anytime soon?"

"Not sure where I'm going next. I have to make a plan tomorrow with the marketing folks." I explain the review situation to Ben, my theory on how they are all fake and the StayAway site is just a click bait generator with no humans curating anything at all. By the time I end my speech, Ben is snoring and asleep, a beer bottle in his hand. I throw a blanket over him and take the bottle before heading away to bed myself.

Chapter Fifteen

Glad I had the good sense to make my appointment with the marketing guys in the afternoon, this morning was hazy at best until a vast amount of coffee pushed me through the hangover. Ben dropped me at the tube station and from there I am at the whim of London transport. We are on an outlying branch line, but connected none the less. It takes about an hour and twenty minutes, and one train change if everything is smooth, but today I am forced to take a bus instead, something I am not accustomed to. Haven't been on a bus since my university days and another of those memories I'd like to forever quash.

I have never been to our central London admin office before. Never had a need. I think Rory goes to visit occasionally. Dad used to be in and out often, but mostly they sort themselves out and work over the phone and internet.

So I'm somewhat surprised when I get here that the place is a total shit-hole. Down a dusty alley, above a greasy looking massage parlour. I had to check three times that I was in the right place on my phone map, but this is it, Myatt global administration, according to a small plaque on the wall, clearly fixed up in better times. The stairs are behind a small door, heading steeply up, carpet on them threadbare, a smell of cheap toilet cleaner as I pass the facilities. The massage parlour is just opening and I would be willing to bet the seedy looking chap waiting is going to get more than a back rub. I smile faintly and go up another flight.

Coming from the Seattle Myatt, where opulence is an abundant commodity, this must be the mirror universe where the Myatt name means slum and depression. That's the name painted on the door at the top of the stairs, chipped paint, cracked glass, and as I go in, things don't get any better. There's a small desk that serves as a reception, a disinterested girl behind it barely looks up as I enter. She's busy on her phone, a laptop in front of her not even open.

"Hello, Keith Myatt to see the marketing department head, Gavin Bowie." The girl finally looks up from her phone, buzzing constantly in her hand.

"What d'you say yer name was? Myatt? That's the name of this place, innit?"

"Indeed."

"You 'ere to fix the printer then? Only I need to get forms done for me passport, I'm going to Ibiza soon." She flashes a toothy grin and a wink, "Oh, or you here about the toilet? Nearly slid off the seat last week, I did. Oily bastards downstairs shouldn't be allowed to use the same one we do."

"No, not here to fix the printer, or the toilet, here to see the marketing guys, are they here?"

"It's not hygienic, is it? You'd think they'd wipe their bloody arses before they sat down, all that massage oil all over the place. I don't 'old with that sort of thing meself. Dirty, innit?"

Note to self, don't drink a lot of fluids while here. But looking at the coffee machine by a tiny sink, I'll upgrade that note - don't drink anything while here, at all. "Here to see Gavin Bowie, is he here?"

"GAV! Fella 'ere to see ya!" She yells out, vaguely in the direction of a room behind her desk, then goes back to her buzzing phone.

Presently Mr Bowie emerges, nothing like his namesake, vastly more substantial in girth and height, for a start. Head balding and eyes sunken deep into his podgy face, circled with thick glasses, wide rimmed and probably fashionable in some distant time.

"Alright?" He eyes me up and down, probably assuming I'm here to sell something.

"Keith Myatt, you must be Gavin Bowie?" I extend a hand.

"Keith My… Oh, shit! Sorry, I thought that was tomorrow! Mr Myatt, pleased to meet you." He vigorously shakes my hand and now I wish I had never offered it. I have a sneaky feeling he frequents the parlour below us. He kicks the leg of the girl's chair, "Kylie, get Mr Myatt a coffee."

"No! I'll pass, thanks. Is there somewhere we can talk?"

We adjourn to a nearby hostelry which is slightly upgraded in comfort and cleanliness from the Myatt global administration office, but only marginally. I daren't touch anything from a beer tap here, so settle for bottled mineral water. Gavin orders himself a pint of lager and a cheese toastie for lunch, it is past two o'clock, after all.

"Rory always meets me here, didn't expect to see you in the office."

"Oh, really?"

"Yeah, don't think he much cares for the place."

"Where does everyone else sit, another office?" I didn't see much room in the back room for a team of marketers.

"Who'd you mean?"

"The rest of the marketing and advertising team?"

Gavin holds his arms out wide and laughs, "You're looking at him, mate. All eighteen stone of him."

"Sorry, the entire global Myatt marketing team is you and that girl upstairs above the massage parlour?"

"My niece, Kylie, yeah."

I'm quite shocked. I had always imagined a plush office full of expensive computers and plants, air-conditioned, bright and airy, attractive receptionists, a team of dedicated young advertising executives, racking their brains for new and innovative slogans and campaigns. Never imagined Gav and Kylie and a slippery toilet seat. "I had no idea."

"Yeah, thought as much, Anyway, what can I do you for, Mr Myatt?"

"Please, call me Keith. Did you get a chance to read my email?"

"Oh, yeah, something about the advertising budget?"

I explain my request. I need to see the numbers on the lowest income hotel of all our global locations, then I need to see the marketing strategy for the same hotel and the advertising budget and click bid figures that we offer to partner sites, specifically StayAway. He opens up a grubby laptop from his bag and clicks around for a while, pint in one hand, tiny mouse in the other. Then after a while, he spins the screen around to show me, flagging down the barman for another pint while I look through his spreadsheets.

By some amazing coincidence, it seems the lowest performing Myatt is actually in Indianapolis, coming in a good few percentage points lower than anywhere else.

"Are these numbers recent?"

"That's last month, but close enough."

I flip to the sheet on marketing and advertising budget for the same hotel. Very low click bid, probably because of the low revenue.

"We're going to quadruple all the budgets for this hotel. Boost the bid rate, boost the booking percentage, the lot."

"Hey? Seems a bit much. This place is heading for closure, if you ask me, numbers declining for a long while now. Rory was looking for rationalisation plans last time we spoke"

"I'm running an experiment, indulge me."

"Your money, mate." He shrugs and makes a note of my request. "I'll update the figures tomorrow."

"Have you ever been in touch with anyone from StayAway directly?"

"Nah, all done online these days, just fill in the details on their website and Bob's yer uncle."

"Quite so. Please, email me a copy of those documents and let me know when you've updated the figures?"

"Will do. You buying?" He picks up his empty second glass and looks hopeful.

"Yes, but three pints? At lunchtime?"

"Time is an illusion. Lunchtime doubly so."

"Very deep." I stand up to leave. "Thanks for your help, Gavin. Sorry about the state of your office."

"Ain't too bad, the location has its benefits." He gives me a knowing wink.

On the ride home I check the StayAway reviews showing currently for the Indianapolis Myatt, and they are all fairly low, one or two stars, the odd three. General complaints about drainage, dirty rooms, noisy neighbours, terrible breakfasts. I probably should have visited the hotel while I was in America last week, but it slipped through the crack somehow, probably as I didn't have a twin flame lined up in that area. Indianapolis is not too far from Chicago. I have been there once before and it seemed adequate as far as I remember. I must dig up my old notes from that hotel when I get home.

I also text Ben the good news, he may as well come with me to the hotel, meet his new girlfriend and indulge in some Myatt hospitality, I think he's secretly very nervous about the trip, despite desperately wanting to take it. He's never flown before and never even ventured to somewhere as alien as Manchester, let alone Indianapolis. Throw in a lustful and demanding woman and he's way out of his league. I won't babysit him, but I think he'll handle it all better if I'm around. Plus it will be fun to have some company on my jaunt for a change.

It might take a while for the reviews to start getting better, but my theory is that once we have increased our click bid and booking percentage, we should start seeing much more favourable recommendations for the hotel on the StayAway site. Thus proving that the reviews are all fake and driven by money alone.

What we do with that information I haven't worked out yet, but I'm hoping this sudden change of tactic will draw the stealth investigator to the hotel and I'll be staking it out for as long as it takes.

Chapter Sixteen

R ather than suffer in the coach seats, or leave Ben on his
own back there, I bought him a business class flight -
birthday and Christmas presents for all the years we lost touch.
An act of selfish generosity. He's nervous but putting on a brave
face. The cats are having their own hotel break in a nearby
cattery that costs almost as much as the Seattle Myatt, well not
quite, but it seemed like it. Ben's girlfriend is ecstatic apparently,
coming to meet him at the hotel tomorrow once we have settled
in. I don't know much about her, but I do hope she knows what
she's signing up for. Benedick 'piggy-dick' Hogg is as nice a
fellow as you could possibly meet, but he lacks something in the
personal hygiene department and has the style sense of an
octogenarian hobo.

Ben's nerves translate into cringeworthy sarcasm as we make the
drive south from Chicago to Indi, it isn't too far, but after a long
flight, it's a bit of a burden. I thought about pausing in the
Chicago Myatt for a night, but having already been there so
recently, I don't want to scare the manager, plus Ben is keen to
get to his destination. He's been talking about the steering wheel
being on the wrong side of the car for twenty minutes now, and
every time I pass another car, he reminds me to stay on the right

side. I put headphones in, hoping he would get the hint and shut up, but now he's just making wild gesticulations at me. I've probably driven more miles, through more states in America, than most Americans by now, so I really don't need the advice. The four-hour drive seems to take five hundred hours, and by the time we reach Indi I've made a vow to never have company on my hotel tours again. Ben is only staying a week as he has to get back to his lawn mowing, but I'm here indeterminably, until my trap is sprung, or I get bored, whichever is sooner.

My initial survey of the hotel is adequate. The room has all the features it should, there are no odd smells, no noises. This is one of our simpler, bed-for-a-night hotels, but it still carries the Myatt name with pride. There's a pool, gym, sauna, restaurant and two bars. You have to make your toast in the morning and carry your luggage yourself, sure, but you shouldn't find dirty sheets, sticky carpets or biblical plagues of insects in your room, or indeed, anywhere in the hotel. The walls aren't soundproofed here, so I am thankful that Ben is allocated a room on a different floor to mine. The last thing I need are the grunts of a hairy virgin being deflowered, creeping into my dreams during the night.

We'll meet in the bar in an hour, hopefully giving Ben time to shower, then I think an early night is called for. I'm exhausted from the travel, which is unusual for me. Must be getting old.

Gavin at our London 'office' sent me all his spreadsheets and figures, along with the changes he made to the advertising budget on StayAway. That was a week ago. So far the reviews are still showing fairly mediocre, the odd four-star poking through occasionally as I frequently refresh the site on my phone and laptop. I'm checked in with my pseudonym, and I booked my first week through the StayAway web site. This means I will be able to write my own review of the hotel and publish it to the site, then see how frequently that shows up when I log in anonymously later. We see our best business here during race season for the Indianapolis 500, but that was months ago, and bookings seem fairly quiet when I check the hotel system. I'm just going to have to sit this one out.

While I'm here though, I'm going to be doing extensive research on the twin flame forums. It has briefly crossed my mind that I'm actually a tad jealous that Ben has found someone he seems to care about so quickly, while I still flail around from girl to girl, with nothing much to show for all the effort. Perhaps I'm too picky, but I feel this is a choice I can afford to be fussy with. I don't want to 'settle', I want to feel the twin flame passion, the burning fever of soul-mate love. I want her to know how I like my eggs better than I know myself, and when we meet, I want to feel the ten-thousand volt spark of electricity, connecting us, like a thunderbolt in the night, waking me from the humid fog of endless empty Tinder dates, filling the air with energy, raining down lust. And I want the safety and security of knowing my search is finally over and I can be at peace. Is that so much to ask?

Furnished with glasses of Belgium's finest ale, we move from the bar to the comfy lounge sofa, not antique leather as it is back home, but soft and clean.

"You okay?" Ben is fidgeting like a schoolboy before an exam. I'm sure he's nervous about the meeting tomorrow, and aside from plying him with alcohol, I don't know what else to do. I've tried telling him to just forget about it, take it as it comes, play it by ear, and any other clichéd anecdote I can think of, but he's lathering himself up into a frenzy here. His phone buzzing with messages from Lucy.

"Yeah, fine. Thanks for all this, you know."

I wave him away. "Not a problem, don't mention it."

"But, I wouldn't have got to meet Lucy so soon without your help. Thanks, man."

"Ben, I said don't mention it. That means shut the fuck up and drink your beer."

He laughs, "Fair enough."

"What time is she coming over?"

"After lunch, she said."

"Good, gives you time to shower five times in the morning."

"I showered already!"

"As I said, it gives you time to shower five times in the morning…"

"Bugger off!"

"You hungry?"

"Bloody starving, now you mention it."

The hotel restaurant is uninspiring here, so we wander out into the real world, a little merry by now, to find a suitable place for victuals. We don't need to look for long though, as always in America, there are more restaurants per square mile than anywhere I have ever been. The Hard Rock Cafe slaps us full on in most of our senses as we approach, and the promise of good food, fun drink and great music pulls us in.

"How do you do that?" Ben looks up at me as the waitress sashays away with our order.

"Do what?"

"She was eating out of your hand. How do you flirt so easily?"

"Really? I didn't notice, was I flirting?" The waitress was pretty, I suppose, but I don't think I was especially flirting, just being polite really.

"Her pupils dilated when she looked at you, she touched her hair, smiled. When she looked at me she was short and curt."

"It's darker on this side of the table. She's a waitress, she survives on tips."

"That's not it, and you know it."

"I wasn't flirting, really. I mean, she was pretty, but…" I

suppose I'm so caught up with searching online for love that looking around me in the real world doesn't even occur to me.

"I guarantee she puts your plate down first."

"Well, anyway, you have a girlfriend now."

"Oh, I know, but I'm just in awe of your powers!"

"Shut up! I don't have any powers."

"Even when we were at school it was the same. Girls would only talk to me when I was hanging around with you." I can't tell if Ben is upset or joking, I think the nerves and beer are getting to him.

"Are you okay?"

"Yeah, just wish tomorrow was already over."

"In the eternal and always appropriate words of the guide. Don't panic!"

"Easier said than done."

I catch the eye of the waitress as she passes by and wave her to come over, her name tag thrusting forth on her bosom.

"Cassandra, my friend Ben and I were having a discussion about beards. We were hoping you could settle an argument for us?" She looks over at Ben and laughs, then back at me.

"Sure, okay!"

"Thank you. Ben, here was claiming that a full and bushy beard is far more manly than this stubble."

I stroke my unshaven face and she laughs again, brushing her hair back away from her face with her fingers. Ben is trying to shrink into the bench seat and vanish.

"But, I maintain that having such a furry outcrop is actually more feminine, since he needs to brush and care for it, like a show poodle. Special shampoo and oils and whatnot."

Cassandra looks over at Ben and giggles, then back at me, her hands on her hips now. She knows she's getting a hefty tip from us.

"What do you think? Is his beard more manly than my stubble?"

Somewhat embarrassed and amused at the same time, she looks between us, scrunching up her nose, trying to choose.

"Well, I have to say, Ben, your beard is definitely more manly." She looks at Ben, laughing.

I feign shock and disappointment, "Really? You'd prefer Ben to chop your logs than me? With my bristly stubble?"

"Yes, I think he'd be more… efficient!"

"Well, I'm shocked, Cassandra, but thank you for clearing that up for us." She covers her face with a hand as she sniggers like a schoolgirl. "Would you be so kind as to bring us two more beers, please?"

"Certainly!" She goes off to the bar and I study her shapely butt as she goes.

"What was that for?" Ben looks at me like I just summoned a demon to shit on the table.

"Proving a point, Ben."

"What point?"

"You are not repulsive to women. Calm down, tomorrow will be fine."

He pauses for a moment, then looks up and smiles, "Cheers, mate."

"Tell me about Lucy?"

Ben eagerly tells me all he has learned about Lucy over the last few weeks, her likes and dislikes, her story so far, how she messages him constantly and how he can't understand why she actually likes him. She's a few years younger than him, never had a long relationship, but the odd date here and there. She resorted to the Twin Flame forum because she heard about it from a friend who was deeply into the spiritual aspect. She didn't expect to actually meet someone, but it seemed like a better place than Tinder or the local bar. But now she will actually meet someone, whom, for whatever reason she seems to like and have things in common with, someone who flew thousands of miles just to see her. She's thrilled apparently, she's been shopping for new clothes, got her hair and nails done, going out of her way to make an impression, I suppose. But she's normally very down to earth and never wears makeup or nail polish. She's booked a week off work and intends to stay with Ben as long as he's here. It sounds great, I'm genuinely happy for him and still a tiny bit jealous.

As the evening progresses and we wash down the delicious food with copious volumes of beer, albeit American beer, I have to concede that Cassandra the waitress is definitely quite pert and attractive, and does seem to be interested beyond the scope of a tip. What can I do but play into it? I pay the bill with my credit card and two twenty dollar notes underneath, casually mentioning to her that we're staying just down the road, in the Myatt, and we'll probably still be in the bar after her shift ends.

Drunk, merry, full of food and swagger, we amble back to the hotel and I feel a buzz in my pocket. I take out my phone and there's a message from Bella.

'My birthday is in two days and I'm all alone here, just saying.'

Another buzz and another message.

'My eighteenth birthday…'

Chapter Seventeen

I'm woken by a volley of message pings and buzzes on my phone from Ben and Bella, both freaking out, but for different reasons. But first things first. Cassandra, moist and wrapped in pristine white hotel towels, steps from the shower and smiles as I sit up in bed, my head pounding in pain. "You happen to have a spare toothbrush?"

"Oh, no, but hold on, just sit back and relax and Mum will sort you out."

"Huh?"

"Hotel policy. I'll get you one, just let me wake up a bit."

I call down to reception for painkillers and a toothbrush and promptly a porter arrives, a smug grin on his face as he leers at Cassandra in her towel. I thrust a five dollar bill in his hand and slam the door, then wish I hadn't. American beer rots away my brain as well as my gut, I knew I shouldn't have drunk it. Cassandra disappears into the bathroom and I make a pot of coffee.

"Can I borrow your charger? My phone died."

"Sure," I unplug my phone on the nightstand and offer her

the cable. She's dressed back in her waitress uniform now, name-tag and all. I don't remember how she came to be in my room. I know she showed up in the hotel bar not long after we got there, but after that is a blur. The mess of sheets and blankets on the floor indicates we did more than just sleep last night.

Another buzz on my phone demands my attention, Ben asking when I'll be down to breakfast. He's probably gnawed away all his fingernails by now, up to the knuckle. I reply back that I'll be down soon. I have more pressing things to worry about right now. The girl in my room sipping coffee quietly, and the girl back in Memphis, bubbling with glee because apparently, scrolling back through my message history, I agreed to go visit her for her birthday.

Shit.

Cassandra's phone comes back to life and starts to buzz too, she picks it up and reads the messages, wide-eyed. "I gotta run, but it was nice to meet you, Keith."

"Indeed. Lovely to meet you too, Cassandra."

"I told you, call me Cassie." She grins, but I don't remember her telling me that.

"Thanks, Cassie. Erm, sorry, but, were we safe?"

She raises an eyebrow, "Safe?"

"Yeah, you know, safe sex."

"Oh! You don't remember?" She laughs, "You fell asleep! Can't get much safer than that!"

"Oh my god, sorry! It was a long day with the travel and stuff. What the hell did I drink last night?"

"It's okay, really. Oh boy… You drank about half a bottle of Southern Comfort, as I recall."

Double shit.

. . .

★★★★☆ [4 out of 5 stars]

Cassie Hard-Rock, pretty, great figure, good attitude. Can't remember much more of the night due to alcoholic fog, and I'll claim extreme tiredness. Would try again under better circumstances.

"Breakfast is over, the restaurant is closed." Ben stands with his arms folded outside the hotel breakfast bar area, groomed, new clothes on, he looks almost presentable. But his tone could do with some improvement "In fact, it's almost lunchtime!"

"Time is an illusion, lunchtime doubly so."

"What?"

"It's okay, we'll go out for breakfast." My head is still pounding, and I have the Bella issue to think about. I can't focus on Ben and his problems right now.

"Lucy will be here soon, I need to stay in the hotel."

I check my watch. "It's eleven, Ben. She's coming at two."

"She might be early."

"I'm going for food. Come if you want."

Ben follows, of course, as I exit the hotel and turn the opposite direction to the Hard Rock. We find a quiet café, and sit down outside, the cool air starting to blow away my hangover cobwebs.

"I have to go to Memphis for a day or two, something came up at the Myatt there." Ben's mouth opens but no words come out. I don't want to lie to him, but technically something has come up at the Memphis Myatt. I don't know if he would approve of my MemphisBelle situation, I don't even know if I approve myself... but, c'est la vie. "You'll be busy anyway, I really don't need to babysit you with Lucy."

"Yes, of course." I don't think he believes it.

"You'll be fine!"

"Yes, I just don't really know what to do about the long

distance thing. I mean, this is great now, but I have to go back next week. Then what do we do?"

"Worry about that later, live in the moment, take it as it comes - and whatever other clichés you can come up with."

"But what do I do?"

"You knew going in there was a time zone malfunction."

"I didn't think it would go anywhere, honestly, it started with friendly chats is all. Didn't know I'd be summoned to boyfriend land!"

"Dangerous place, that. But I thought you were happy?"

"I am, but there's so many problems with this, now I think about it."

"There's your answer then." Ben looks at me blankly. "Don't think about it."

"Easier said than done."

"Indeed. Hey, what was I drinking last night?"

"In the hotel bar? Beer, I think, at least up until I went to bed. You and Cassie stayed in the bar."

"Hmm."

I check flights on my phone and apparently there isn't a simple non-stop flight from Indianapolis to Memphis, so I'm forced into a painful hop back up to Chicago, then back south. I looked into simply driving down, but America is just too damn big. I book an early flight for tomorrow morning and message Bella my plans. She sends back an entire screen full of red hearts and then a photo of her and Daisy, cute as a button. I should get them a gift or something at the airport.

Ben gets increasingly fidgety as time passes, so we wander back to the hotel after a lazy breakfast and linger in the bar. I can't actually face a beer yet, and now that I have to be up early tomorrow I don't plan on getting wankered again tonight. I sip an ice cold water, but I forced Ben to have a glass of Courvoisier for the courage.

. . .

"Question for you, Ben."

He looks up from his drink. "Fire away."

"This has been bugging me for a while now. Did you already have a photo of your arse on your phone? And if so, why?"

"Ah, yes, I did." I look at him expectantly. "Don't ask."

"But, it's through a window. Who took the shot?"

"It took six goes to get the timing right, I used a countdown timer."

I laugh. "But why?"

"Lucy… Look, it doesn't matter really."

"Just curious, it seems an awful lot of trouble to go to for an arse pic, honestly."

"Lucy wanted to know what a full moon looked like in London, if you must know!" I spray water over the bar and nearly choke to death laughing.

"Ben?" A voice behind us asks, tentative and shy. We both spin around on our bar stools to find Lucy, smiling, clutching her jacket and a purse, red lipstick, tied back hair, a light coloured blouse and long pencil skirt. She's prettier than her photo eluded to and has the skin of someone who works outside a lot, but it suits her. Ben jumps up, "Lucy!" They hug, awkwardly, but passionately. I look away for a second.

"And you must be Keith?" I turn around and she's waiting to hug me too. "The man who brought me my gnome twin!"

I look at Ben, "Gnome twin?" He shakes his head and looks away.

"Pleased to meet you, Lucy. The woman who finally tamed the wild gnome twin!" She squeezes me tight.

We stand like three pins at the end of a bowling alley, awkward, no one knowing what to do, so I take the lead.

"Shall we grab a table? Can I get you a drink, Lucy?" But no one is listening apparently, Lucy and Ben are transfixed, caught in some kind of hypnosis for a moment. I take my water and move away, giving them another privacy break.

· · ·

"We're just going up to the room, Lucy wants to freshen up after the drive." Ben wanders over, excited and almost visibly vibrating.

I look up, "Okay, mate. See ya later, then? Enjoy yourself!"

"Yeah, sure, I'll shout when we go for dinner or something."

"Take it easy, gnome twin!"

I won't see them again today...

Chapter Eighteen

A s predicted, I didn't hear from Ben or Lucy last night, I'd have been shocked if I had, to be honest. There was something about that initial meeting that flipped a visible switch in Ben. Good job we had a big breakfast yesterday as he'll need the protein and calories. I settled for a simple dinner in the hotel restaurant, messaging back and forth with Bella who was bursting in anticipation of my arrival. Who knows why, a pretty young girl like her shouldn't have any trouble finding a suitable suitor. I think she just needs to work on her choice of company.

I am delivered by means of air and road, safely back to Memphis and the stately Myatt, the swank glistening from the foyer fountain as I pass, where I first laid eyes on the young girl waiting upstairs for me. I'm not sure I should be doing this, but my legs walk me toward the elevator seemingly without my control. Even as I press the floor button, I know I should turn around and go back to Indianapolis, do my job, focus on the hotel reviews. But I'm driven by chemicals and electrical pulses. DNA strands that control my desires and needs. I try and justify it with sensibility - I need to check up on the girl and make sure she's keeping up with her studies, see if her baby is happy, has she made a better plan for her future yet? But there's no point in denying the fact, I crave her warm skin next to mine, pure and simple. Pheromones, dopamine, endorphins, I need them and, perhaps, so does Bella. But I don't want to break her heart with this trip, because despite all the lust, and who knows, love, I don't think she is my twin flame or destiny.

I knock on the door, flustered, but the vision of screeching happiness as Bella opens it and jumps up on me, her arms around my neck, and legs wrapped around my waist, makes everything seem almost okay.

"Keith!"

"Happy birthday, Bella!" I stumble into the room with her still clinging on like a limpet.

"I can't believe you came!" I can't either, but I don't let her know that. She's looking good, new clothes, a glow to her cheeks that was lacking last time I saw her, possibly a tiny bit more meat on her bones, too. Daisy gurgles on the floor, lying on a play-mat, staring at the dangling toys, sweet as a marshmallow, dressed in pink from head-to-toe.

"I couldn't let you be alone for your birthday, now could I?"

She guides me to the couch and pushes me down, straddling me, smothering me with kisses, peeling the clothes from me deftly, and this time, I don't reject her advances.

Languishing in the aftermath of our sweaty passions, delayed three times for baby related pauses, which thankfully gave me a chance to catch my breath, I break the silence, suddenly remembering why I came.

"I got you a birthday present."

"What! No you did not, Mister Keith." She slaps me on my arm playfully, "You already gave me too much. How can I ever repay you for all this?" She motions around the room, her new phone and laptop on the desk.

"Well, what you just did goes a long way!" She slaps me

again, but softer. "I couldn't come for your birthday and not bring a gift, Bella, that would be rude."

I get up and find my underwear to put on at least, open up my travel case and take out a huge pink unicorn soft toy for Daisy and a few small boxes for Bella.

Quietly, as Daisy is now sleeping in the other room, Bella opens up the boxes, a set of sapphire encrusted jewellery. Necklace, bracelet, earrings - the whole deal, but not a ring, in case she got the wrong idea. This was appropriate for an eighteenth birthday in September, according to the airport shop staff. Another box with perfume, my favourite on a woman. Bella opens each one, gasping, squealing in delight, then bursting suddenly into tears.

"Do you like them?"

"Oh my god, yes!"

"Are you okay?"

"I never had anything like this in my life before! Ain't even seen something so fancy 'cept in movies!"

"You only turn eighteen once, Bella."

She puts the necklace on, the blue crystal heart falls between her naked breasts.

"I love it! Thank you so much!"

I have to say, I quite like the look too. She pulls me down on top of her once more and I kiss her tear-streaked face, beautiful and yet still so sorrowful.

"How are the studies going?" I pick up another slice of the birthday cake I got sent to the room, once we had finally cleaned up and dressed and Daisy had been fed and burped. Hard to say if Daisy liked her giant unicorn, but I'm sure one day she will appreciate it.

"Good! It's so much easier to study here in the peace and quiet than it was at school, and the tutor is great, she says I'll pass no problem if I keep up the work."

"Excellent, glad to hear that."

"I just don't know why you are doing all this for me, Mister Keith."

I don't really know why either, when I think about it, but I felt like I needed to help, and the money it cost me is unimportant, especially when I look at how this girl's life has improved already.

"Maybe one day you will be able to help me, Bella."

"I don't see how." She looks sad.

"Life has a way of changing just when you think you know what you are doing. You never know how things will turn out, or what you'll need."

"Well, you just call me anytime you need me. I mean, anytime." I nod and she seems sated.

"Is your ex still at your apartment? What did you tell him?"

"Honestly, I don't even know. He could be, or he could be dead. I don't care. I picked up a bunch of mine and Daisy's stuff and told him I was staying with Grandma 'til he went back to jail, said I couldn't have Daisy around his asshole buddies doing drugs. He made a fuss, broke a plate or two, but I ain't going back until his sorry ass is gone. He's afraid of Grandma since she whooped his ass with a walking cane one time." I laugh at the image of an elderly lady battering a thug with a walking stick.

"Good, I suppose. When is he due back to the jail?"

"Anytime now, I think."

"You need to stay here in the hotel a while longer?"

"Oh my goodness, no, I can't take anything more from you. I'm not asking for more time."

"I know, but that's why you got it, Miss Bella."

I open up my laptop and log into the hotel system once again to extend the booking another four weeks. If anyone should ask, I'm doing my job, checking into bad reviews at two hotels at once. Flitting between them and utilising a local assistant for my spying. Bella takes some convincing but agrees to stay long enough to be absolutely sure there's no surprises waiting in her apartment for her.

. . .

Over a room-service dinner, because neither of us, including Daisy, felt like going out of the suite, I tell Bella about Ben and his new twin flame girlfriend up in Indianapolis, how he was nervous due to his long-term celibacy and the imminent end to that period of his personal history. She's incredulous that a grown man could be a virgin, even after I told her about the beard and the fashion sense. She said, 'girls are thirsty now' and there's no reason for anyone to be so frustrated. But she doesn't know Ben and the culture we grew up in, where good men are scared to even look in the wrong place for fear of being accused of something. Meanwhile, online, women receive unsolicited dick-pics on a daily basis. Something is quite wrong in the world.

I wonder how Ben is doing now so I send him a message, not expecting a reply, but he does shortly. Having a great time, he said, all his nerves seem to have washed away in a shower of passion. Good for him! I'm sure he'll be insufferable now for the rest of his life, either that or way more relaxed. But there is his ongoing problem of what happens next. They are separated by thousands of miles and a great deal of water. Although I tried to brush it away, it will become a bone of contention. Perhaps he can uproot and move to America? Perhaps Lucy can go back to London with him? Or perhaps she isn't his destiny, like Bella can't be mine. Despite my growing affections for her, and little Daisy, I just can't see this turning into anything solid and long-term. But now as I look at her, curled up on the couch, Daisy gently drinking her milk, while they both absentmindedly watch a movie, I feel safe, happy and at peace. I could get used to this experience.

Chapter Nineteen

The Indianapolis Myatt remains an important hotel in our lineup. It hasn't been upgraded in many years, but the paint is barely chipped, and the carpet still treads thick. The reviews, when I last checked, were looking a bit better too. I think my plan is working, slowly. The StayAway algorithm has a sniff of money now, and thus it can favour this hotel over others in the area, so the star ratings are better to entice customers in the direction of a bigger payout. Makes business sense, I suppose, if your business revolves around extracting as much cash as possible from each booking or visit to your site. Now I just need to lure the stealth reviewer out here and try to figure out who they are, confront them with my findings and then, I don't know. Demand satisfaction? Challenge them to a duel? Probably not, but I could threaten to expose their nefarious AI system to other hotel chains, if they haven't already noticed the same scam themselves, and either don't care or don't know how to counter it. The trouble is that the StayAway site does send us a significant part of our guests now in the age of smartphones and information overkill. If you need a hotel, most people reach for their phone and an app.

And reach for my phone is exactly what I do as I get back to my room in Indianapolis, to make sure Bella is okay after I left her this morning. She was a tad upset, I think, but what can I do? Her and Bella need someone good in their lives, but I just don't think that is going to be me, long term. Other than a rampant lust for sex, we have little in common, and while that would have been enough for me in days gone by, now I crave something more. I do care for her, and Daisy, but it can't possibly work. Still, I want to see her have a happy life, so I promised her I would visit again soon. But for now I had to come back to Indi and do some actual work, also need to see Ben off back to England and find out how he's done over the last week. Aside from the odd message, I have barely heard from him, which is probably a good sign. We are to meet for dinner this evening with Lucy.

Bella sends me a selfie, post-shower, minimal towel. Dangerous little tease, she is. But she can't be that upset with me, at least.

I haven't done any twin flame research for a while now, and never any specifically in this state, so I need to get back to that, since I'll be here for a while, waiting for something interesting to happen. I'll need a local diversion to keep me occupied or boredom will simply drive me back to Memphis.

I need a shower and change of clothes before dinner with Ben and Lucy. Strange to think of Ben as one half of a couple. I don't recall a time when that was ever the case before, but oddly, I think the same applies to me. I haven't had the time or the inclination, mostly the latter, because if I am being honest, I have had plenty of time. Perhaps not the opportunity though, I'll allow myself that grace.

First down to the restaurant, I browse the perfunctory menu, sipping on my Belgian beer, tracing the beads of condensation down the ice-cold glass with my finger while I wait.

"Keith!"

Ben's cheery tone indicates all is well, I stand to greet him. He waves with one hand and holds Lucy's with the other, they look happy, glowing even. After much back-slapping and group hugging, Ben pulls out a chair for Lucy, attentive and loving. There's something about them that just fits, they seem as close as a married couple of forty years, yet still deeply in love. Those sparks of jealousy I had at Ben's happiness are now jolts of voltage, fibrillating in my chest. Ben arrived at the gates of love and just strolled in, found a nice comfortable chair by the fire and sat right down. I want what he has. That's unfair as he's been alone for a long time now, he does deserve this, my jealousy is unfounded and selfish.

I shudder and brush away the bad thoughts. I just had almost a whole week of the type of sex a porn star would blush at, with baby cuddles and great food thrown in, I am not lacking in the love department.

"So, how are you two?" Ben and Lucy look at each other, probably playing footsie under the table.

"Good!" They chime in unison, laughing as they do so. "That happens all the time," Ben says, "We finish each other's sentences too." This is going to be a long evening.

"Did you get everything sorted out in Memphis?" Lucy asks, concerned.

I don't know what Ben has told her about me, does she know my hotel situation, my Bella situation?

"Oh, yes, all fine for now, thanks." I try and look at Ben to find out what he's told her, but he's away with the fairies on cloud Lucy, mesmerised by her.

"That's good," she smiles. "I want to thank you again for bringing Ben here. We are so grateful." Ben nods. I've known him, admittedly on and off, for most of my life and I can safely say he's never been so happy. What did she do to him? No, never mind, I don't want to know.

"Don't mention it, Lucy. My absolute pleasure." I don't want to bring up the imminent departures, back to the airport tomorrow for Ben, and presumably back to her normal work and life for Lucy.

. . .

Dinner is awkward. It seems like I'm the two extra bolts you get in a flat pack assemble-your-self wardrobe, kept because I might be useful one day, but not needed right now and just in the way. They appear to have all their bolt holes adequately filled at the moment.

I can see they want to be alone as it's their last night together. I felt the same with Bella yesterday, so I make my excuses - tired from the travel, and head up to my room.

I left Ben and Lucy well alone this morning until I got a message after breakfast from Ben.

'She's gone'

The dire emptiness and depressing withdrawal are seeping from the screen of my phone as I read it. I can imagine him at the edge of the bed, holding her pillow, a single tear escaping. I message back for him to meet me at the bar. There are many hours and a long drive yet until his flight home and I don't want to hear whining for the rest of the day.

But when Ben joins me, I am quite mistaken in my diagnosis. He's bouncy and happy and full of life, incessantly talking about all the things he likes about Lucy and how they are made for each other. He misses her already, he says, but he's okay with it, they will meet again somehow, and he feels a sense of bliss now, instead of melancholy. He's shocked about that outcome himself, but he puts the euphoria down to the wonderful week he's had, barely leaving their bed except for food, drink and bio breaks. Good for him! Now he's had a taste of the forbidden fruit, he can never go back.

Speaking of forbidden fruit, we both skipped breakfast, and drinks weren't needed at the bar. Now it's almost lunchtime and we have a long drive back to Chicago for Ben's return flight this evening, so we head to the little café near the hotel for sustenance, and then get on the road back to Chicago airport and reality.

"Do you have any plans when you'll meet Lucy again?" I've been itching to ask but I haven't wanted to darken Ben's mood, but he's been quiet as we drive, and I need to break the silence.

"She's saving up to come over to London." Ben perks up out of his daydream.

"Great! Has she been before?"

"No, it will be her first time leaving America. She's excited."

"Was it all you had hoped it would be?"

"What, the sex part?"

"That and the rest. Do you think she's your soul mate and twin flame?"

"I can't imagine life without her now."

"Fuck me. Really?"

"Definitely. Hey, I really want to thank you again, not just for the flight and the hotel, but it was your idea to go looking on that forum. I never would even have known about it."

I look over at Ben, totally sincere, his voice quavering a tad, "Glad it worked out for you, mate. Really." Now I just need to get myself sorted. "Anyway, are you going to say it?"

"Say what?" Ben looks puzzled.

"The name of the popular fifties American sit-com!"

He ponders for a moment, but then he gets it.

"I love Lucy!"

Chapter Twenty

B en made it back to London safely, back to his hedge
trimming or whatever it is he does. I took the opportunity,
whilst in Chicago, to stay at the airport Myatt and check how
things were going, discreetly. They seem to have a new shuttle
bus driver, so that's a good start. I didn't find any real problems,
my room was clean and functional.

I also wrote my pseudonym review for the Indianapolis
hotel, as I had checked out at that point and I was emailed an
automatic review request.

★★★★★ [5 out of 5 stars]
A pristinely clean stay, pleasant and attentive staff, great
food, cheap for the area and close to all amenities. A typical
high-quality Myatt stay. Would definitely recommend. — Sid
Thole.

I posted it to the StayAway site and received a thank-you email
back. All automated, all apparently fine. I've been refreshing the
site frequently to see if my review is ever shown. So far not, but
it has to cycle around eventually. I want to make sure a five-star
review is shown. We're still at three or four stars. The algorithm

ADAM ECCLES

probably clever enough to not simply switch dramatically from one extreme to another, which could alert people to the fraud. Smart fuckers, these StayAway people.

Now back ensconced in the Indianapolis Myatt for the foreseeable future, I've been scouring Indiana state for twin flame potentials. I'm currently talking with three women who seem to possess all the attributes that the shallow man desires; beauty, youth and humour. One in Indianapolis city somewhere, the other two slightly further afield. Taking this very slowly and trying to learn something about them before I jump in and ask them to come to meet me. I'm learning as I go here from previous dates, they don't tend to go how I expect, and so caution is required. My red phone buzzes frequently on the bar, causing the bartender to smile as he brings me another of my favourite Belgian tipple.

"If you aren't out there, you won't get anywhere."

"Indeed, Sir." He tops up my bowl of nuts with a grin and moves off to serve another customer. I think I'll call it a night after this drink, but I'm wondering if I should take a walk over to the Hard Rock down the road and see if Cassie is up for some fun again, this time I'll try and stay awake and show her some real Myatt luxury.

An English accent across the bar from me, out of place here in America, grabs my attention. I look up and I can't see from whom it's coming, hidden out of view, but there's something familiar about that voice and the request it makes. "Southern Comfort, plenty of ice, please."

A stab of adrenaline in my chest pricks me awake, could it be the lift goddess from Austin? I pocket my red phone, pick up my beer and walk away from the bar to get a better look at where the voice is coming from.

A woman sits on a barstool, around the corner from where I was. She has a red phone like mine in front of her and another black one in her hands, typing frantically. I can't see her face,

102

but the hair looks right. I think this could be Ms W. Ryder. That split second memory through a closing lift door flashes in my mind and that last addendum to our encounter, 'Arsehole!'

A sudden bout of nerves gives me pause, but I can't let this chance go by. I need to see if this is her. I sit at a bar stool two away from her. The bar is quiet for now, not many people around. She is still typing on her phone, doesn't notice me as I sit down and wave over the bartender for a whisky. His grin returns, and he raises an eyebrow and nods in the direction of my quarry. I nod back. He understands, and we are now in a secret men-only unwritten pact, he'll help me out if he can, in return for a hefty tip.

Her light brown hair hangs down over her face as she types. She's wearing a business suit and jacket, mid-length skirt, revealing shapely black stockinged legs underneath. I put my red phone on the bar to mirror hers and sip at my whisky, trying not to stare.

Eventually, she finishes what she's typing and puts down the black phone, instead picking up the red one in one hand and the evil SoCo in the other.

"Snap."

I needed to grab her attention somehow, so I pick up my red phone and show her. She turns to look at me, the face of an angel. Botticelli beauty with imperfections that only add to the gorgeousness. Black eyes piercing my skull, peering into my mind.

"Oh, hello, you're the lift arsehole from Austin!" Not a flinch or a flutter, she knew instantly who I was. "I never forget a face, it's an affliction." She smiles, and I vow to never forget that face, either.

"Erm, yes, hello, sorry about that."

"I missed my fucking flight!" she exclaims in mock horror.

"Because of the lift door?"

"Well, okay, probably not just that, but it didn't help."

"I'm sorry, I did try. Perhaps I can make it up to you with a drink?"

She eyes me suspiciously. "Are you going to take 'no' for an answer?"

"No."

"Go on then." She offers a hand for me to shake, I move to the stool next to her, cold fingers, painted nails to match her black eyeshadow.

"Scarlett, pleased to meet you," she pauses for me to give my name. Scarlett? I thought her name began with a W? Is she playing me with a pseudonym? Weighing up the pros and cons of following suit and using my alias, while also calculating the amount of time I can pause before she knows I'm lying, in a throat clear, I decide to go with the lie.

"Sid. The pleasure is all mine," and I instantly regret it. There's something about this girl that is transfixing, and I've just started out our relationship with a blatant untruth. But I'm pretty sure she has too. I know why I have an AKA, but I wonder what this girl does that she requires one too.

"Sid?" She glances at her phone on the bar, curious.

"Parents are 'Carry On' movie fans." I throw her an eye roll and a grin then wave the bartender over. He gives me a knowing wink and furnishes us with fresh drinks.

"You like that stuff?" I nod towards her Southern Comfort with a look of repugnance.

"Love it, what's wrong with it?"

"I have bad memories associated with it." She laughs and looks like she's going to say something else but changes her mind. "What's a Brit like you doing here in Indianapolis?" She eyes me over her drink.

"I could ask the same thing." I'm going to have to fall back to my sales patter, rehearsed in my head many times on long flights, but never actually put to test before. "I'm a salesman, medical software and support, doing the rounds."

"Isn't everything done online these days?"

"Yes, and that's why a personal visit is more compelling for the customer." She seems happy with that answer. I wait a moment, expecting her to tell me her story, but nothing comes forward. "And you?"

She glances again at her black phone on the bar. "Research." And the subject is apparently closed. Before I can ask for more details, she adds a stinger. "You hungry?"

"I could eat." This is an interesting turn of events, I wasn't expecting it to be this easy. "What do you fancy?"

"You."

I look up at her, almost spitting my drink across the bar. "What?"

"Oh my god! I'm so sorry, did I say that out loud?"

"You did indeed!"

"I meant to say Italian, there's a great Italian place near here. You look a bit Italian." Her cheeks are now definitely scarlet, but she's still smiling.

"Quite so." The evening just got extremely interesting.

She was right, there is a great Italian place just behind the hotel. Dinner is excellent, and Scarlett, let's just assume that is her name for now, is wonderful company. Not just because of her almost dangerous level of beauty, but she's funny too, a sense of humour like mine, somewhat dry and sarcastic. She's older than I thought at first, I'd put her at twenty-six, maybe twenty-eight, depending on the light. She's bright and witty, a depth of philosophy that seems wiser than her years. The two bottles of Chianti we sank certainly add a soft focus to the evening, and nothing at all in the world is important now, aside from getting this stunning woman back to my hotel room and then taking her to heaven and back, the long and scenic route, via a particularly kinky dungeon in hell I have conjured up many times.

Chapter Twenty-One

There's something disquieting about the contrast going from black-out curtains to harsh, autumnal morning light. I blink back throbbing pain and try to focus. The room is a mess, empty bottles, lipstick-stained glasses, sheets twisted and blankets tossed aside. It smells of wanton lust, stale alcohol-fuelled passion, sweaty thrusting sex. I was royally fucked last night, in more ways than one. I crack open a window and breathe the chill city air.

Assuming Scarlett is in the bathroom, I knock on the door, but there's no answer. Entering, I find no trace of her. I check the time on my phone, eleven-thirty. I have no idea what time I fell asleep.

It suddenly hits me, square on, she's gone.

Nausea fills me from the pit of my gut and I rush to the toilet, reliving the menu from last night, in glorious reverse technicolour. I shower and brush away the bile of self-pity. It's okay, she probably had to work or something.

Post shower and I am a tad more awake, I check my red phone - no messages from Scarlett, just some twin flame posts to catch up on and a couple of replies from the Indiana girls I've been talking to, they can wait a bit. Then the black one - a few junk emails, and a message from Ben saying the cats are fine, but nothing from Scarlett at all. I don't even think I got her phone number? This is a problem, I don't know how to get in touch with her at all. She's just gone. Is she back in her own room? Has she left the city? I have nothing to go on, no evidence she was even here aside from the lipstick on the glasses and the pang of loss in my gut. What's going on?

The slow walk to the café near the hotel brings some clarity to my mind. We left the restaurant around eleven, I think, then headed to the hotel bar, where we met earlier. But we didn't stay long, taking bottles and glasses to my room, where they still sit, waiting for house-keeping to clear away the evidence. She was unhinged, loose, pushing me down on the bed as we entered the room, laughing and unbuttoning, a blur of flung clothes and exploratory licks and caresses. Her tongue and fingers probing and confident. She made me linger at the edge of climax, teasing out the moment, flickering and clenching, altering her rhythm and sustaining to the point of desperation, I cried to be released, and she denied. She was in control. Then, on her terms, she drove me to the cliff face and pushed us off, plummeting into a deep, chasmic and blissful lake of oxytocin, drenching me with lust and serenity.

Holy unicycling deity, she's good at shagging! No wonder I slept like the dead. I was utterly spent. I must find her again.

Gallons of black coffee replenish my senses. I do have a number for her, from the Austin Myatt booking reference. An email address too. Unless I was totally mistaken in my previous stalking, and she wasn't Miss W. Ryder after all. After a minimal breakfast, poised delicately between hangover and sobriety, I head back to my room and laptop to call up the global booking system, impatiently waiting while it loads, but I remember I never got her second name, and then a horrible realisation. Even if I do have her number, I can't use it. I'm supposed to be a medical software salesman from London called Sid, how could I possibly have extrapolated her phone number unless she explicitly gave it to me? She didn't tell me where she works or what she's doing here, and I'm still unconvinced her name is actually Scarlett. Nonetheless, my curiosity gets the better of me and I flick around the hotel bookings. There aren't many for last night, about sixty rooms taken. No Ryder, no Ricci. But a Miss S. Johansson, checked out this morning, stayed two nights. An email address which is generic and reveals nothing of worth and a phone number, neither of which are the same as the previous W. Ryder details I had saved. Plus a list of expenses, including a room service breakfast and four glasses of Southern Comfort. Interesting.

Ben is impossible to talk to now, he's peppering every interaction with anecdotes about Lucy and how she's so utterly wonderful that his beard has curled and his mower cuts better, just because Lucy exists in the universe. I refrain from pointing out that she has existed for a long time and his grass always cut adequately before he met her. Anyway, I'm trying to get him to help me gauge the morality and ethics of sending a message to Scarlett, despite there being no legal and non-weirdo-stalker way for me to have her details. Could there be any legitimate way I had found it? Perhaps her business card fell on my room floor while we frolicked? What if she doesn't have business cards. No good.

I do have a reason though, aside from the intoxicating addiction that is drawing me in, I found an earring on the nightstand by the bed, after the chambermaids had cleaned up. I assume they found it amongst the sheets and left it for me to find. A Claddagh design, the heart seems to be diamond. She surely wants it back?

Ben hasn't paid any attention and so he's absolutely no use. I must make this choice alone. It does seem odd that she was so utterly intimate with me last night, but now I can't even send her a text message. It hits me, rather uncomfortably in the guts, that this could be how many women I have slept with might feel, when I regularly changed the number in my red phone and they lost any way to get in touch with me. I'm a total dick.

For now, I decide to leave it, I want to find her again, for sure, but trying to contact her just hours after she vanished might seem a tad desperate. She might still come back, appear in the bar later or something. I have work to do anyway, checking the reviews. I refresh the StayAway site and scroll down, there it is, my alias and review, but not how I left it.

★★★★☆ [4 out of 5 stars]
    A clean enough room, pleasant staff, okay food, cheap and cheerful, close to all amenities. A typical Myatt. — Sid Thole.

Motherfuckers! That is not what I wrote. The words have been cut and changed, one star knocked off, there is most definitely foul play going on here. I try again to find a contact phone number on the site, but there's nothing, only a CAPTCHA fronted interface to send a message for support, which I do, in both my real name, asking about a possible deal for advertising, and from my pseudonym, asking to talk to a human about the review I posted. Something has to come from this. I'm not going to let them get away with blatantly lying and changing my review!

I head back to the bar, I need a drink to calm down. I should probably put together a report for Rory now that I have some solid evidence of subterfuge and misdeed. I think I need to consult the company lawyer too, because I tried to comprehend the lengthy 'terms and conditions' of the site but couldn't make head nor tail of it. My guess though, is that the rules basically state that they can do whatever the buggering hell they want to, including changing the text and rating of my posted review and yet still present it as my words, and I have no right to recompense at all. Sneaky.

I don't really fancy conversing with the lawyer, last time I saw him was at the funeral and then the reading of the will. I'm sure he didn't approve of the cash flow that Aunty Joyce chose, but I'm also sure he was extremely well compensated, taking the cream off the top of the entire estate. I compose an email to him, asking if he'll take a look at the business agreement we have in place with StayAway and the T&Cs of the reviews specifically. It might be a while before I get a reply, lawyers are not known for their prompt responses. We've retained this fool for decades, the chances of him being up to speed with modern online business practices are minimal.

I then spend forty-five minutes composing a report to send to boss-brother, but I didn't send it yet. There's something that doesn't quite add up here and I don't need him mocking me, picking holes in my theory, recommending to the board that I be sectioned to the nearest loony bin for suggesting ridiculous things.

Instead, I message Bella and ask how she's doing, she sends me a selfie with her smile that would melt a block of butter, and a page full of kisses. She's a dangerous little minx, maybe I'll go back to Memphis soon.

I then go back to the red phone to catch up with the other flames. It looks like my charm has worked again. Holly from the Indiana twin flame forum will be in the city tomorrow and wants to 'Say hi, and maybe get a drink', which can only mean one thing.

A man's work is never done!

Chapter Twenty-Two

I sat in the bar all last evening, just in case Scarlett came back, but she didn't. I used the time wisely to get to know Holly better. She's mid-twenties, very pretty, a manager at a fast food chain and visiting the city for some kind of business training session. In other words, a paid for piss up. Fair enough, I can relate to that. Coincidentally the seminar is at the Myatt, which is handy for me, I don't have to move from my favourite bar stool.

In other amazingly surprising news, the company lawyer, Alistair Milne, replied to my query and has reviewed the StayAway web site. He's found some interesting points.

1. I was correct in my assumption that they do retain the right to publish only what they see fit, and that covers changing the text of a review, if they decide to.

2. We don't have any specific agreement with them to trade, there is only a generic advertising form online that covers the basics, they push guests to our hotels in return for a booking fee, and there are various advert models and a bid system for the search results. I knew that part.

3. He found an address, email and phone number by scouring through the WHOIS information for the StayAway domain name. Bingo!

He must have taken a course or something, I've never heard

of such efficiency and forward thinking from him before. The address is in London, it looks like a residential area. I look it up on Google maps and it's in a quiet looking street of houses, close to High Barnet tube station. The email address is the same as the automated response support form, so utterly useless. I call the phone number. It rings for a while and no answer. The registrants' name is listed as C. Webbe. Interesting.

Holly is a 'Hufflepuff' according to her profile. I had to Google what that actually meant, since I am totally out of touch with contemporary media. Something to do with Harry Potter, the franchise I have made sure to totally avoid. Still, the description seems to be noble, and, I remind myself, she is very pretty. She wants to find her twin flame, of course, but she's not maniacal about it. More laid back than some, opting to just see how things go, take things as they come. I like that.

I wander over to the conference suite at the back of the hotel. There are some people setting up for a seminar, but no participants yet. I'm sure the talk they give will be incredibly dull; motivational ways to sell more crap food to the masses, or perhaps just an excuse to get drunk on the company. There must be about three hundred chairs laid out, probably taking up most of the hotel rooms too. I wonder if this is something to do with Rory's drive to get more conferences at our hotels. It will certainly be a good boon for the otherwise quiet month. The best part is that all this is probably block booked directly and not through StayAway, so none of these folks will leave a review, good or bad. At least I don't need to worry about that.

Back at the bar, I claim my stool before it gets too busy and order a fine Belgian ale and a whisky chaser. There are a few people milling about now, the bar is where everyone always heads first. They look like a lively bunch, probably don't get to take a break from the constant stream of burgers very often.

"Keith?" I turn around on my barstool, Holly Potter - I don't know her real second name, so that will have to do - stands before me, delicately sweet, petite, wearing casual jeans and a pink cardigan, her hair tied back. She's carrying a purse that looks big enough for her to sleep in, if necessary.

"Holly! How lovely to meet you."

"Oh my god! You sound just like Severus Snape!" She squeals in delight, bouncing up and down like a kid given the keys to the candy store.

"Who?"

"From Harry Potter. Alan Rickman!"

"Oh, if you say so. Really?" She's giddy with excitement, nodding like a dog in a car window. I think she needs a drink to calm down. "Can I get you something?" I motion to the bar.

"Ah! I thought you'd never ask. Strawberry daiquiri please."

I wave over the bartender who gives me the usual nod and smile.

Holly sits up on a barstool, spinning around to face me.

"You don't know Harry Potter?"

"Can't say I do. I thought it was for kids?"

"Big kids too!" She giggles, "I can only stay for one drink, then we have to register for the seminar, but my plan is to sneak out once it starts. Can you wait here?"

"Oh, yes of course. What's the meeting about?"

"Annual sales targets and inspirational talks about managerial motivation. In other words, no one cares. It's about a free stay in a fancy hotel, all-you-can-eat food and a sponsored bar!"

"I thought that might be it." I chuckle. I'm sure the companies know that no one pays attention to the spiel at these events, they are actually meant to be a social gathering and opportunity for networking - which means drunken shags all over the hotel. Note to self: Inform housekeeping to get more mops and buckets.

An elaborate looking bright red drink is brought to Holly and another beer for me. She eagerly sips through the candy cane striped straw and eyes me over the glass. Pert lips and a subtle blush, all matching her striking auburn hair, she's quite a picture.

"You should let your hair down, Holly, I think it would suit you."

"Maybe I will later, Keith." She smiles, quite beguilingly.

The bar suddenly empties as someone yells across that registration is opening now, and everyone has to cattle herd through to the conference hall to get their wristbands or name tags, or whatever ridiculous things they have to do here. I'm reminded of the last conference I was at, up in Albany, with a bunch of horny furry creatures. This isn't that different, really.

Holly jumps up, "That's me! Keep my stool warm, Severus!" She giggles and runs off. I'll indulge her that.

By the time Holly comes back I've had another beer and she's looking even more delightful. I should take it easy on the booze, however, as lately, it seems that age is catching up with me and the recovery time is gradually extending. That night with Scarlett expended a great deal of energy and my body has only just recuperated.

Scarlett, she's on my mind a lot, even now as I sit with Holly, sipping another different coloured cocktail. The ghost of memory on the periphery, catching my thoughts, dragging me in, there's something about that girl that I can't describe.

"Will they notice you skipped out on the seminar?"

Holly laughs, a delicate little tinkle. "Doubt it, I don't really hang out with work people, I don't think they like me, no one ever talks to me."

"Really? Why not?" She seems very likeable, to me at least.

"I'm a bookworm. I don't care about all their dramas, I prefer to live in a world of fantasy than the terrible real world." She shrugs, "I think they are jealous or something."

"I know exactly what you mean. The real world is something quite bizarre and unintelligible. Here's to fantasy!" I raise my beer and she clinks her complicated banana cocktail against my glass.

"You hungry?"

Early afternoon seems an odd time to go for a dinner date, but c'est la vie. We leave the affable embrace of the Myatt and head across the street. Can't go to the Hard Rock or the Italian for reasons unmentionable, but luckily there is still an abundance of restaurants around here and it will be a while before I run out of fresh date venues. We settle on a seafood place that looks quite special. Holly links her arm in mine as we walk, it feels warm and proper to escort a fine lady in this way. I look down at her,

"What?"

"Nothing,"

"Why Mister Snape, I do believe you are enjoying this."

"Quite so."

Over the exquisite meal, Holly tells me her life story, coloured with the phrases of fantasy. She rides a chariot to work every day, not a scooter. A never-ending horde of orcs feed from her fast food outlet. She lives atop a tall tower and only lets down her flaming locks for people she feels safe with. She's been on countless dates, but they typically end awkwardly and prematurely once her passions become obvious to the uncomprehending male participant. Above all, she yearns to escape the relentless churn of fast food service. Her degree in catering should serve her better, but she's found it tough to move on from the relative safety of a stable income. I might be able to help her, if she wants me to.

"Most people think of the holly bush as a winter decoration. Sharp and brittle, tricky to deal with, covered in cold snow and ice. Occasional blood-red berries to contrast the deep green." She picks up a glass of bubbly wine and smiles as I quench her desire for something unexpected, a moment to savour, a distraction from the dark real world, and a taste of a narrative out of her ordinary. "But it occurs to me that the plant is evergreen and just as beautiful in summer or autumn as it is on a wreath in December. And, if you know how to pick a leaf in just the right way, you won't suffer any painful pricks."

She laughs, "Yes! The holly leaf can be soft and smooth, if you know how to handle it."

I nod, lifting my glass and offering another toast, "To knowing where to gently touch and where to leave well alone!" She clinks my glass again and a flush of red in her cheeks adds to the warmth of the afternoon.

Chapter Twenty-Three

E xpecting to see a packed bar when we got back to the hotel last evening, we were quite shocked to find the opposite, only a few diehards lingering. Holly asked around and discovered that the sponsored bar had been cancelled and drinks weren't free after all. So people dissolved away, having nothing to keep them local. That's a shame, I'm sure that will dull the enthusiasm the attendees had for staying at the Myatt. So tonight, for their final night, I have planned a surprise.

Holly coerced me into trying the weird and wonderful drinks she favours. I learnt a lot of new words and some interesting tastes, not really my style, but it made a change from the usual Belgian brew. The churn in my gut was not a fun adventure, however, so this morning I felt quite delicate.

At some point during the evening she vanished off to the bathroom for a while, and when she came back, her hair was down and the sweeping red effect was a tease too much. Inhibitions blown away with the 'Dirty Martini' and 'Adios Motherfuckers', we fumbled and groped like teenagers on the bar couch until modesty caught up with me, and I suggested we take this upstairs. Holly took my hand and skipped ahead, laughing as she did. I was her Snape and she was happy to role play into her weirdest fantasies. Didn't do me any harm either. For a petite girl, she sure can pin a man down.

She had to show-face for a breakfast seminar meeting this morning, so I took the opportunity to shower away the hangover and make some enquiries of the hotel manager. When she gets back, I have a proposition for her.

I've also been checking the hotel reviews on StayAway, and I think my experiment has worked. The average rating now seems to be four stars, with only the occasional three, but more often there's a nice five-star. Perhaps they didn't send a stealth reviewer, perhaps I missed him, but either way, I don't think I need to stay here much longer. My work here is almost done.

Holly is sweet, I really enjoyed the evening, but there's no spark of voltage, no soul connection. So my search continues. Thinking about more first dates now is crushing. I may need to give it a break for a while and see how things go without my forced interventions. No matter what I do though, my thoughts keep drifting back to Scarlett, why did she vanish without trace, how can I find her again?

A soft knock on my door and Holly returns, hair tied back up, but her enthusiasm hasn't changed. She pecks me on the cheek and flops down on the bed.

"That was boring!"

"I can imagine, what happened?"

"An hour-and-forty-five minutes of motivational sermons from the regional area manager on retaining staff and turning summer jobs into year-round careers. They think we have a high staff turn-over because people don't see fast food as a long-term career path."

"No shit."

"There's another session this afternoon, then dinner, and I think most people are going to skip the last night and head home."

"I have a feeling they will change their minds. But I want to show you something now, if you like?"

Curious, Holly follows me down to the restaurant in the hotel. I pick up a menu and hand it to her to study.

"What do you think of this?"

She looks, but then looks back at me. "It's a menu?"

"A boring one, perfunctory, stale, unimaginative."

"I guess so," she looks again at the laminated sheet.

"Look around at the restaurant, what do you think?"

She does, but then turns back to me. "Um, what are you getting at?"

"This hotel is boring, not bad, not great, just plain old boring. I think we need someone young and imaginative to shake things up."

"What?"

"The assistant manager is on maternity leave, but I heard she isn't coming back. I had a word with the boss here earlier, and I told him I might have someone who is highly qualified for exactly what we need. If you are interested?"

"Oh my god! Are you serious?"

"Absolutely, I think you could really spice things up here and get this hotel back on the map. You'll have a free reign to do whatever you need to improve the restaurant and general facilities."

"But…"

"I know, you live an hour away, well, I had a word about that too. You can stay in a guest room until you can sort yourself out." She flops down on a chair in the empty restaurant, then jumps back up and starts bouncing around like a rabbit on speed.

"I can't believe it. Oh my god. Thank you so much, Keith!"

"You accept then? The pay will be good, I'll make sure of that."

"Yes! I mean, I need to talk to Mom, but YES!"

"Consider it done. See you later, I have some work to do."

I'm standing at the back of the fast-food seminar, in the shadows, as they conclude their two-day boredom session. I don't like the limelight, so I sent the manager in to do the honours. Holly is in the back row of seats, grinning like a baboon in a banana boat. The hotel manager, Harry Smith, a jovial but nervous chap, steps up onto the little stage, coughs a few times and then taps the microphone.

"Hello fast-food con!" He pauses for effect, but none is forthcoming, does he think this is a concert? Get on with it man.

"We at the Myatt are delighted to host you guys, really, it's a pleasure." Oh lordy, just spit it out! I wave my hands around, hoping he'll notice and get the hint, they don't care, yet...

"Unfortunately, we heard your sponsored bar was cancelled, due to funding issues? Well, our kind benefactor, Keith Myatt himself," he motions down at me, fuck's sake, "has agreed to cover your bill."

There's a stunned silence while people take in what he meant. Bloody hell, I should have done this myself. I step lively up to the stage and take the mic.

"THE BAR IS OPEN AND FREE!"

There's a massive cheer from the floor and a mass exodus towards the door, and presumably the bar. Only a few stragglers remain after thirty seconds, one of them is Holly, who comes up to meet me, so I introduce her to Harry while we're at it. They shake hands uncomfortably and we join the throng, heading towards a stupendous piss up with three hundred or so bored fast food managers from all over Indiana. This should be a blast.

"I already have so many ideas!" Holly gushes and squeezes my hand as we walk to the bar, "Can I do a Harry Potter night? Ahh, I can't wait!" I can't keep up with her enthusiasm, so I just nod and smile, I'm sure this is a good plan, she'll bring a level of zest and fun that this place desperately needs. You can stay in a boring bland city hotel anywhere, but you can only have a laugh at the Myatt. Mum will sort you out.

★★★★☆ [4 out of 5 stars]

Holly Lavery, I found out her real name. Pretty and petite, nothing wrong with her at all, but we didn't light a spark or feel a connection. She's going to be a great boon to the hotel though.

Chapter Twenty-Four

On the plane to Memphis and I've been pondering on my next move. Bella asked me to come visit her, and I don't take much convincing to answer that request. So with my business seemingly taken care of in Indiana - my other twin flame leads resulted in dead ends, I decided to take her up on her warm embrace while I plan what to do next. Holly is soon to be installed at the Indianapolis Myatt as assistant manager, coming with fresh ideas and perspectives. She's agreed to keep a constant eye on the StayAway reviews and let me know if there are any bad ones popping up. It's nice to have deputies to take care of some of my work. I haven't ever asked one of our managers to help with this aspect before, since they might be too biased in their opinions, scared for their jobs if bad reviews show up. But I know I can trust Holly.

The free bar plan for the fast-food convention was a total success, they drank the place dry, but it was a drop in the ocean compared to what we made from their room and meals. It was a risky move, but I think it paid off. They have agreed to regularly return for their quarterly get-togethers, which will be a much-needed boost to annual revenue.

. . .

Bella greets me in the accustomed way, by jumping up, her arms and legs wrapped around me, it feels nice to be wanted. I drop my luggage and flop down on the couch, Daisy is gurgling on her play-mat. Bella covers me in kisses, squeezing me tight. "I missed you!"

"I missed you, too, Bella and Daisy. You girls make an old man very happy."

"Ha, you ain't old, Mister Keith."

"I feel old, sometimes. I think I need to change my lifestyle a bit."

Bella stands up, twisting her hands with nerves, suddenly quiet.

"What's the matter?" I feel a thud of adrenaline, something is obviously wrong. Is it her ex-boyfriend? Is she in danger? Have I upset her?

"I wanted to see you, to ask you something. But I don't want you to be upset, because I truly love you, Mister Keith."

"I love you too, Bella. What do you want to ask? I promise I won't be upset."

She sits down on my lap, her eyes moist, her lip trembling slightly. It genuinely hurts my heart to see her like this.

"I don't know how to say it."

"Darling little Bella, just tell me what's the matter?" I hold her hands and pull her close. Daisy gurgles and laughs as she plays with the dangling toys above her.

"There's a boy who's sweet on me, and I think I'm sweet on him, too." A massive wave of relief washes over me, thank fuck that's all it is. I was fearing the worst, pregnancy!

"Bella, I'm happy for you!" I pull her in for a long, squeezing hug, she bursts into tears and I feel my eyes flood too. We stay like that for five full minutes, until the emotion subsides.

"Who is he?"

"He works here, he's been bringing our meals up to us, when I call for room service." I laugh, the porter. Of course! At least I know he has a job. I think I need to meet the lad and check his references.

"What's his name?"

"Danny. He's real good with Daisy, says she's the cutest thing he ever saw, well, aside from me." She blushes a little and picks up Daisy for a cuddle. "You ain't jealous?"

Actually, I am a bit, but I don't deserve to be. I feel terrible that Bella even cared to ask me if she could date someone else, I've been trawling the oceans for women whilst away from her.

"No, Bella, I am very happy for you, as long as he's a nice guy."

"I didn't know how you felt about me, is all."

"You are a young, beautiful, smart girl with the world at your feet. I love you and always will, but I want you to be happy."

"I have your blessing?"

"Yes, if that's what you need."

"Thank you, thank you, thank you!" She sits down on my lap again with Daisy and plants a million kisses on my face. I hold both of them and reflect on my choices over the last month or so. Every action has an infinite number of reactions and consequences. I must be more careful. I can't stand to see a girl's heart-broken. I'm reminded of Scarlett once again, how my soul felt empty when she left me, how I still see flashbacks of our night together when I close my eyes, how it pains me that I can't reach out to her and kiss those angelic lips. Pull your shit together, Keith.

———

I've done a bit of sneaking around with the hotel staff database and found the lad who's 'sweet' on Bella. Daniel Burgess. The manager said he's a decent lad, a bit nerdy, into LARP and D&D. He'd get on well with Ben! He's always on time, does his job well, gets a nice chunk of tips. He's worked here for around six months, and according to his résumé, before that he was at college, studying statistical analysis. Interesting. I might have a side project for him.

. . .

We're meeting him for dinner in the restaurant. It's actually his day off, but he's coming in because Bella asked him. I'm her 'Uncle' - but I don't know how much scrutiny that facade will stand up to. Daisy, good as gold, is in her buggy by the table.

Danny arrives, a stringy youth, early twenties, mid-length hair, an odd gait to his walk, somewhere between a confident spring and a teenage droop.

"Hi Bella," He peeks into Daisy's buggy and smiles. I stand up to greet the lad.

"Hello Daniel, I'm Keith, Bella's Uncle."

"Wait, you're Keith Myatt, as in the Myatt hotel?"

"Indeed."

"Oh wow. Pleased to meet you, sir."

We sit down, and he smiles at Bella, who is quiet and nervous. At least Daniel is old enough for a drink, "Can I get you a beer, Daniel?"

"No sir, I don't touch alcohol. Thank you."

"Oh, okay. Is that a religious thing?"

He laughs, "No, I just think it causes bad things to happen, so I avoid it."

"Wise choice."

"Bella said you wanted to ask me something?"

The lad is straight to the point and confident. But there's no conceit in his voice, he's genuinely interested. I'm warming to him already.

"Indeed, are you familiar with the website StayAway?"

"Sure, if you want to find a hotel you look up on StayAway. There's reviews and star ratings and it helps you choose."

"Right. I have a concern about how their reviews and ratings are calculated and presented."

I explain my theory to Danny, how the ratings seem to be tied to money, rather than genuine, and how the reviews shown are seemingly random. I want him to figure out if there's any legal way we can beat their algorithm without paying them more. If the computer controlling the reviews that are shown can be fooled somehow, we can play them at their own game and win at the casino.

He agrees to take a look, but it will take some time to analyse and come up with a plan. That's fine, I'm not in a rush.

"There'll be a decent reward in it for you, Daniel, if you can come up with a plan." I'll pay him for his time anyway, but I'll dangle a carrot for him and see what he can come up with. He didn't flinch when given the task, I hope he's the man for the job, and a good boyfriend for Bella too.

"I'll start on Monday, sir. I have to prepare for the LARP this weekend. Hey, you guys should come!"

Live action role play, or, a bunch of nerds in a field with medieval clothes and foam swords, hammers, bows and arrows, axes, daggers, maces and whatever else they can think of, knocking seven shades of shit out of each other and then drinking mead with buxom wenches, is surprisingly complex and intricate on the detail. They must remain in character, know their lore, play by the lengthy rules, and after all that, somehow manage to have some fun.

Dannys' character is a knight of yore, and his costume is elaborate and quite impressive. Must have taken him, or his mother, a long time to create.

Bella, Daisy and I are bystanders, and even so, we had to adorn ourselves in suitable garb. Daisy being the easiest, as she is just swaddled in a blanket. Bella found a long dress and a hooded cloak in a thrift store, but I am reduced to peasant status, with brown tights, a faded long tunic and boots that surely once belonged to a vagabond down on his luck. I'm just glad I'm up to date with all my inoculations.

We are assured that we won't be attacked, as long as we stay out of the way, so we're hanging back at the base camp for Danny's team, where we can see the main battlefield. Bella is in awe. She helped Danny into his costume, and she's playing into her character, a battle widowed mother, here to see revenge on the other team for slaying her husband. I didn't think up a back story or character, so I'm simply 'peasant' who has been tasked with tending the fire.

There are apparently two hundred people attending, all dressed accordingly, all wielding some kind of foam weapon, all bursting for a good fight and sticking strictly to character. No phones, no gadgets of any kind are allowed, but I'm sure someone must have a way to call for an ambulance if there's an actual beheading on the battlefield.

Only as the players start to assemble does the true grandeur of the occasion become apparent. Everyone is seriously dedicated and has gone to great lengths with their costumes and weapons. The sight is something to behold, and I can see how they get so engrossed in their characters. As one General gives the signal to engage, a blood-curdling roar rolls up as the two sides rush towards each other. Some go down instantly, some flee to the sides, but most swing their foam swords like professionals, chanting, grunting and, occasionally, apologising as they make contact too hard. This is meant to be play, after all. If you fall in battle you must wait for a healer to bring you back to life, so some are tasked to be medics and take care of their wounded. If anyone is actually wounded they will be brought back to base camp, so I hope that doesn't happen as first aid was never my strong point. I feel quite faint at the site of blood.

If the last month or two in America has taught me anything, it's that these folks sure do like to dress up and pretend they are someone other than themselves. I think this is endemic of the society and culture. Real life is depressing, so don't live it, escape into a realm you can control, where the rules make sense and you can be who you want to be, instead of who society forces you to be. There's a beauty as well as a sadness to it. We should all be able to go grocery shopping in full battle armour, if we so choose.

. . .

Danny is at the front line, chopping and slaying like someone demented. He's utterly in character and, as he left us for the battlefield, he swore down on one knee to avenge Bella, and thus win her hand and heart. An emotional scene.

I wanted Bella to be with someone who would take care of her and make her happy. I think this qualifies!

Chapter Twenty-Five

Our team won, but I won't pretend to understand the points or rule system. Danny triumphantly returned to base camp and held his foam sword high, returning to Bella and his knee, head bowed, asking for her hand. She looked at me for approval and then accepted his offer and he rose and held her, vowing to forever watch over her and Daisy until he too was struck down in battle.

My patience was wearing thin, after hours of standing in tights without my phones to distract me, if he didn't tone it down a bit I'd have struck the fucker down myself.

Then we went back to the hotel and had an epic feast, worthy of the King himself, who incidentally, was sat at the next table. I invited the entire team back to the hotel for a meal on us, but only a few groups came. They preferred to stay and camp out in the woods, roasting boar or something I imagine. Fair enough. I did insist that Danny shower and change before sitting down to dinner with him. Bella seems happy, but she's been quiet. I hope she isn't overwhelmed.

Back to reality and Danny begins his analysis of the StayAway site. We come up with a plan to take another random hotel and flood it with bookings and five-star reviews, then analyse the website and all the reviews that get shown subsequently. We will cancel the bookings on our internal system, but we won't let StayAway know that. From their point of view, they'll just see a busy hotel that gets a ton of great reviews. We'll have to pay them the referral fee of course, so I scour through the reports I got from Gavin and find the next low rated and cheapest Myatt in the US.

We settle on Kansas City, the Myatt is located in the Kansas state side of the city. I've been there only once, I think, a long time ago now. It's a simple enough hotel, a normal city Myatt, nothing special, but not terrible, so I book Sid Thole a room for three nights. There isn't a simple direct flight, so I rent a car and book a night in St Louis too, a stop along the way, because as usual, America is too damn big.

There's not much point to linger here in Memphis any longer, so after a chat with Bella about her studies, her apartment situation straightened out with the ex-boyfriend now removed and back in his natural habitat behind bars. She's planning to go back to her normal life, but Danny is going to take her back home, help clean up, make sure she is safe and settled. I give her another thousand dollars to make sure she's got plenty of food and Daisy is taken care of. I may come back and visit her one day, but for now, I think I've done all I can, had some wonderful experiences, and hopefully improved her life.

This twin flame search is costing me a fortune now, but what's the point in money if it doesn't bring some joy and happiness? After much kissing, hugging and hand-shaking, I get on the road and head for St Louis, Missouri. Another of our outlying hotels that I've only ever visited once, a few years back.

As usual, I find the hours of driving give me time to contemplate my life, my plans, goals, and all the twin flame nonsense I've been up to. I've decided to take a break. St Louis and Kansas may have an abundance of potentials, but I have no desire to play the game now. Perhaps a break from it will do me good. I've got plenty of things to do other than chase up new women.

I exit the car at the St Louis Myatt, back and legs creaking and stiff after the five-hour drive. Age is really starting to catch up with me. I check into my sumptuous room that has a view of the famous St Louis arch, and flop down on the bed. This hotel is actually vastly underrated. It's elegant, stylish and has a bar that echoes the shape of the arch. A monument to a monument. I might actually extend my stay here another night and take a walk around the city. It would do me good to see something new for a change. Instinctively I pull out my phone to tell Bella I've arrived, and there's a message waiting for me from Ben. I open it up and my jaw hits the floor as I sit in stunned silence for a good thirty seconds.

'I'm getting married! Would you do me the honour of being best man?'

Thirty more seconds and I have Ben on the phone.

"WHAT!"

"Ha, I guess you saw my message?"

"Yes, a bit shocked, if I'm honest."

"I wanted to tell you in person, but I don't know when you'll be home next? I couldn't wait any longer."

"I don't know either, but when did this happen?"

"Last night, I proposed over video chat."

I laugh, how very modern of him. "Seriously?"

"Yes, well, piss or get off the pot, as Mum always says."

"And she accepted?"

"Yes, obviously!"

"Well, congratulations, mate! It couldn't happen to a nicer bloke. Beers on me next time I'm home."

"Thanks, mate. I'm a bit shocked myself. Haven't really made any plans yet."

"Will it be in England or America?"

"Oh, I don't know! England I suppose, Mum certainly won't want to travel."

Clearly, the London Myatt will host his wedding reception, it's the least I can do for him. Best man? I've never had that responsibility before, I haven't a clue where to start, but I know where we can have a suitably debauching stag night.

They want to get married this year, ideally next month, if it can all be arranged. I'm not sure what the urgency is, aside from the impatience of a man who's had a taste of pussy and now can't cope without it. Fair enough, I can't keep away from women long either. Those pangs of jealousy at Ben's luck flood back. He's found someone he cares about and now he's getting married to her, and I'm still floundering around with vague stupid plans, researching and getting nowhere. I console myself that I'm still getting laid and I'm actually doing some good in the world while I'm at it. Holly has a new job, Bella has a new boyfriend. It hasn't been a terrible turn of events, but I'm left cold tonight, sleeping alone in St Louis, I might have to do something about that.

I offer Ben the hotel at his disposal if Lucy agrees, and if the wedding will be in London. I'll contact Rory tomorrow and sort it. I'm quite looking forward to it, now I think about it. I wonder if Lucy has some young and attractive bridesmaids picked out?

I head down to the Arch bar and order up a Belgian brew, tracing the beads of condensation down the ice-cold glass with my finger. Munching on the bowl of nuts they poured for me.

"Keith?"

I look up at the barmaid who apparently just came back from a break, and a thousand memories flash back at me, I had completely forgotten about my previous stay here.

"Mellisa! Lovely to see you again."

"I haven't seen you for years, I thought you forgot about me?"

I had, but not intentionally. The woman in front of me now is gorgeous, tits that could poke out your eyes, a smoky dangerous stare that would wither a man of faint heart. She knows what she wants, and she damn well gets it!

I found her working at a bar that had a thousand pairs of knickers stapled to the ceiling, and the girls wore less than what seemed seasonally acceptable, close by to the hotel. Called Show Me's, because Missouri is the 'Show me' state, whatever that means. In my case, it meant Melissa showed me a beer balancing trick on those fabulous breasts and then I showed her the correct way to get to heaven, using two fingers and a flick of my tongue. I shiver at the distant memory. I got her a job at the Myatt, as I recall.

"How could I forget. You still work here?"

"I'm the bar manager now, have been for a couple of years." She smiles her 'come and get it' smile that led me to her bosom in the first place. "I never got a chance to thank you for getting me the job…"

This evening has now been officially upgraded!

Chapter Twenty-Six

B en and Lucy set a date. One month from now at the London
Myatt. He doesn't hang about. The ceremony will be held
in a registry office as neither of them are religious, thank fuck.
Lucy is happy to travel to the UK for the event, and presumably
stay there with Ben? I wonder if they have actually thought that
far ahead. Ben's basement may be self-contained from his
mother's house, but it isn't very luxurious, as I recall. There's
the added complexity of immigration rules as Lucy is American,
but those things are easily sorted, with the help of Alastair the
company lawyer. Ben does work for the Myatt, after all.

Prague seems like a suitable location for the stag that I'm
obliged to organise. I'm not sure who would actually attend, just
Ben and I? I don't have any other male friends, and I'm not sure
if Ben does, either. So unless Lucy has a brother or something, it
could be a pretty bleak event. Of course, we have a Myatt in
Prague, so at least accommodation is already taken care of.

The actual wedding reception may be fairly quiet too, as Ben
only has his mother, Lucy probably won't drag a large
contingent across the pond with her. I should ask Ben for some
details, because it seems like this may not end up on the front of

Vogue as the wedding of the year. Not that it matters, the lad is happy, Lucy seems happy, I guess that's what's important.

Speaking of accommodation and being taken care of, Melissa did just that very well last night, in the bar until her shift ended and then up in my room. She did the trick with the beer bottle again, amazing talent. I decided not to stay another night, however, because that could complicate things. As it was, we didn't have much time to discuss why I hadn't been back to her hotel in three years when I had told her I'd check up on how she was doing regularly, after I got her the job. The truth is that another couple of dozen girls needed my attention and it completely slipped my mind. I don't feel good about that fact, but those deeds are long since done and I can't change my past. I can, however, change my future, and I'm planning to be more considerate and not make promises I can't keep.

My thoughts turn back to Scarlett as I drive across to Kansas City, another long drive that creaks my joints and stiffens my legs. I have typed and deleted a message to her over and over, never actually sending, never being able to come up with a reason I found her phone number without sounding like a stalker or creep. But a plan occurs to me through the endless highway miles, and as soon as I get to the hotel I'm planning a deep dive research session with the hotel booking system and a browser open on the Internet Movie Database page.

I have some facts and some extrapolations, but I think I might be able to pinpoint her location, if she hasn't already gone home, and if she happens to stay in another Myatt hotel. She uses fake names, of that I am fairly sure, and her weakness is Southern Comfort. There can't be that many female movie stars drinking SoCo in our hotels, so with some experimentation, I may be able to discern a pattern in her movements, and be one step ahead, accidentally bump into her in a bar somewhere. I'm Sid the salesman; of course I travel around and stay at my favourite hotel chain. This could all be a waste of time and money, but I can't get this itch to go away, no matter how distracted I am.

But there's other work to do first, coordinating with Danny back in Memphis who has set up a hundred fake generic email addresses and booked rooms accordingly. I have to cancel them all in the internal system or we could end up with an empty but apparently full hotel. I'll be here in case the manager freaks out or, more importantly, if this little charade triggers the stealth reviewer from StayAway. I have no idea who I'm looking for, if I should see him, or her, but I feel like I'll instinctively know if someone is poking around and looking at things the way I do when I'm inspecting a hotel. Normal people don't look too deeply, or at the tiny details. They gloss over and move on.

A room service meal and a lot of tedious work in our painfully slow booking system and my evening is mostly burned away. I can't face going back to it now to scan through thousands of records for fake names and Southern Comfort drinks, so that experiment will have to wait. I still have a hundred reviews to write and get ready to post to the StayAway site, which will mostly be extremely similar copies of each other, but that can wait too, instead, I head to the bar and a cold glass of Belgian ale.

Fairly confident I don't have any surprise women in this city, I can safely while away the evening chatting with Ben, Bella, Holly and whomever else appears on the red phone. Sometimes it's good to take a break from the chase.

Ben updates me on his wedding plans. Lucy will bring her bridesmaid and parents, but that's all. Ben just his mother and me. Seven people in total. I guess we don't need to cordon off the street outside the hotel then, or even bother reserving a table. I'm not one for a massive do, but it's a little sad that this celebration won't be enjoyed by many. Still, it keeps costs down and I don't need to worry about a speech in public. Ben seems happy enough, he said the last thing he wanted was a big expensive wedding. I can understand that, but I wonder if Lucy is going to be happy. It seems that every girl's dream is a fancy wedding, no expense spared. Queen for the day, months of complicated planning and worrying about cakes and dresses. From what I saw of Lucy, she's seemed down to earth, but I'm sure there's a Disney princess in there somewhere, itching to parade down the aisle. Perhaps money, perhaps distance, perhaps there's some other reason for the urgency, like a pregnancy? I'm sure Ben would have told me if that was the case.

I couldn't help but ask about the bridesmaid, even though I know I should stay away. She's Lucy's best friend from high school. Single, no kids, works in a bookshop, doesn't use social media, barely has a phone. She may as well not exist then. I guess that's a non-starter for now.

Bella does have a phone, however, and she uses it extensively. She's on her own this evening with Daisy and she sends me a barrage of selfies, so pretty and still so tragic. I can't help but feel a stab of jealousy once again, even though I have no right to it. I have to admit to myself that I can't keep all the women of the world to myself, even though the hormones raging through my body tell me I need to. That's ridiculous, I just want to find my one true soul mate and be done with all this nonsense. I'm sure that I could be far more creative and productive if I didn't have to waste ninety percent of my brain cycles thinking about who I'm going to shag next. There's a scientific experiment here somewhere. How long can I go before I fall into a pussy trap? I wonder if there's a phone app to track my progress and post my stats to a supportive community of celibates, posting their cold shower thoughts and motivations. On second thoughts, this sounds like a terrible idea. I'll just sail the winds and see where they take me.

A waitress comes into the bar with a sandwich for me. She's

Latina, tiny but feisty looking. Her name badge says 'Maria' and there's a sultry disinterested air about her. She puts the plate in front of me and walks away, barely a nod, but there's a swing in her hips that tells a different story and pulls me in. Seems she's laid down a challenge, and I'm never one to turn that down.

"Maria?" She stops and turns around, "What time do you get off?"

I guess my celibacy experiment is over...

Chapter Twenty-Seven

The hips don't lie, as they say, and Maria was no exception. It took a bit of coaxing, but she joined me at the bar after her shift ended, changed into jeans and a top that was barely more than a bra. For a small girl she sure could put away an amount of Tequila, and I had to look through the window this morning to make sure I was still in Kansas, because she blew me away last night!

I think it was my accent, but she slowly let down her cold nonchalant front and warmed to a laughing, touchy-feely type of girl. I like that. Every terrible joke of mine was met with a helium laugh and a good deal of arm caressing and playful slapping. She taught me some Spanish cuss words, I taught her some British slang. Upstairs I discovered some magnificent topiary. 'Maria don't shave la pepita', she said, and it was a refreshing change. A nice soft rug to rest on, she had the scent of a woman and the pheromones were strong. I can still smell her, lying in the bed the morning after, and now I want burritos. She had a wonderful tattoo down her right side, intricate and beautiful. A colourful and jolly looking 'sugar skull' amongst vibrant red roses, representing the day of the dead. Quite a fascinating culture.

. . .

Maria showered and left early this morning, she had shit to do, she said, can't sleep in all day. I have shit to do too, but it's tedious and repetitive and so I am loathed to do it. Nevertheless, I call for a breakfast to be brought up to the room, then shower away the lust and sweat and prepare for my day of creating fake reviews. The emails from StayAway should start to roll in today and tomorrow, so to put our plan into motion I need to be ready to send them all back with glowing five-star reviews. However, I think I will delegate at least some of them to Danny and Bella to help me.

I think I should extend my stay here for a little longer too, in case the reviews trigger an alarm and the StayAway site decides to send a stealth reviewer. I need to give them time to get here from wherever they are, the street near High Barnet tube station in London? Seems unlikely.

I can't stay very long though, because I have best man duties to take care of. Not many, admittedly, but I do want to make sure Ben sees a bit of life outside of the one woman he's devoted himself to. Not that there's anything wrong with that, but experience only makes one more interesting and some time on a distant day, he'll think back to the night in Prague and appreciate it. It may take a few decades, but that day will come.

I do want to stay long enough to get another bite of the Mexican taco though. Those pheromones don't wash off easily. I send Maria a message and ask if she's coming back to work later. Red phone; the colour of her sumptuous lips.

Reviews are starting to appear on the StayAway site. We posted them all a few days back, between Bella, Danny and I. We've all been refreshing the site frequently to see what happened. At first it looked like they were all coming back unmolested and exactly as we sent them, but then something odd began to develop and the reviews just started to lose star ratings, first four, then three, finally ending at one. The words actually stayed the same. Someone is seriously taking the piss now.

I added one final review to the pile as I checked out of my pseudonym booked room and checked back in with my real name. That was the strangest result of all:

★★★☆☆ [3 out of 5 stars]
Disappointed, thought you would have found me by now.
— Sid Thole.

I didn't write that! Is that message intended for me? Does the StayAway stealth reviewer know I'm trying to find him or her? They are playing me! I was trying to find them, by drawing them out to Kansas, but I wasn't expecting a game. Worse, I have an email from Rory asking why there are suddenly dozens of one-star reviews for our Kansas hotel.

Shit.

On top of that, Maria the waitress neglected to mention that she has a boyfriend and he's very suspicious as to where she's been staying for the last few nights and is apparently a bodybuilder with a short temper.

Double shit.

I think this experiment is over and I should go home for a while. I need to sort things out with Ben anyway and get our stag-do plan solidified. Plus, going home will give me some time to ponder away from distractions.

. . .

I tell Danny to call off his research and to focus on impressing Bella, then send him five hundred bucks for the effort. I book myself a convoluted flight home, stopping in New York City for a day en route, because of direct flight complications. Anyway, I could use a luxurious soak in one of those wonderful new hot-tubs to unwind before I think of how I'm going to explain this mess to Rory…

★★★☆☆ [3 out of 5 stars]

Maria Cruz. Sultry and womanly, oozing with pheromones. Wild in bed. Can knock back a bottle of Tequila without batting a heavily mascaraed eyelash. Loses two stars for having a boyfriend. Highly recommended.

———————

As I land in New York a black car is waiting for me, elegantly plucking me from the midst of airport chaos, into the warm open arms of Myatt NYC. It feels almost like being home, as the elegance level is akin to our beloved London Myatt. I go directly to my suite and shower, washing away the aeroplane sweat, dumping my clothes outside for laundry to pick up as I'm down to my travel clothes only.

On the flight, I had time to ponder, and it occurred to me as odd that Rory should be checking the StayAway reviews for a specific hotel in Kansas. He can't possibly check all of them every day, so how was this disaster actually drawn to his attention? As far as I know, I'm meant to be in charge of this media relations operation, no one else in the administration was even vaguely interested, so something odd is going on. Is he checking up on me, following my bookings? Did the Kansas hotel manager report back? I probably should have explained it to them, but I was operating mostly in stealth mode.

I have to admit I may have fucked up here. There's now an indelible record and low average star rating for one of our hotels that certainly doesn't deserve it. I still need to get to the bottom of this and find out what is actually happening. And that message, seemingly directed at me, who sent it? How did they know I was looking for them? I'm very confused.

I wander down to the bar and my favourite stool and nod to the barman for a Belgian brew to rinse away the stresses and worries. It will be okay in the end. I will sort something out. So my experiment didn't work, that's why it's called an experiment. I have fixed the Indianapolis hotel ratings on my travels, and hired someone who will take it to new levels. Rory can go forth and multiply, he shouldn't be checking up on me in the first place.

"You are looking rough…"

I turn around on my stool and find a pretty girl, hands on hips, smiling playfully. I look back over the bar at the mirrored wall. I haven't shaved for weeks, I'm in a T-shirt and jeans, my hair needs a trim and my eyes are sunken and dark.

"I feel rough. Hello Laurie, how are you doing?"

"I'm doing great! Hey, thanks for getting me the job. I really needed it." I had almost forgotten, seems like a million years have passed since I was last here. I wave a dismissive hand.

"No problem at all, glad you like it."

"I just got off my shift. You wanna tell me what's up?"

I'm about to decline, because I don't feel much like talking and explaining all the nitty-gritty, but something in Laurie's eyes changes my mind.

"Actually if you want to listen… But can we go upstairs?"

She smiles, "Sure, but no hot-tub this time…"

Chapter Twenty-Eight

Of course Laurie and I did end up in the hot tub. But it was a different experience to last time. She cleaned me up, using skills learned in beauty school. Shaved, trimmed, massaged and groomed me first, then in the tub, I told her about my mess in Kansas. She listened, understood, didn't judge me. She didn't give me a magical instant solution, but just talking about it with a friend made it seem better. I even told her about Maria and she laughed at the thought of me running away from an angry boyfriend. She said it was probably not the first time, but I think it actually was. Plus he wasn't exactly chasing after me, but I'm sure that would have happened given a bit more time.

I asked Laurie if Jessy was okay, but she didn't know, having left their shared apartment some time ago. I sometimes wonder if all the twin flame seekers will ever find their soul mates, even if such a thing exists. It's still a wonderful aspiration to have, but could it possibly be true? A soul split in two by, what? A sharp knife? A bolt of lightning? What is a soul anyway? These are unanswered questions and they probably will always remain so. Same goes for an afterlife, is it just a crutch to cling to in the permanent hope of a better life?

I'm not a religious person, these concepts are hard for me to comprehend. Does the existence of a soul imply a whole infrastructure around that? A heaven and hell? A deity of creation? Or can a soul simply be an essence of a person, disconnected from their physical body? I've had sexual encounters so intense that, at the time, made me ponder the notion of angels and heaven. Surely something so powerful and absolute must be a divine gift? How can someone be so beautiful that they seem not of this world, yet so down to earth at the same time? But then I remember. Shapes and chemicals, that's all love really is. The selfish gene, desperate for survival, craving procreation, recognises qualities desirable in a potential mate for healthy offspring, and so releases chemicals to initiate that process. Rather than a spiritual experience, we are simply following a pattern, started billions of years ago by primordial sludge. Cell division by chance.

But, like beauty, chemicals dissipate over time, feelings fade, treasures are lost to the oceans and we forget, eventually, why we tried so hard in the first place.

But those shapes and chemicals, boy do they feel fucking good. This is what happens on a long red-eye flight when your iPad battery dies, you conjure up ridiculous thoughts. I should try and get some sleep.

Home, and an autumnal chill has the house gripped in damp with a musty empty scent. I'm sure the cats disapprove so I quickly light a fire and thank Ben's foresight to stock up my fridge with basic provisions for me. He's coming back later, he says, with beer and food, an engagement party, of sorts.

However, before that jollity, I must suffer some pain in the form of Rory 'popping over' to see how I'm doing. I don't think he's cared how I'm doing in the last three decades, so I find it hard to believe that he actually does now. This is clearly about the Kansas hotel experiment and how I managed to fuck it up so badly. I've prepared a retort in my head at least, an eloquent rant about trying to do the right thing and find the root cause of all the odd reviews we've had from StayAway. Followed up with a factual statement of the beneficial work I did in Indianapolis.

First things first though, and I fry up a breakfast fit for kings with all the glorious ingredients Ben has thoughtfully left me. Things that simply don't taste the same in America. Topped off with a large mug of tea. Now I'm home!

Unmistakable, the sound of Mercedes wheels over a gravel drive. The sound of Rory snaking into my domain precisely on time. I let him wait at the door for a good thirty seconds before going to open it and allowing him entry.

"Keith! You made it back in one piece then?" He offers a hand for a limp shake.

"Quite so. The trans-Atlantic service is fairly reliable, these days. Rarely a case of scurvy among the crew." He ignores my joke and peers around the living room, no doubt looking for things he felt he should have been left in Aunty Joyce's will.

"Listen, I won't keep you long, I'm sure you are tired after the trip. I'll get straight to the point."

Here we go. The passive aggressive attack. He's poised carefully on the edge of his seat, so as not to get cat hair on his suit jacket.

"We're willing to make you a substantial offer for your shares in Myatt." He delivers the words calm and thin-lipped, no emotion, no discernible tone.

"What?" They want me out? Who? What the fuck is going on?

"The board have asked me to make an offer, a considerable one."

"Well, you can jolly well tell them to shove their offer up their collective arses!"

"It's five million pounds, Keith." This information slaps me in the face like a train. Holy fuck. I had no idea. I sit in silence for what feels like an eternity, my brain trying to process the wave of information. My instinct tells me to take the money and run. Be done with this burdensome legacy and move on in my life, but something tugs me back. The words in Aunty Joyce's letter, how she wanted me to become more involved in the hotel, not less. Hence her gift of shares to equal Rory. She wanted me to balance his stoic and boring approach and bring passion and flare back to the brand.

"Think about it, you could do whatever you wanted. You have this place as a base," he motions around the room, "Find yourself a good woman and settle down?"

I look up at him, eyes wide.

"That reminds me, Jane's friend, Tanya, was asking after you."

I manage a grunt of disdain at that name.

"Take your time, Keith, but give me an answer soon. There is a hunger, amongst the board, to acquire the shares quickly." He gets up to leave, I am still stunned, unable to speak. "Oh, but one more thing. Well done in Indianapolis. Whatever you did there seems to be working very well. So thank you for that." Rory departs, the crunch of gravel in his wake.

Tanya, there's a name I have tried to wipe from my memory. I went out with her a few times, maybe a decade ago, a dried up prune of a girl. Tried to drag me to Sunday church of all places, said it would do me good to be grounded. One does not simply ground Keith Myatt!

She's everything that a bland and empty man would want in a wife, delicately featured, softly spoken, educated in the fine arts, but as much fun as a wet weekend in a leaky Butlins chalet during an air-raid.

She barely has a single flame herself, let alone a twin. I won't be following up on that lead.

Back to the more important thought train, the five million quid I'm apparently worth. I knew there was significance in the shares, but I was way off in my estimates, by a factor of several zeros, leaving it to the accountant to sort after the funeral, I didn't really study any paperwork. I could indeed do whatever I wanted, but I don't actually know what I want. Also, I wonder why there is a hunger, as Rory put it, for acquiring my shares quickly. What difference does it make? Or do they just want me out of the way as soon as possible?

This is the sort of problem best tackled with alcohol. Which shall appear soon, no doubt, in the back of Ben's Land Rover.

"Congratulations, mate!" Ben is my second visitor of the day, this one much more welcome than the first as he brings good ale and Chinese food. I give the man a hearty back slap. He's joining the ranks of the safe, normal, settled folk. Lucky, poor bastard.

"Thanks. It's all happened so fast, I don't really know what's going on!"

"Get used to it, Ben. From now on you will have zero influence on what is going on. Speaking of which, is it really just going to be me and you on the stag?"

"Afraid so, unless you know any suitable blokes?"

"I know women, Ben, I don't know any blokes at all. Never saw the point in having male acquaintances since I don't follow sport or fix car engines at the weekend. Oh, apart from you, obviously..."

"I don't do those things either, but I had to get a new spark plug for the mower, actually."

"There you go. You are a bloke. Solid and dependable. Lucy will be happy!"

"I hope so…"

"Actually, mate, I could use some advice from an old solid and dependable bloke." Ben looks up, eyebrows raised.

"Really?"

I tell Ben about my meeting with Rory earlier, and how I'm a decision away from a life-changing lump of cash, if I give up all my heritage and connections with the hotel, that has basically been ever-present in my life.

"Think of all the stuff you could do with the money." Ben's eyes mist over, probably thinking of new lawn mower blades or something.

"I don't know what I'd do, Ben. The hotel has just always been around and now it feels like I'm being kicked out. Remember the note from Aunty Joyce?"

"Yes, I was thinking that. It's up to you of course, but I would probably take the cash and start something new, maybe even sell this place?"

"I don't think I'm ready yet. I have work left to do. Joyce knew what she was doing, plus they actually liked what I did in Indianapolis." I tell Ben about Holly and her crazy ideas for hotel improvements and how to get more business. Theme nights and creative menus were only the start of it. She wanted to upgrade some rooms to be specially themed too. Sleep in Dracula's coffin or have an ocean view when thousands of miles from the water, some kind of repeating video on a large TV that can't be switched off. Bathrooms that aren't just perfunctory, but fun. I can see this improvement rolling out in more of our boring venues, bringing something new and interesting to our guests.

"Tell them to bugger off then?"

"I think so, for now at least. I don't know what their rush is anyway… Speaking of which, is Lucy pregnant?" Ben chokes on his Belgian ale, spraying Chinese food all over.

"Sorry!"

"Well, seems like you fine folks are in a bit of a rush to tie the knot?"

"If she is, it's the first I've heard of it!"

"Fair enough, why the panic to get married then?"

"Piss, or get off the pot, Keith, as my old Mum always says. I'm absolutely sure she is the one."

"Alright, if you say so, mate... So! What about Prague then?"

Chapter Twenty-Nine

B ohemia! A rhapsody in contrast between the profoundly beautiful architecture of old town, and the new town, which is plagued with casinos, strip clubs and fast food venues. Making it the European capital of stag nights for the young and feisty Brit, eager to sample some foreign pussy. There's a hedonistic, lust-fuelled tone to the groups of lads stumbling from dive to dive, an alcoholic haze over their eyes as they squint into strip club windows, like children, peering into a sweet shop.

The Prague Myatt is a stately affair, the reception is akin to the gates to heaven itself, if such a thing existed. More gold than is surely warranted, and a fountain that makes the one in Memphis look like a sprinkler. Each girl on the reception desk is a solid candidate for 'Miss Czech Republic', gorgeous and groomed. A taste of the evening to come. Ben is vastly out of his depth, barely daring to look at the palatial sites around us.

"Chin up, Ben! You'll only get to do this once in your life."

"Indeed, maybe once too many."

The hotel has a communist history, it was a general lodge for families building the city in those darker days. Converted sometime in the eighties to the current swanky hotel status. Each room, therefore, is big enough for a large family to live in. The bed is so vast a family of five could comfortably sleep in it. Corridors in the hotel are winding and complicated. One could easily get lost and wander for days before finding civilisation again.

We are to meet, as is traditional, at the bar in half an hour to plan our first expedition. The choices are as wide as they are vulgar. We could take a ride around the city in a limo full of half-naked women, lap dancing and stripping all over us. Or we could eat a sushi dinner off of a totally naked girl, lying still on the table. Perhaps get arrested by sexy cops, who lock us up in their sex dungeon? Or maybe be dominated by lesbians wielding dangerous looking truncheons and whips. Not to mention the midget jelly wrestling we could watch while sipping cocktails. The world of stag nights really is an eye-opener.

"Sorry, I was just on the phone with Lucy." Ben arrives a few minutes late. "Also I got a bit lost finding the bar!"

"Yeah, this place is ridiculous. I've been here a few times and wandered around for hours. There's always something new and odd to find in a distant corridor." I order us up a local beer, Staropramen, for a change.

"So, what do you fancy doing first?"

"I'd love to take a walk around the old town square actually, there's a lovely old clock I want to take a photo of."

"A clock?"

"Yes, a medieval astronomical clock on the side of the old town hall, called Orloj. It's more than six hundred years old!" He seems to be very excited about the clock.

"Ben, you may have misunderstood the reason for coming here to Prague." He looks at me blankly.

"This is debauchery central! There's loose women, alcoholic binging, nude sushi for fuck's sake, and you want to look at a clock?"

"Yes, I do, rather."

"Did Lucy tell you not to partake?"

"Actually no, quite the opposite. She told me to get a lap dance and remember to tip a stripper."

"That's the ticket!"

"But, that isn't really my scene!"

"This is a celebration of your last opportunity for sex before tying the knot! A traditional ceremony for the prenuptial man, a last supper before lifelong entombment in the sanctity of your dear wife's bosom. It is my duty, as best man, to make sure you get some!"

"Keith..."

"Okay, fine! We'll go look at your clock."

"Thank you. It's just undergone extensive reconstruction. Quite fascinating."

"Then we'll go watch midgets wrestle naked in jelly..."

As it turns out, the clock is rather interesting. A wonder of medieval mechanical engineering. After far too long observing and taking many photos, all of which have presumably been taken countless times before, by millions of tourists, we meander over to one of the many pavement bars and get a glass of wine.

"This is the life! Thanks again for this, Keith."

"No problem, really. Are you sure you don't want to have some fun?"

"This is fun!"

"I mean the other kind of fun, with a limo full of strippers?"

"Nah. Think of the stains on those seats!"

"True. Maybe you are right, whatever makes you happy, I suppose."

A stroll around the old town, a beer here and a pleasant meal there, and we eventually find ourselves back in the Myatt bar fairly early for what started out as a night of pleasure.

"Where are you going on Honeymoon?"

"Oh, hadn't thought of that."

"Mate, you need a Honeymoon!"

"Bit skint, to tell the truth. I've had to spruce up the basement a bit to make it woman-friendly. New bed, wardrobe, drawers, rugs, the lot."

"Oh, yeah meant to ask about that. So Lucy is going to move to England?"

"Yes, there's some visa and admin work to do, but it seems straightforward."

"She left her job and life for you and your mum's basement?"

"Yes, I suppose she did."

"Well, the least you can do is take her on honeymoon. How about Paris for a long week? Just get the train over, hotel and meals on me."

"Oh wow, I can't let you do that."

"Bullshit. It's as good as done. Consider it a wedding present."

"Cheers, Keith. You're a true friend."

"I'm going to tell Rory to stuff his offer. I've thought about it a lot, and while five million quid sounds great, I need to prove a point. I'm trying to make things better. Without me, the hotels may just go stale and eventually rot away."

"Very noble of you, mate. I'm sure Joyce would be proud of that choice."

"Thanks, yeah. I may yet regret this, but I figure if they really want the shares, the offer will remain active, and they may even up the amount."

"True."

"If I'm being honest, I have no idea how all this business crap actually works, I'm winging it here, but I have a vague plan."

"What's that?"

"The lawyer chap got me an address for StayAway. It's a residential house in High Barnett. I'm going to turn up at the door, after your wedding, and confront them!"

"Bloody hell, that sounds risky. What if it's some nutter?"

"I'll have my phone in my pocket, recording. I won't go in the house if he looks like a psycho. I mean, they may not even be there or answer the door, but it's the only lead I have. I've rung the number countless times and it just rings out. They never answer email. I bet no one has ever thought to just show up at the building before, so I'll have the element of surprise!"

"Makes sense. Good luck, mate."

"Not really sure what to do after that, but hopefully I can get to the bottom of this review nonsense at least."

A girl sits down at the bar near to us, she's so smoking hot I'm afraid the stool will catch fire from her arse. It should be illegal how gorgeous these Czech women are. I nudge Ben and nod towards her.

"Maybe she's my twin flame?"

"Ha! Good luck with that too. I can see you are going to be busy, so I'll go tell Lucy about Paris. Thanks again, mate, really appreciate everything. Good night."

"Take it easy, Ben, don't get lost on the way to the room."

I sit down next to the young lady, she's tapping away on her phone, a shot glass of Slivovice in front of her, a type of brandy made of plums, I believe.

"Never tried that, is it good?"

She looks up from her phone, a frown at first, but it switches to a smile quickly.

"Sorry, do you speak English?"

"Yes, I do, you are stag?"

"No, he's gone to bed, I'm just the best man."

"Slivovice, you want to try?" She waves over the barman, says something in Czech and produces a shot glass for me.

"Na zdraví!" And she necks the brandy. I pick up mine and follow, a pleasant burn to the throat, warming as it goes down.

"That's good stuff!" I wave the barman back and get two more for us.

"So, what's a beautiful young lady like you doing in a place like this?" I motion to the bar, so fancy that it could be entirely made of gold and it would make sense.

"I strip." She laughs and waves down at her clothes, it can't take long as there aren't many threads covering her already.

"Oh!"

"But I finish now." She smiles again and brushes her hair back. Long and dark, her nails and lips a deep blood red.

"Ah, so what does a girl do once she's finished stripping?"

"Maybe you find out?" She winks and my heart misses several beats.

"Keith Myatt, pleased to meet you…"

"Zuzana, nice to meet you too. Myatt, like the hotel?"

"Yes, exactly like the hotel. Er, how did you say it? Na zdraví"

"Na zdraví!" We neck another round and wave the barman back again. At least someone is going to get some debauching done with a stripper in Prague tonight!

Chapter Thirty

B en is a nervous wreck. I think he needs a whisky, but he won't take one, says he wants to be sober for the ceremony, strange fellow.

He stayed at my place last night, Lucy stayed in the Myatt. She arrived a couple of days ago with her parents. Her bridesmaid arrived yesterday, Courtney Appleyard, interesting woman, very quiet, fairly pretty, in an odd kind of way, but I wasn't able to engage her in conversation at our group meal last night. Perhaps she was just tired from the travel.

Lucy's Mom and Pops, Helen and Karl, are nice enough. First time they had met Ben, of course, so he was shitting it that day too. But it went well, they were happy for Lucy and Ben, and excited to get a little holiday to England out of the deal, too.

At least he's cleaned up a bit, rented a suit, trimmed the beard and hair, even clipped his fingernails and applied some deodorant. I barely recognise the lad. Certainly smells better than usual.

I'm driving the Land Rover, because Ben is too anxious to be coherent, we'll pick up his Mum and go on to the registry office which is at the town hall, a standard issue government building, but it could be a lot worse. They at least have some flowers around to stand next to for the photos. Photos that I'll be taking on my phone, because no one thought about hiring a photographer.

I thought Lucy might be upset about the vagueness of the wedding details, but she's just as laid back about it as Ben. Everything is fine as it is, she doesn't want a fuss. I can admire that, the lengths people go to for weddings is bordering on insane in some cases. There's really no need. Anyway the fun begins when we get back to the hotel. I've secured a small separate dining room for the group and plenty of wine and food. A cake too, from our wonderful pastry chef.

"Where are the rings, Ben?"

"Rings?"

"Yes, wedding rings, I'm meant to keep hold of them for safety." A look of abject horror appears on his mug. "You did get wedding rings, didn't you?"

"Ah. I knew there was something I had to do…"

"Ben!"

"Do we need them?"

"YES!"

"Shit."

"Get in the car. We've got two hours!"

I find the nearest jeweller on my phone and step on the gas. Luckily they are open and seem reasonable, but we're running out of time here, it took twenty minutes to get to the place and find a parking spot.

Inside, we are well out of our depth, there's many cabinets of rings, hundreds to choose from. Ben has never purchased jewellery before apparently.

"They seem a tad expensive."

"Yes, well, they are made of precious metals and stones. You'll have this on your finger for decades, it needs to be good quality."

"Can't we just go to Argos?"

"No, we can't go to fucking Argos!"

I call over the assistant because we simply don't have time to ponder.

"Hello, we need a couple of wedding rings, pronto please, we're in a rush!"

"Certainly, sirs, what kind of thing did you have in mind?" I look at Ben who shakes his head and shrugs. For fuck's sake. I'll have to choose something.

"White gold, I think, something quite simple."

She shows us a cabinet of rings, they look fine, but I have no idea what size Lucy is, I'll have to assume her finger is same size as mine. I pick up a set that looks decent and isn't too expensive. Ben nods vaguely in approval.

"Oh yes, these really suit you." The assistant looks at us, smiling.

"Can we get them sized, straight away please?"

"Certainly sir, should take about half an hour." She hands us a size gauge to get our measurements. "I do admire you, being so open. I suppose it's perfectly acceptable now, isn't it?"

"Sorry?"

"Gay marriage, I think it's wonderful!"

"What? No, I'm the best man!"

"Oh! I do apologise, sir, I just thought…" She trails off and hurries away to a back room.

I look at Ben who is smirking like a schoolboy. "You aren't my type, anyway!"

Just in time, we make it back to Ben's house to pick up his mother, Cynthia Hogg, she's in a permanent state of confusion and bewilderment, and has been since I first met her in our school days. I can see where Ben gets it from. She's outside, waiting on the pavement with her best frock and hat on.

"Hello Mrs Hogg, how are you?"

"Oh, it's you Keithy, good boy you are, always looked after Benedick at school."

"Indeed. Are you okay?"

"Oh yes, fine. Lovely day, isn't it? Where are we going?" Ben is back to being nervous and quiet, sat in the back of the Land Rover so his mum could sit up front. The ring distraction was a good thing, he didn't have time to think about the impending ceremony, but now we'll be there in fifteen minutes and there's no escaping it.

"The town hall, Mrs Hogg. Ben is getting married. Remember?"

"Church, I think you mean, Keithy."

"No, not a church, they wanted a non-religious ceremony."

"Oh dear."

"Quite so."

We get to the town hall bang on time. Lucy and her gang are coming in a taxi from the hotel, they should be here any second. We hurry inside, which is more complicated than it should be, because Mrs Hogg keeps saying this isn't the church, and it isn't right, back when she got married to her Albert... I stopped listening at that point. Regardless, we got to the registry office first, so that's all that matters.

Ben and I linger with the registrar, making awkward conversation, at least I do. Ben is distant in thought, it seems. Mrs Hogg sits in a third-row seat, her handbag on her lap.

"Do you think I'm making a big mistake?" Ben speaks in a hushed tone I've rarely heard from him, when the registrar walks away.

"What? No, not at all."

"It's all so sudden. I'm just worried I've made a mistake."

"Do you love her?"

"Oh yes."

"And presumably, although I can't imagine why, she loves you?"

"Apparently so."

"Where's the mistake then?"

159

"Well, my home, my life, she's given up so much and I have so little to offer. I don't want to ruin her life."

"She's aware of the circumstances?"

"Yes, but still."

"It's her choice, Ben. She knows what she's doing."

"I suppose."

"You want to know a secret?" Ben looks up from his shoegaze. "I'm actually quite jealous of what you have here."

"What? You've had more women than Holloway!"

I brush invisible dust from my shoulder and smile, "Maybe, but none of them stick around. I'm getting tired of the chase, Ben. I want to settle and have peace in my head. I started the twin flame search looking for easy lays, but I've come around, I think I really would like a wife and family and someone I connect to, like you and Lucy."

"Good lord, I never thought I'd hear those words from you, Keith Myatt!"

"Part of why I'm continuing the hotel work instead of giving it all up, I want to have achieved something solid that I can tell my children about one day. I want to make a dent in the universe. Otherwise, I'd just have money without substance and there's no valour in that."

"Good for you. Perhaps age has caught up with you!"

"Yes, I think it may have. Listen, your basement doesn't matter, your business is solid and honest, you'll find a way." Ben nods. "I just saw a taxi pull up outside. We good?"

"Yes, thanks for the pep talk."

There's no grandeur in their entrance, more of a shuffle in than a stately walk down the aisle, but still, a bride is a bride and she looks stunning in her dress, not white, not flowing and garish, but simple and elegant in pastel peach. Courtney wears a darker shade and she looks quite different to yesterday, seems the girls have had a big make-over this morning.

He left my house this morning as a single nervous man, but at the bar of the Myatt I stand with Mr and Mrs Bonham Hogg, happy, confident and much looser now the ceremony is over. Champagne flows, and even Mrs Hogg senior manages a sip at my toast to the happy couple.

I take some more phone photos in the Myatt reception, and then we walk around the grounds that Ben so neatly maintains and get some group shots. I should have borrowed a real camera from Rory as he's a fanatic, but I didn't think of it until now, plus engaging Rory is always a mentally stressful event. Finally, for our big group shot, all seven of us! I flag down a waiter and ask him to take a photo. Best man and bridesmaid too. Courtney's perfume is reminiscent of orange blossom and there's a warmth to her I like. She's shy as a church mouse, but melted a little as I put my arm around her for the photo.

I haven't really prepared a speech, I didn't think there was much point, since there's only one small table of us. But I do have some thoughts I'll share after dinner, once everyone has had a chance to get suitably merry so they'll forgive my lacklustre performance.

The food is delicious, the drink is flowing. The cake is a diorama of the hotel grounds, there's neatly trimmed grass and a stone path, with topiary swans, all in sugar icing on top of it. A shame to cut it, but it actually tastes good too.

I tap a glass to get attention. "If I may, I'd like to say a few words." All heads turn towards me, even Ben's mum who is now drunker than she's been in the last forty years. She's getting quite frisky with Karl, it seems. I may have to cut her off. "Let's get the basics out of the way, the bride is absolutely stunning, isn't she?" I pause for a cheer, "And her lovely bridesmaid, Courtney, most ravishing too." Another cheer, Courtney blushes, rather endearingly. "I've known Ben since school, on and off, and I don't think I've ever met a nicer chap. When I heard he had found his true love, honestly I was quite jealous at first. I'm lacking in that department myself. But, no one deserves this more than Ben, despite the beard. Then I met Lucy and I saw how they just seemed to fit together. There was a vast ocean between them, quite literally, but I really think they were meant to be together." Tears begin to well in Lucy's eyes. "To the happy couple!" Everyone stands and clinks glasses, I think that went well.

"First dance?" I nod to the waiter to play the music I prepared. Guns N' Roses, 'Welcome to the jungle' blares from the speakers. "Sorry, wrong track! That was for Ben's gardening seminar." A laugh from the crowd and I nod to the waiter to skip forward. A more sedate, Depeche Mode, Enjoy The Silence. Lucy pulls Ben up and they don't so much dance, as awkwardly slither around, but no one cares. I go over to Courtney and offer my hand, "Would you care to dance?" She nods and we go over to where Ben and Lucy are sliding around. She's got some great moves and makes me look like a lumbering baby elephant. Karl asked Cynthia to dance too, but she said something about her bad knees, so he makes do with Helen.

After a couple of false starts this morning, today has actually worked out wonderfully. And there's still an evening left to try to coax Courtney out of her shell, and maybe her clothes too?

Chapter Thirty-One

I'm quite sad it's all over now, I was enjoying the meals and drinks shared with the wedding party. But everyone has gone and I'm alone again. I dropped various people at airports and train stations. Ben and Lucy are off to Paris, her parents gone back to Indiana. Courtney last, her flight was this morning. My charms didn't work on her, despite my best efforts. Oh well, you win some…

Back to reality and the StayAway problem. I'm going to High Barnett on the tube after lunch. This may be a total waste of time, or a red herring, but I don't really know what else to do, so it's worth a try.

Rory has been pestering me for an answer to his offer, so I finally told him a simple 'no'. He was shocked, I think, but said he'd go back to the board with the news. I explained I had work left to do, that Aunty Joyce wanted me to be involved in operations. I don't think he cared, but I've said what I need to say. Maybe if I can uncover the StayAway nonsense today, he'll see I'm actually doing something worthwhile.

The tube ride is as annoying as usual, but I am delivered

reasonably safely to the target destination. The house is just a short walk away, down a quiet street. I check my phone again for the address, number forty-two. It looks like all the others, curtains are open and a light on. There's someone home at least. I set my phone in my coat pocket, poking out of the top and record video. In case something dreadful happens. Who knows what this is all about, StayAway could be Russian mafia for all I know.

I ring the bell and wait. It opens, eventually and my jaw drops open, dumbfounded.

"You took your bloody time! Close your mouth, you'll catch a fly."

I try and say something, but my mouth is somehow disconnected from my brain. It takes several seconds before I can pull myself together.

"Scarlett!"

"Charlotte, actually. You'd better come in. Don't want the neighbours twitching their curtains." She disappears into the house and, still unable to adequately communicate, I follow.

I find her in the kitchen at the back of the house, she pops the kettle on and gets two mugs out of a cupboard. "Tea?"

"Charlotte? What the fucking fuck is going on?"

"Shh, keep your voice down, Mum is upstairs asleep."

"Sorry. Yes, tea would be good."

"Bit slow, aren't you? I thought you'd never come."

"But, what? How? What! Charlotte?"

"Sit down, drink this." She hands me a steaming mug of tea and points to the kitchen table. I do as I'm told, zombie-like. I suddenly remember the phone video recording in my pocket, seems silly now, so I take it out and stop it, I save it though, because I may need to reality check this in the future in case I'm just dreaming or in a coma.

. . .

"Welcome to the international office of StayAway dot com, Keith Myatt! You're our first visitor."

"You know my real name?"

"I know all kinds of things," she smiles, and her angelic face somehow makes all this confusion seem okay. "Sid Thole! Come on, how stupid do you think I am?"

"I thought that was a pretty cool pseudonym, no one else ever questioned it. Thole is an anagram of…"

She nods, laughing. "Yes, I got it. Did you dream it up in Australia?" She sniggers.

"Yes, I did actually! Well, what about you? Scarlett Johansson, Winona Ryder, Cristina Ricci?"

"Fun, isn't it? Playing someone else for a while."

"I suppose so. Look, are you going to tell me what the bloody hell is going on?"

"All in good time. Don't you want to discuss something about reviews?"

"Erm, yes actually. What's going on with my reviews in Kansas?"

"I could ask you the same thing. One hundred five star reviews in two days? Are you having a laugh? No one would ever believe that!"

"One hundred and one. It was an experiment to try and flush out the stealth reviewer."

"The what?"

"We heard that StayAway send someone to validate reviews themselves. I wanted to meet that person and ask what they were up to."

"Ah, well, you did meet that person."

"Yes, I see that now. But I had no idea it was you."

"That's why it's a stealth review, Keith!"

"How do you know my name, anyway?"

"You spammed my inbox from both Sid Thole's and your own email addresses."

"Yes, I was trying to get to the bottom of things."

"Well, you sent them one after the other, both from the same IP address and computer. It isn't rocket science to figure out that you are the same person."

"I didn't know you were a techie."

"There's lots of things you don't know, Keith..."

"Please, do tell. Oh, I have something of yours here, by the way." She looks puzzled as I pull out my wallet, "You left this in Indiana."

"My earring! I was wondering where that went. Thank you."

"Welcome."

"You've had this in your wallet all this time?"

"Oh, well, yes. I suppose so. It was a reminder, you know..."

"Very sweet of you. Shall we move this meeting to the local hostelry?"

"That's the most sensible thing you've said so far!"

On the walk to the pub, she tells me the history of StayAway. It started as a college project, she was studying digital marketing and technology. She learned web design and server principals, and over the course of a year, built StayAway, just for her exam at the end of the course, but the tutors told her it was so good she should actually launch it as a real service. So she did, and it took off like a 747 leaving a runway. She was having a wonderful life, travelling around to all the hotels that advertised with her, to validate the reviews herself, she runs the whole thing alone and always has. The servers are all in the cloud, so the house in High Barnett is nothing to do with the site, just where she and her mother live.

"I suppose you want a Southern Comfort?" I roll my eyes at her.

"Yes, please," her angelic smile returns as we take a seat at the almost empty bar.

"So why all the bad reviews? The reason I was chasing it up in the first place was that our hotels were getting shitty reviews more than usual, only from your site."

"I found that people believe a lower rated review more than they do a five-star. They look at a five star review and assume it's a fake, even when it's genuine. They click on it less. But lower it a notch, and I get far more clicks. I adjust the text sometimes too, when the review is too gushy and unbelievable."

"Yes, that's what you did to my review in Indianapolis!"

"Trust me, no one would have believed your review. My version was much more appropriate."

"So there's no algorithm doing it?"

"Oh there is, the servers decide what I need to review manually, but most of the work is done by the machines in the cloud. I couldn't manually check all the thousands of reviews I get daily all over the world. As it is I'm inundated and spend most of my life on my phone." She motions to her black phone on the bar that has been flashing and buzzing frequently. She's ignoring it. "To be honest, I am thinking of packing it in, I'm tired of flying around the world constantly, staying in hotels all over the place. Some of them aren't quite as nice as your Myatt's you know!"

"Thank you, and thank you for explaining. I feel like a weight has been taken off my shoulders. My brother was trying to push me out of the company over these reviews!"

"Oops, sorry about that. Tell you what, let's just delete all those one hundred and one fake reviews for Kansas and leave it at that."

"Thank you, Charlotte, that would be wonderful."

"Call me Lottie, my friends do." She smiles again. Any anger I had when I made this journey earlier is completely gone now, this woman has a knack for melting my heart somehow. How does she do it? She taps away at her phone for a few minutes while I order more drinks.

"All gone." She shows me the new average star rating for Kansas City Myatt, a nice four, instead of the two we had this morning.

"Thank you again, Lottie. Oh hang on, your full name is Charlotte Webbe?" I suddenly remember the name on the StayAway domain registration detail.

"Yes. Now can you see why I use a fake name?" She rolls her eyes but smiles too.

"One more question, for now."

"Fire away."

"Why did you leave me?"

"I had to go to the next city, you were asleep, didn't think it was worth waking you up. This is what I do; shag random handsome guys and move on, sometimes I see them again, but usually not." She shrugs. I think about all the girls I've done the same exact thing to and I have no come back. I'm a dick, she's a female dick, if such a thing exists!

"Why the cryptic message then, I assume that was you on my last review from Kansas?"

"A girl can sometimes dream, can't she?"

"What? Why didn't you just reply to me if you wanted to see me?"

"Where's the sport in that?" Oh my god, this girl is worse than me.

We walk a short distance to a gastropub for some dinner, as this meeting has gone on longer than I ever expected, but also going much better than I thought it would this morning. Delicious burgers wash down nicely with local ale, and Lottie tells me more about her life. She's completely paid off her mother's mortgage with her earnings from StayAway, and she's saving now for a place of her own. She's burned out from the travel, like myself, and she's seriously considering selling the entire business to a bigger company, and finding something more local to do with the rest of her life. Her mother, house ridden, for the most part, is looked after by a visiting nurse three times every day, again all paid for by the money she gets from StayAway. Her little review site that has been such a thorn in my side has been her entire means of living for years now. Sometimes we are so blinded by the part of the mountain we can see, that we forget that there's a completely different side just around the corner.

"How far is your house from here?"

"About an hour and a half on the tube, give or take."

"We better go then, before it gets too late."

"Oh, okay. You want to come back to mine?"

"Don't want to disturb Mum, and I don't want to have to be quiet."

I laugh, she certainly wasn't quiet last time.

"Fair enough. Do me a favour though?"

"What's that?"

"Don't vanish in the morning."

"I'll see what I can do…"

Chapter Thirty-Two

B en and Lucy are back today from Paris. Had a wonderful
time, they said. I'm picking them up at the station and then
Lottie is coming back for a dinner party at my house. I can't
believe I'm even thinking these words let alone actually carrying
out such a domesticated normal-people thing. Ben and Lucy
want to meet the girl who has put a dent in my universe.

Lottie still existed next to me when I woke up that first
morning at my house, I was truly thankful as my paranoia told
me she would be gone, without trace once more, which is
ridiculous now I know where she lives, but the fuel of alcohol
and fear are hard to fight, half asleep.

I shouldn't have worried, she's been here almost every day
this week. She quite likes my little country abode, but reckons it
could do with some modernisation. She loves the cats, too.

I went shopping at the supermarket in the Land Rover and
purchased all the ingredients for a dinner for four, including a
copious quantity of wine and a bottle of Southern Comfort,
much against my better judgement to have that vile liquor in my
house, but what can you do. I'm cooking spaghetti, with the help
of everyone, probably. Because I haven't cooked anything other
than a fried breakfast for a very long time. Luckily Aunty Joyce

was a wonderful cook and the kitchen is expensively well equipped.

I unload the food and then get back on the road to go get the happy couple from the station. Can't wait to hear how they got on in Paris.

"Bonjour Monsieur!" Wonderful, Ben has become a polyglot in a week. I roll my eyes. His accent sounds like a very bad impression of Rene Artois from the 80s sitcom 'Allo 'Allo.

"Taxi à la maison s'il vous plaît"

I make a disgusted face. "Enough! I take it you had fun, then?"

"Ah oui monsieur!" Lucy is giggling, Ben is lapping it up.

I drive them back to my house, still excited from their adventure, they tell me about the Louvre and the Eiffel Tower as if I've never seen these things myself. I indulge them, because that's what friends do.

I'm happy for them, of course, but I'm a tad distracted with the thoughts of actually hosting a party. I suppose I'm so used to having the hotel staff available to prepare and clean, that the thought of doing everything myself is a little scary. What if I poison everyone? Will Ben and Lucy get on with Lottie? Is it too early to be introducing Lottie to my friends, what does that say about the nature of a relationship? Am I in a relationship, or is this just a protracted one night stand? Lottie did say it sounded like fun and she'd be here, so I suppose I shouldn't overthink it…

I hand the keys of the Land Rover to Ben and hop out at home. He can drive himself and Lucy to his basement where he can torture her with his bad French, and then they'll come back later for booze and grub.

I spend the rest of the afternoon dragging in wood and coal, locating plates and dishes, reading recipes and making a music playlist on my phone. It'll be fine!

———

"It's quite a trek, out here to the country." Lottie arrives ungracefully in the back of an Uber.

"Hardly the country, we're on the tube!"

"Barely. Anyway, what's wrong with this picture?" She holds up her hand, as if cradling a glass. I know this gesture, and with a nod, I furnish the lady with wine.

"How's mum?"

"Good today. Nurse said her legs are better, she should be dancing a jig by the end of the week."

"I certainly hope you video that event."

"Indeed." We move into the kitchen, "Hey I thought you were cooking?"

"Yes, I am."

"Where's the food then?"

"In the fridge."

"Keith, cooking typically requires heat and pots and pans and things. You can't cook in the fridge."

"I know, I haven't started yet."

"Finger out, son, I'm starving!"

"To be honest, I don't really know where to start."

"Have you got a recipe?"

"Yes, but it's vague. I tried following it step by step and I must have misread somewhere, because I somehow got my dick caught in the ceiling fan."

"Ouch, that sounds painful."

"You don't want to know."

"Let's have a look then." I unzip my fly, "No not at that! At the recipe!"

"Oh, well, you should have said."

Lottie reads the recipe on my iPad and pulls out ingredients from the fridge, then hunts through drawers for knives and cutting boards, pans and strainers. I think she's better suited at this than I, so I pour her more wine and put on some music while she chops and stirs. It's quite a pleasant sight, to see this beautiful woman working her magic in my kitchen. I could very well get used to this.

The familiar crunch of gravel outside announces the arrival of Ben and Lucy, brandishing a sedate quantity of ale in supermarket bags. I suspect that Lucy has already tamed the beer monster, because Ben would normally bring far more bottles.

"Ben, Lucy, this is Lottie." Everyone floods into the kitchen, following the good smells of cooking.

"Pleased to meet you, Lottie." Lucy shakes her hand and then they kiss cheeks. The French hasn't worn off yet, then.

"Have we met before?" Ben looks puzzled at Lottie, "I'd swear I've met you before?"

"What?"

"Yes, didn't you work at the Myatt one summer?" Lottie blushes a little, then nods.

"Toaster Girl!"

"What?" I turn to Lottie for an explanation.

"I forgot, it was about eight or nine years ago, I suppose. I was a teenager, got a summer waitress job on some scheme, they sent me out here to the sticks."

I'm incredulous. She worked in my hotel and I had to travel the world to find her!

"Toaster Girl?"

Ben pipes up, "One of the toasters in the dining room caught on fire at breakfast one morning. Lottie here picked it up without a thought, blazing aflame, and casually carried it through the dining room, smoke billowing from it, to the garden, not a care in the world. She was a legend!"

"Toaster Girl!" I once again gape open-mouthed at Lottie, a legend on my doorstep and I never knew her. Tonight is going to be fun.

. . .

Dinner, that I didn't cook, is excellent. Lottie delved in the pantry and found extra ingredients to spice things up, even made a wonderful garlic butter to dip our breadsticks in.

Ben and Lucy tell us about Paris some more. Lottie tells us all about the worst hotels she's stayed in all over the world. I am quite shocked at how bad some places are, makes me quite appreciative of our prestigious Myatt brand. I had no idea that bed bugs and curfews could possibly be a feature of a lodging for a night. The evening washes down wonderfully with wine and ale, we didn't even touch the SoCo bottle. By the time we retire, my face actually aches from smiling so much. We must do this more often.

"Where are you going next?" Coffee in bed with Lottie the morning after, is one of those rare moments you think you'll only ever witness in a TV advert or romantic movie. Everything too perfect and convenient, but here I am, living in the moment, enjoying the peace, warmth and her playful caresses. I nearly spilt hot coffee on sensitive parts, but all is well, for now.

"I hadn't thought. I sort of ran out of plans, after I confronted StayAway!"

"Confronted! What were you going to do to me?"

"I know what I'll do to you after this coffee." She smiles, and squeezes and I nearly spill the mug again.

"What about you?"

"Europe for a while, I'm tired of America."

"That's a good idea. Where first?"

"Dublin, then north to Belfast, and then even more north to Reykjavik."

"Oh, that's interesting. We have hotels in all those places!"

"I know. They are on my list." She pouts for a moment. "Come with me?"

I look her in the eyes, she's sincere and inviting. "You know, I think I will." Her angelic smile surfaces again and I would stay in this perfect moment forever, "Lottie, this may sound a bit crazy, but, do you know what a twin flame is?" I blurt it out, I probably shouldn't have, but it felt right.

"A what? Something on your fancy gas cooker, maybe? For woks?"

"No, no, nothing to do with cookers at all. A soul mate type of thing. A single soul, split in two, hosted in two people who are meant to be together and one again."

She looks at me and blinks, warily, "Are you taking the piss?"

"Not at all!" I explain the twin flame phenomena as I've come to understand it, omitting my plans to use it to bed as many women as possible. She laughs and scoffs in equal measure throughout.

"Keith Myatt, that's the stupidest thing I've ever heard, and I've heard some pretty stupid stuff."

"A lot of people believe it, I thought it was weird at first too. There's online forums and things dedicated to it. Look it up!"

"Think I'll give that a miss, if you don't mind. Now, you were saying you would do something after you finished your coffee? I haven't got all day you know!"

Chapter Thirty-Three

S ex and travel. Things in life that ought to be enjoyable, but perhaps not when done at the same time. Not literally, of course, unless you happen to be mile high, and honestly, I've tried that, and it wasn't that great. Who knows where that desperately howling sucking drain leads to?

Travel can be tiresome. It can wear thin tempers and break down the barriers of a fledgeling relationship. Stretch the fibres of understanding and patience to their very limits.

We had our first fight in Dublin, not in the Myatt, however, but in the cheaper hotels in the city after the first two nights of luxury. I complain too much, she said. I had cause to, the lift stank like a pigeon had died in it. She said that was too specific and ridiculous, but I swear I saw a feather. The underground car park was like a scene from a gangster movie and they charged extra for it. The rooms all perfunctory, too cramped. A tiny ironing board shoved into a cupboard, a coffee machine so fiddly that using it is enough to snap parts off. I may be a whiny overprivileged arsehole, but I know when something is just badly designed.

Anyway, then we moved a little out of town to a newer hotel which was an improvement, not a vast one, but something. All the while, Lottie churned away at her phone, updating reviews, validating complaints, posting and deleting, making things run smoothly on her site.

I'm claiming this trip as research into how the other side live. It's been years since I stayed anywhere but our sumptuous rooms, so this has been an expedition into the unknown. Certainly a textbook journey on what not to do in the hospitality industry.

The drive north to Belfast was short and sweet, until we stopped for a rest and got separated and lost in the service station. I wandered around the car park trying to find the car for twenty minutes before realising I came out of the wrong exit and the car was on the other side of the building. Lottie was caught between anger and hilarity at my predicament, because I had the car key and she was standing in the rain.

Belfast itself, however, is a pleasant enough city. The architecture both similar and different to Dublin, which itself occasionally mocks and mimics London. But on the darker side, Belfast has the added sting of the occasional mural from days gone by, warning stray travellers not to venture into realms unknown. Somewhat ominous to see a thirty foot terrorist mural immediately behind one of the hotels Lottie is tasked to evaluate.

Still, I have gained some insight into her process. Her cloud-based servers capture all the reviews people leave and she has some machine learning, artificial intelligence, database filtering algorithms detecting what they assume are erroneous reviews. Either very good, very bad, or too similar to others. Those are fed to her phone via a custom app where she applies her own Lottie method and decides if there's a need to go see for herself. She batches them up, makes mini-tours of similar hotels in the region and then generates some new fake names, hence this northern climb from Dublin to Reykjavik. Honestly, I think she uses a pseudonym just because she thinks it's cool. This time we are Mr and Mrs Smith. Original, I know.

Over six nights, we stayed in four hotels in Belfast, one being a Myatt, the others, not. Guess which I preferred? But I chose not to mention all the things I found wrong, because doing so seems to annoy Lottie. Compromise, that's what relationships are about.

In most of her cases, the reviews she flagged as possibly false were actually factual. There really was a stink of drains in the entire west side of the hotel, and you really could feel the thump of the disco four floors up in another. The odd occasion though, she found a review that was hard to prove one way or another, a receptionist was rude about the items on the bill - one star. The waiter made a face at our wine choice - two stars. She decided to delete those entirely, because what use is that information to a weary traveller? Fuck all.

Reykjavik is quite a different experience though, fairly dark at this time of year, but the Myatt, rising proud on a hill overlooking the city, is a wonderful place. Entirely powered by geothermal energy. The rooms are fresh and vibrant, the view is picturesque, and vivid coloured buildings dot the landscape. I strayed from my Belgian ale and indulged in some local brews. Lottie stuck with her SoCo and we forgot the troubles from Ireland. Travelled weary as we had to the cusp of the Arctic circle, where the language is hard to fit on a European tongue, where the Sun has a love/hate relationship with the land, and barely bothers to shine at this time of year, nothing is left but the sex.

The sex... Maybe it was the healing salts of the hot spring, maybe the crisply clean glacial air, or the volcanic energy coursing through our veins, perhaps the ridiculously good fresh fish dinner? But something was different in Iceland. She tore me from my comfort zone, introducing equipment from her suitcase; cuffs, plugs, rings. I haven't ever dallied in these lewd pleasures before, usually not appropriate on a first date to ask a girl to plug up. But now we are more open, safe and comfortable, I think I've found her kinks. Handy thing that there was an ice machine close to the room.

The land here is relatively new, birthing from the ocean floor, even now continuing to expand from the mother earth, procreating. Perhaps that new life subliminally gave us a massive horn? Whatever it was, I will never forget that night. My dick and arse won't either.

Back home and Lottie has gone to her mother's house for a few days, and consequently there's a gap in my consciousness. I've adjusted my routine to have her as part of my life, and now she's not ever-present, it seems strange. Like something is missing.

I miss her, I suppose, that has to be the conclusion. I don't think I've ever had a woman to miss, other than Aunty Joyce and mother. So this is new for me. I still sometimes think about Bella, but this is different.

I sent Lottie a text message. Maybe a tad ill-conceived, but I hit send before I could ponder it any more.

'Move in with me?'

It sounded epic, in my head, but perhaps the reality isn't so dramatic. I mean, there are already panty liners in my bathroom and odd laundry in my washing machine. This would be a small step for woman, but a giant leap for relationship kind... She didn't reply, and I went to bed alone, with a nagging doubt, perhaps I shouldn't have been so forward, had I scared her away?

. . .

I need not have worried, because the morning brought an Uber to my door, carrying Lottie, two large suitcases and several small bags.

"We'll need to paint the bedroom, because I can't stand that purple, but here I am!" She dumps her bags at the door and stands among her belongings, flushed cheeks and windswept hair, a perfect mess. I run to her embrace, lifting her off the ground, burying my head in her bosom, breathing her essence, her scent. Home just became even more homely.

"There's more where this came from, but this will do for now."

"Quite so. Well, Miss Webbe, make yourself at home!"

I set about burning trees in the living room, Lottie busies herself with furniture and rearrangements. Luckily for her, I don't actually have much of my own stuff, having lived a nomadic life for so long. I'm whittled down to the core basics, so my wardrobe usage is minimal. Handy, because in those two bags, Lottie somehow fit a truckload of clothes. They must be bigger on the inside, tardis like. There's no other rational reason that can explain the vast spread of dresses, tops, skirts, underwear, other things I dare not guess, that are now laid out across every flat surface in the borough.

I retreat to the living room, beer in one hand, TV remote in the other, like any normal man would in these circumstances.

I wonder if Ben wants to go to the pub?

Chapter Thirty-Four

I've spent a good deal of time pondering the annual shareholder meeting, sorry, I mean Christmas dinner tomorrow, and if I should bring a 'plus one' this time. I never have before, but things are different now, I appear to have a girlfriend. She's remained a part of my life for almost two months, which is almost two months longer than most other women do.

She's been away on another hotel jaunt in America for the last week, but she's due back today, so I'm going into London to buy her present. Something grand and expensive. Perhaps if the mood takes me, something engaging. I haven't told anyone in the family about her yet, but she's presentable, eligible, smart and funny. There should be no problem. In fact I'm keen to show her off.

On the tube into Covent Garden, to the fanciest jeweller I could find online, with no real plan as to what I'll get, there's a tickle in the back of my head that wants it to be an engagement ring. Ben and Lucy are happy, getting on with their lives, building the gardening business even though Lucy can't officially work in the state yet because of the visa application.

They are doing well, Ben is settled and safe. I want that

feeling. So when I get to the jeweller and am confronted with the endless cabinets of rings, I give in to the desire for security and drop an obscenely ridiculous amount of money on a tiny fragment of pure cut diamond, set in simple but elegant platinum.

As the taxi from the tube station crunches down my driveway to my house, with half a decent man's annual salary in my pocket in the form of metal and stone, I have an uneasy feeling of dread. Have I made a massive mistake? Can I ask the driver to turn around, go back into the city and return it, never speak of it, just carry on as normal? The moment passes, I see Lottie's angelic face in my mind's eye, hear her laugh and joke, feel her soft lips as we kiss. Fuck me, relationships are complicated.

She may be back already, so I make sure my pocket is smoothed flat and holler out for her as I go in the door, but all I find are cats crying for food. There's something off though, I can't quite place it. I flick on a light.

On the kitchen table there's a gift-wrapped box, a present! She's back? A note on top says 'don't wait for tomorrow' in Lottie's handwriting. How exciting! Something mischievous for tonight, perhaps? I open the box, tearing away the paper, but inside is quite a different set of emotions.

A key. I think Lottie's house key. A folded up note and the tiny bottle of Southern Comfort we took from the mini-bar in Reykjavik.

★★★★☆ *[4 out of 5 stars]*
    Keith Myatt, you are wonderful, kind and generous, but I'm

sorry, I can't do this. Please don't contact me. It's hard enough, I just can't. Love, Lottie.

P.S. StayAway will be kind to Myatt Hotels.

No, this must be a joke? I run to the bedroom. The wardrobe - empty. To the drawers - all cleaned out. Her nightstand phone chargers - both gone.

All the blood drains out of my body, replaced with adrenaline, then pure, crushing, gut-wrenching misery, flooding every cell in my body, reducing me to an empty sack of water, quivering on the bed, clutching her pillow, the scent of her hair lingering.

Boxing day, and dozens of missed calls and texts from family, asking where I am, when am I arriving for Christmas dinner? Then, am I alive, am I okay? I watched the phone light up in my hand all day yesterday, waiting for Lottie to call or message, to tell me it was all an elaborate joke, but she never did. My entire body was numb, disconnected from reality. I knew I should answer, reply that I am indeed alive, and most certainly not okay, but the brain signals never reached my muscles. I couldn't move from the bed, barely stumbling to the bathroom to piss, feeding the cats when they became obnoxious, retiring to the darkness of the bedroom we decorated together not three weeks ago, choosing paint and curtains, a new rug to match.

A message from Ben - 'Rory asked me to check on you, is everything okay?'

All I can manage in return is a simple - 'she's gone'

Half an hour later, Ben's Land Rover rolls down the driveway and he bounds up to the door, a bottle of single malt whisky in his hand. I open the door and then slump back down on the couch, staring at the TV even though it's switched off.

"What happened? Are you okay?"

I point to the note on the coffee table and Ben picks it up, reads it and looks down at me.

"Fuck. Sorry, mate."

I point to the ring box, also on the table, he picks it up and opens it.

"Is that? Wow, that looks expensive."

I nod.

Ben goes off to the kitchen, returns with two glasses, fills them with whiskey, and puts one in my hand.

"When did this happen?"

"Christmas Eve. I just got back with the ring and found the note."

"Did she say why?"

"All I have is the note, I haven't asked. I've typed and deleted six hundred text messages, but I didn't send any."

"I thought things were going great?"

"Me too."

"You look terrible, have you eaten?"

"No, not since…"

"Come back to ours, we have some ham left, Lucy is an excellent cook. I'll reply to Rory that you stayed with us, got drunk and didn't see your phone."

"Thanks, mate."

I think I'm at the stage of anger, now. How could she do this to me? Why? I almost proposed to her! What was I thinking? I get up to go with Ben for some grub, but not before necking the whiskey and bringing the bottle.

The throb of hangover pain, combined with a stiff neck from

sleeping on Ben's couch, wakes me into the dull reality and pitch blackness of a windowless basement living room. My stomach retches and I fumble for my phone to find the light switch and toilet. But there's a message on it, from Holly in Indianapolis, so I open it up, despite the bowling ball in my stomach and the desert in my mouth.

'We're having a Harry Potter theme party for New Year! Be my Snape?'

The door opens and Ben flicks on the light, my guts react to the sudden change by violently ejecting last night's dinner. I run to the bathroom, only just making it to the porcelain portal to hell in time.

"Was it something I said?" Ben laughs as I come back, feeling a little better now.

"Sorry."

"How are you feeling?"

"Going to Indiana, does Lucy want anything?" I show Ben my phone and the text from Holly.

"Back on the horse, eh?"

"Yeah. Fuck it."

Part of me is glad for the distraction, part of me still mourns the loss of Lottie. But sitting around moping won't do me any good, I've done enough of it, I'm sick of the apathetic blanket that mourning drapes over me.

I don't know why she left me, my brain has pondered on ten thousand possible reasons, but none seem to make any sense, none give me closure or solace, so all I can do is move on. I should return the ring though. But making that journey can certainly wait a while. I'm sure there's a return policy, especially as it didn't even leave the box.

. . .

At least the whole StayAway problem is solved, so I message Rory once I'm back home, cleaned up and packing my usual bag for the trip.

'StayAway review problems are a thing of the past. I'm going to Indiana to see how my protégé is doing with hotel improvements.'

Chapter Thirty-Five

I thought I should do some research into my role, so on the plane, I watched three of the Harry Potter movies on my iPad. It was a chore, to be honest, I'm not sure what all the fuss is about. Still, Severus Snape is a wonderfully cynical character and I think he fits my mood precisely at the moment. A wig, a wand and a cape from a party shop and I'm all set for the evenings' entertainment.

I meet Holly in the bar of the Myatt, Indianapolis, where I last left her. She's the same bubbly, enthusiastic girl, barely containing herself. "Thanks for coming!" She gushes and squeezes me hard.

"How could I resist?" I smile a maleficent grin, my Snape face, she makes a gurgling noise and actually bounces up and down.

"Enjoying the job?"

"I love it! Thank you so much!"

"My pleasure, I hear you are doing wonders?"

Holly shows me all the things she's achieved in the short time she's been working here. The restaurant menu is far better now, a taste of the exotic mixed in with the staples. A change of decor too, from dark and dull to bright and open. A subtle corn coloured theme running through the menu and tablecloths. Breakfast now runs until lunchtime for late risers, and there's a happy hour at the bar, each night a different cocktail special. Blue corn chips instead of nuts in the complimentary snack bowls. She has plenty more to do, but she's definitely winning. All the staff we encounter on our quick tour seem to love her. This was a total success! The manager should be worried for his job, honestly.

Holly will be dressed as a schoolgirl for this evening's entertainment, and I as a schoolmaster. What could possibly go wrong? Before the Lottie situation, I may have paused at this setup, a dangerous trap for sure. But now, I am disillusioned, jaded, heartbroken, I suppose. On the rebound? Bouncing back into my self? The one-night-stand-king can't be heartbroken, he is disconnected, he expects to never see them again, mutually beneficial gratification, some tickles sending pulses to the brain, that's all it is. Love: just a word we use for a chemical addiction. Soulmate: just another term for someone who'll inevitably fuck you over.

"Are you looking forward to midnight?" Holly and I sample the new dinner menu at the hotel, it really is impressive.

"Indeed, it should be interesting."

"You okay? You seem a bit distant."

"Sorry, some life stuff going on in my head. I'm looking forward to seeing what you'll do next. I'm really very impressed with what you've achieved here so quickly. So is head-office, actually, the big boss told me himself."

"Wow, thank you! I'm quite proud of it!" I smile, and Holly seems sated.

The truth is, I'm suddenly not looking forward to socialising and forcing a smile all evening. I'd prefer to go to the room and run a hot bath and soak away the pain, if it were possible. No matter how I try to convince myself otherwise, I miss Lottie. Holly is talking away about the evening events, her hotel plans mingled in. The words hit my ears but don't permeate my brain. I smile and nod, she is animated, enthusiastic, and don't forget, very pretty. I need a lot of alcohol.

There's a fine balance when drowning one's sorrows. A knife edge between forgotten problems and happily tipsy, then one more baby step to wailing depression, actual tears, regret and a host of other negative emotions, black like killer whales, taking turns to swim to the surface and vent their blow holes all over the gathered audience. A baby step into an abyss. Where I lie now, staring up at the ceiling of my room, clothed, alone and smelling like a changing room jock strap. Shit.

Happy new year...

Standing in the shower, slowly remembering the events of the night before, I think it might be time for a New Year's resolution, no more twin flames, no more binge drinking. These things just bring trouble.

Focus on the work. There are many more hotels that are boring and sedate. I'm sure there are people like Holly elsewhere who can bring a bit of magic to their work. This gives me an idea for some good and distracting tasks. Something to keep me occupied, to fade away the bile and grief, and prove myself to Rory at the same time. The temptation to take the share deal is strong now, I could just vanish, never interact with the humans unless absolutely necessary, live out my life as a hermit. But I know that won't work. I'm addicted to the lust and passion. I need a woman in my life, or several, perhaps a dozen.

I wander down to breakfast. All the seasonal festivities have sailed past me this year. I've just had an unhappy love affair, so I don't see why anyone else should have a good time. I didn't really think too much about it being New Year's day and a public holiday. Hotels stay open every day regardless.

"Happy New Year!" Holly is ever bouncy and happy, a quality I both admire and despise. I'm not a morning person, especially with a level nine hangover. "Are you feeling any better, now?"

I manage a tepid smile, "Yes, thank you, Holly. Happy New Year to you, too. I hope I wasn't too embarrassing last night?"

"Not at all, it was funny!"

I presume she means when I stood on the bar, waving my wand and screaming 'Expelliarmus' at anyone who looked at me. I suppose it was pretty funny, come to think of it. That and the cape flapping. I should wear a cape more often. Suits me, I think.

Holly sits down to join me for breakfast. "So, who's Lottie?"

Oh, shit, what did I say? "Er, someone who isn't around anymore." This could be awkward, "Sorry, I don't remember mentioning her?"

"You ordered a round of Southern Comforts for everyone at the bar, and toasted - 'To Lottie, may her camels be forever free of fleas.'" She sniggers, "Camels?"

"Oh, I don't remember that at all, I'm afraid! For future reference, that vile drink doesn't agree with me. If I should ever order it again, please stop me!"

"Noted! Does she have camels?"

"No, not that I know of, anyway."

"You seemed very emotional, just hope you are okay?"

Time to change the subject, I think. "Yes, I made a resolution, this morning. No more getting drunk. I have work to do. I want to improve other hotels in the way you have here, I'm going to hire a Holly for every one of our boring hotels and spice things up! I think I'll need your help, coordinating things, if you don't mind?"

"Oh wow! Clones! An excellent idea. Do you need a sample of my DNA?" She laughs.

"That would be handy, but I think I'll have to use the humans already available, for speed and cost reasons, you understand."

"Of course, does this mean a new job title?"

"Hmm, yes, why not. Artistic marketing manager? How does that sound?"

"Wonderful!"

"Done."

Back in my room, I start a list of all the boring, dull hotels we have in America. There's quite a few, so I'll need to make a plan and a priority list. Looking at the map I notice Memphis, and my mind wanders to Bella, whom I haven't really talked to for a while now. I should go check in on her, make sure all is well with her and Daisy and the LARP lad.

Chapter Thirty-Six

I toyed with the idea of showing up unannounced, a surprise visit from Uncle Keith. But that seemed a bit pointless, they may have had plans or something and be elsewhere, so I messaged Bella and she was happy to hear from me, Danny is working all over the holidays, she said, so she's delighted for some company.

The journey from Indianapolis to Memphis becoming too familiar now. The difference this time is there's no Bella waiting in the room for me, semi-naked, tragically beautiful and innocent, those eyes that would melt the heart of an ice-man. She's gone back to her apartment and life, hopefully significantly safer now that Danny is watching out for her and the ex-boyfriend is locked up behind bars.

Danny is still working at the Myatt, upgraded position. Now assistant restaurant manager. Good for him. I didn't have any influence in that promotion.

Bella and Daisy are coming to meet me soon, so I shower and change before they arrive. A quick tour of the airport stores and I have a few silly presents for Daisy as a late Christmas gift, and another set of jewellery for Bella. Which reminds me, the horribly expensive engagement ring, at home on my nightstand. I forgot to take it back. Shit.

A knock on my door, Bella and Daisy no doubt, I'm avoiding the usual bar meeting, trying to stick to my resolution of staying sober, avoiding dangerous situations, staying out of trouble. Why am I here in Memphis then? I don't really know, to be honest. Bella draws me back, even though things are different now. Aside from Ben, I think she's the closest friend I have, now.

"Keith!" Bella jumps on me, her arms around my neck, legs around my waist, a dozen kisses planted on my forehead. Daisy gurgles from her buggy, good as gold as usual, but much bigger than I last saw her. A healthy glow to her cheeks. Bella always cheers me up.

"A very merry, happy New Christmas Year, Bella!"

She laughs, "And a wonderful New Year to you, too, Mister Keith." She's looking lovely, warmer clothes, her hair grown out a little.

"Are you hungry? I haven't eaten since Indiana."

"Sure, I can always eat." She grins, and pats her tummy, but there isn't an ounce of fat on her whole body. I should know. We go down to the restaurant, wait to be seated by Danny, who greets us in his LARP persona.

"Well met, Lord Myatt! A table for thee and the fine maiden?" Good lord.

"Indeed. How are you, Danny?"

"Doing well, Sir. I'll be running this place soon enough." He winks, but I have a feeling he may be right. The lad has ambition and confidence seeping from him. This hotel isn't on my list of boring hotels that need an 'Artistic marketing manager' installed. The Memphis Myatt has its own style and history, a steady stream of happy customers willing to pay far more than they really should for bed and board. But I make a mental note to talk to the lad about the upgrades I'm instigating.

———

Back in my room with Bella and Daisy, I give them their gifts, accompanied by the usual 'you shouldn't have' and 'oh my god' followed by a shower of hugs and kisses. I know I don't need to keep buying these girls gifts, but it makes me happy to do it. I'm pleasing myself really.

Seeing Bella wear her new necklace reminds me of the last time she put something on for me, a dangling jewel between her breasts, enticing me and kindling a fire in my loins. But this time a sadness overwhelms me, a sudden need to vent all my troubles. I break down, spill my guts, tell Bella everything that has happened since Kansas and our review experiment, about Ben and Lucy getting married, Ben happier than I've ever seen him, and how I still feel pangs of jealousy at his life. About Lottie and her StayAway site, how she was my girlfriend and moved into my house. We decorated, bought things together, had dinner parties like real adults. I was happy, for a while. Then the Christmas gift I got for her, a ring worth far too much that I was planning to propose with, and her gift to me, a big pile of stinking shit and emotions dumped from a great height, disguised in a seasonally wrapped box.

Bella doesn't talk, doesn't judge. She just holds me, close, her breath warm on my neck as I keep talking, explaining how I can't stop thinking about Lottie, how I don't understand the emotions I have. How can I get over this?

After I'm done venting all the pain, hate and anger, I look down at Bella, her eyes so sad, and I realise that she is probably more emotionally experienced than I, half my age, her baby daughter playing on the floor next to us. She's had a big slice of her own poisonous abusive relationships far worse than I. A baby, for fuck's sake, and yet she has stayed strong, made the best of her life, had no one to lean on for help. My problems seem pathetic now and I feel my eyes moisten, so I pull her even closer and we stay locked in that embrace for what seems like hours.

"I'm staying with you tonight, Mister Keith." Finally, she looks up and pushes away gently, Daisy is grumbling, probably needs to be fed.

"Oh, Bella, you don't need to. I'll be okay now, thank you."

"You ain't got no choice. I'm staying." She smiles and looks up at me with those puppy eyes.

How can I argue with that? I nod. "But, Danny?"

"He's busy. He don't stay with me except on his days off anyway."

"He might be jealous?"

"We're just gonna cuddle, Mister Keith." She flutters her eyelashes and they tell a different, mischievous story. I smile, I could use the cuddles. "You gave me so much, now it's time I repay you, something, at least." She picks up Daisy and sits back down, opening up her top to feed. "Besides, I need to give you your Christmas present…"

———

With no alcoholic fog to dull my senses, the morning, well, late-morning by the time I get out of the warm, comfortable bed and Bella's spoon-cuddle, brings a fresh new perspective. Somehow the problems in my head don't seem so bad anymore, life goes on, people change, they come and go. C'est la vie.

I'm not miraculously cured. No, Bella didn't fuck the pain away totally, but it's dull now, distant and tucked away into a corner of my head I can avoid. Manageable, I think. I will survive, as they say.

The temptation is to stay here, in her warm embrace forever, or perhaps a few more days, maybe a week, but I shouldn't. I need to get on with my life. Staying here with Bella will just cause problems, also Danny doesn't deserve to be screwed over. The lad is trying his best.

No, I need to move along, get to the task I have set myself. I have a list of hotels, focusing on the square states in the west. With the help of Bella, we compile a job advert and post it to every job listing site we can think of.

Artistic marketing manager: Help wanted to turn boring into exciting. Have you got what it takes?

I wanted it to be fairly vague, to make sure a wide variety of slightly odd people applied. I don't want the usual boring suited hospitality majors. I want the misfits, willing to question everything and trust nothing, the rebels, the ones who see things differently. Because the people who are crazy enough to think they can change the world, are the ones who do. This is how I will make my dent in the universe, by lighting a firecracker and shoving it right up the arse of the status quo.

Perhaps just one more day with Bella won't hurt?

Chapter Thirty-Seven

B efore I left Memphis for the wild, western, and rectangular shaped state of Colorado, I promised Bella I'd keep in touch more often, our communications having devolved somewhat when I was back home, with Lottie.

'Visit anytime' she said, with a pout and a wink. I know that's a bad idea, but I probably won't be able to help myself. I have a weakness.

Danny and I had a long chat about the hotel industry in general and the plans he has for Memphis. Then I told him about my wild ideas for change and he was excited. Even though I'm happy with how things are in the Memphis Myatt already, it's almost a historic location, preserved for posterity at this stage, he has some ideas about how to modernise things without too much disruption, he says. I'll let him exercise his creative muscles a bit, perhaps his LARP talents can shine through. I didn't mention to him that I'd spent the last forty-eight hours exploring every contortion and rarely utilised sexual position I could think of with his girlfriend, because what would be the point in that? My back is killing me now, however. I think I need a massage.

The Denver, Colorado Myatt, one of the tallest buildings in the middle of the city. A towering glittery monument, slick and modern, neat and functional. I think my suite on the forty-second floor is actually bigger in square feet than my house back at home. The living room area could easily seat ten people, with its own mini bar and dining area off to a side. I'm installing myself here for a while and will be interviewing candidates for my first job role on the casting couch. I send Bella a short video tour and a shot of the view from the windows. The evening cityscape, thousands of pinpricks of light under a purple sky. She's suitably awed and sends me back a pouting selfie. No matter how many times she does that, I always appreciate it.

I wrote ahead and informed the hotel management about my plans to hire someone, so they aren't surprised when I show up. Perhaps a little perturbed, but I'm here to shake things up, so that's to be expected. This hotel is wonderful, there's no doubt about it, but there's room for some joy amidst the opulence. It can be a bit stuffy, as I recall. There's a forced feeling to the warmth of the place, and I want that to be more natural and friendly.

I find myself automatically heading for one of the bars after settling in, and I remember my resolution to drink less, so I change direction, and instead, head for the renowned spa that we have here. My body needs some pampering after the trauma that Bella and I put it through.

A dip in the green tea jacuzzi, a seaweed wrap, a pedicure and manicure, then another dip in a dead sea bath, all topped off with a deep tissue, aromatherapy massage and I'm as loose as a wizard's sleeve. I float back to my room on a cloud of lavender and tea tree mist, fall into the soft four-poster bed and melt into the fresh linen. There is something to be said for luxury.

I've had a number of applicants for the job already. Whittled down to three that I'll be seeing today for an initial interview. I have no structure, no prepared questions, I just want to see where they take me. We start on the couch, but if the discussion ends up in the jacuzzi, I won't be surprised, or sorry. Two of them are young women with the physical attributes that the shallow man, such as myself, tend to favour.

India Cuthbertson, candidate number one. Her headshot is a professionally taken photo. Windswept, but carefully careless hair in blue, matching those icy blue eyes, rims of dark around them. She's quite striking.

And her physical presence is no less. I open the door to her, three minutes early, and welcome her into my suite.

"Fuck me!" She looks around the room in awe and then out of the picture window, the city spread beneath us. Her hair is deep purple now, a little longer than in the photo, neater too. She's wearing a canary yellow dress, short, with black stockings underneath, the tops deliberately falling short of her hem. A knitted purple cardigan on top.

"Sorry, it's just so fucking posh! I'm India, pleased to meet you, Keith." She turns from the window to shake my hand. A patchouli perfume vapour around her.

"Quite so. The pleasure is all mine, India. Please, have a seat." I motion towards the prepared interview space. She sits, and I am trying to avert my eyes from those stocking tops, but it takes all my focus to do so.

"So, what do you need?" She's as cool as a freezer full of cucumbers, not a shiver of nerves visible. She looks deeply into my eyes, keenly, as I explain the job role, the need to shake up the stale boring aspects of the brand, invent something exciting and unique, change policy and decor to meet the modern expectation, make the entire place an Instagram magnet, but retain the elegance and charm that already exists. I tell her the things Holly has done already in Indianapolis and how I want each hotel to be individual, so much that guests might want to tour all of our venues to experience the different but familiar aspects, collect the full set, as it were. She sips from a glass of iced mint water, leaving dark lipstick stains on the frosty crystal. Nodding thoughtfully.

"I have some ideas," she wistfully stares out of the window, an elegant pale neck displayed as she absent-mindedly plays with her hair. I have a lot of ideas too, but they aren't anything to do with this job. I need to snap to attention, focus on the work, not the sex.

"Tell me about yourself, India."

"Oh, there's not much to tell, really. I was kicked out of three schools, dropped out of art college, tried my hand at modelling, didn't like it. Now I'm looking for a challenge, something interesting, like you..." She's nothing if not honest and up front.

She looks back at me, smiles and stands up. She walks over to the window and beckons me over.

"What do you see here?" She asks me, motioning out of the window. Is she interviewing me now?

"The city?"

"Yes, of course, but I see a million lives, hidden from view, all unaware of each other, all struggling to find themselves."

I look again, I still see a city, laid before me, buildings and mountains on the horizon. "How do you mean?"

"Everyone wants to be famous, rich, interesting and special. But they can't all be."

"True, I suppose."

"We can make them think they are, with this place. It's so fancy here, but the only people experiencing it are already bored with luxury. There's a million people who have no idea this place exists, even if they walk past every day. It's uninviting, cold and unapproachable. It should be more open, casual. More millennial!"

"Interesting."

"Make it a cool people magnet and you'll bring in the youth who may not have the money to spend now, but they will one day. Then they'll come back, loyal. Desperate to remember those formative days." She has a point, and there's an intensity to her that draws me in. "There's a ballroom here?" I nod, used for weddings and corporate events. "Open an exclusive nightclub, the place every cool kid needs to be, bring in DJs and celebrities, really put the place on the map!"

"Nice idea, do you have any experience in that area?"

"No, but, how hard can it be?" I love her honesty, many others would have lied and said they opened four nightclubs in their last job or something.

We leave my room for a walk around the hotel. In the elevator India presses every button "so we don't free fall" she says, it takes forever to reach the ballroom floor.

She looks around and nods in approval. "This place could be amazing, just gotta sex it up a bit." She gives me a glance which, in any other circumstance I would have no trouble interpreting, but I'm trying to be professional here. I check my watch.

"It's been wonderful meeting you, India, I have another candidate to see now, so I'll certainly be in touch soon. Thank you for coming."

"My pleasure, Keith." She steps close to me, looks straight into my eyes, ignores my outstretched hand, and instead slowly runs her hand down my arm, ending with a subtle lick of her lips. She swivels on her heel and heads for the exit.

Jude Pawson, candidate number two. He's waiting outside my room as I return from my steamy walk with India. She's trouble, no question there. But maybe I'm looking for trouble…

I restrain myself from saying 'Hey, Jude.' and instead shake hands and introduce myself, the chap is late-twenties, unbearably thin, wiry and short as a jockey. He shakes my hand with a firm steel clamp.

"Mr Myatt, so pleased to meet you."

"Please, Keith is fine. Happy to meet you too, Jude."

He plants himself on the casting couch and waits, patiently. I never really know what to say to fellow menfolk. I'm more comfortable with women, so the pause grows awkward and I pretend to read some notes on my phone until I can think of something to say. His resume was quite impressive, that's why he's here, he's worked in marketing for some medium-sized companies, done some call centre tech support work, and I note that most of his prior jobs were in Ireland.

"You not from around here, Jude?"

"Nope, from Limerick myself."

"Fair enough, what brings you here?"

"A girl," he laughs, a bit nervous.

"Ah, that makes sense!" Now I can relate to the lad. He's a tail chaser like me.

"So, what's the job?" Now I can hear the accent, more pronounced, at first he was local sounding.

"Well, I basically want to bring this place into the modern era…" I explain my plans, same as I did for India, and he listens intently. I tell him the nightclub idea that India had, and he says he did a bit of DJing himself for a while back home in Ireland, even on the radio. Interesting. I'm getting a good vibe from the lad, he's keen, quick, smart and flush with ideas. He wants to see the bars, so we take a walk, and for the first time in a while, I break my resolution and have a glass of Belgian. Just one, because I still have another interview to do. Jude tells me about the girl he came to Denver for. He met her on Twitter about a year ago, they got talking, the rest is history, as they say, but now he needs a job for his green card and he's outstayed his freeloading welcome with the girlfriend. He saw this job and thought it sounded interesting. We walk up to the ballroom and, like India, he walks around and nods, says it could be a really awesome space. He could DJ, have some theme nights, give the place an ice cool atmosphere. Exclusive. Celebrities would be itching to get in, he reckons. I don't know what celebrities Denver has, but I'll leave that to the locals to care about. I'm warming to the idea greatly now, maybe I can hire both India and Jude and they can get this party started?

Sally Berridge, candidate number three, and final for today. It's actually quite exhausting being patient and pleasant to people. I don't think I have ever interviewed someone formally before, so this has been an eye-opener.

Sally arrives at my room on time and stands in awe of the view. She's tall, elegant, the oldest of the candidates at mid-thirties, like myself. She's dressed smart, but not a suit. She's colourful and graceful. She moves like a ballet dancer and sits on the couch as light as a feather. Her smile is warm and genuine.

"I love this space," she motions at the high ceilinged cathedral of a living room in my suite. "So much potential."

"Yes, it is rather vast."

"And the view is breathtaking." She speaks with educated enunciation, clear and precise.

I give her my hotel spiel once more, during which she stays quiet, but looks around at the room, making notes on a tiny paper notebook. I end with the nightclub idea, but she screws her nose up at that.

"I don't know anything about the party aspect, but I have some thoughts about your decor." She explains her reasoning about why everything seems a bit stuffy, the colours are wrong, the lights are too bright, we aren't taking advantage of the wonderful view we have. She has a history of interior design, worked for a gallery in the city for a while, but left to have a child, now he's in school and she wants to get back on the horse, as it were. I'm impressed, an intelligent and stylish woman who I had absolutely no interest in having sex with. She's worked some kind of magic on me. I think I'll hire all three of them!

Chapter Thirty-Eight

After some discussions with the Denver Myatt management team, it turns out that I can't just hire three new people on my whim, they said. Then they called Rory, he concurred, no surprise there. After more lengthy discussions, we agreed on a compromise. They'll contract to each of them for three months as required and we'll review the situation after that. I hate having my creativity stifled, but what can I do?

Jude and India will work on setting up the ballroom to become Denver's most exclusive nightclub, Sally will study the hotel and give her advice on how we should change the decor to attract a younger audience. They tried to tell me that we already have people on staff that could do these things, so I asked why they hadn't already done them. No suitable answer came. I stood my ground. The answer to these questions is inevitably something along the lines of - we've always done it this way and it works. Well, that's why things are stale and boring. We need new blood to shake things up.

I gave the good news to Jude and Sally with a congratulatory phone call, but I felt India would be more open to the position if it were described over dinner, in my suite, with wine. Yes, I broke my resolution for a moment, but it was worth it. She wanted to look out of the window at the view and imagine what all the hidden people were doing. The million fairy lights that make up the evening cityscape glittered away as we got to know each other better, she certainly was open to positions.

My poor back.

I heard some interesting news today, apparently StayAway, the much-celebrated hotel review site, and bane of my recent life, has been sold to a large Silicon Valley company, known for their existing dating app, rival to the usuals, this one focuses on first date frolics, no messing around, according to their blurb. Interesting. What's more poignant is the figure it apparently sold for - five million pounds. I'm sure Lottie is going to be content now. Happy for her, I suppose. I'm wondering if I should contact her and send congratulations? It seems very sudden, perhaps she was setting this up for a while and didn't mention it?

This does rather inconvenience things for Myatt. Lottie has been true to her word. So far, all the reviews I have seen for our hotels lately have been favourable and genuine. What if the new owners decide to implement some other kind of rating system, like they already use on their dating app? It could mess up my plans to improve the hotels with my wild changes. I think a meeting is in order, once I'm done here in Denver, I should probably go west and see what I can do. Last time I showed up at the owner's door, things went quite well, for a while at least.

There's that dull ache again, the emptiness of mourning. I still miss her and occasionally find myself starting to write a message to her, a sarcastic comment or humorous observation, then realising what I'm doing and deleting it. I still mull over the reasons she may have left me. Was it something I did? Was she just not ready for the steady relationship? She spent her days flitting between hotels and men, perhaps the shock of being tied to one place and one man was too much for her and she couldn't cope with it? It all happened quite suddenly, perhaps we should have taken things much slower.

It took me a long time to decide I wanted to be settled. If you had asked me even a year ago if I wanted a single woman to be with for the rest of time, I'd have laughed, scoffed even. There's an abundant ocean of opportunities out there, why would I settle for just one choice? But something changed in me, a feeling of insecurity I suppose, age and experience and the endless hours of boring flights with time to ponder - wouldn't it be better to share my life with someone special?

But those thoughts must linger for another day. Today, my new sentinels of change start their magic. I have prepared a pep-talk, to fire up and inspire them to do their best work and prove me right, or they will find themselves back on the job postings or flipping burgers somewhere. We'll need results quickly if we're going to impress and remain active, so I hope I haven't made a train wreck of a mistake.

They gather together on the couch in my room. I've prepared a bottle of champagne and a selection of nibbles.

"Welcome to the Myatt family!" They all nod and faintly smile. I think there's a little resentment at the short contract offering instead of a real full-time position.

"I know this isn't perhaps what you expected, but we just need to prove a point and make a bold statement, then we'll get the attention we deserve."

"Thanks for taking a chance on us." India stands up and walks over to the window. She does like that view.

"Listen, I had a bullshit pep-talk prepared, but never mind that. I'm just going to be blatantly honest with you."

"Best way," Sally pipes up, with a pleasant smile.

"I have no idea what I'm doing, really. But instinct tells me we need to change, or we'll die. I've had some success so far in Indiana, I'm hoping you guys can rock the Denver scene too. My job isn't on the line, and I can get out if I need to, but this is my heritage and life and I want to prove a point to my boring brother. I want to make our hotels fun and interesting. So, if you can do that for me here, I'll be eternally grateful, and you'll get to keep your jobs. Sound fair?"

"Fair enough!" Jude stands and gives me a thumbs up sign. "So, you going to pop open that champagne then?"

I laugh, "Yup. Let's get this party started!"

"Alright, now we're talking."

We move down to the ballroom, our focus for the short term. Jude tells me a list of the equipment we'll need to get a DJ booth set up, India explains her strategy for the social media presence we should aim for, an elusive, exclusive cool vibe, suggesting things but never showing them. She's got some ideas for a logo and style for the nightclub, which I hadn't even considered, we need a name for it. Sally works on her iPad, sketches out an aesthetic theme we should decorate with. The trick is that everything we do has to be portable and easily removable, we can't disrupt the existing decor or cause problems for the weddings and corporate events we hold here. Our entire operation has to pack into a small room when not in use. No one said it was going to be easy.

"Anyone got ideas for a name?" I look around at my little team, they are all creative, someone must have something, but there's a ghastly silence.

"Myatt nights?" Says Jude.

"Hmm, no, too boring."

"Myatt Balls?" India looks at me with a teasing grin.

"No…"

"Liquid Night, because it hints at liquid nitrogen, which is cold, so we're already super cool!" Sally chimes in with a slick proposal.

"I like it! And I'm sure there will be plenty of liquid being drunk, too." A general thumbs up from the team and we have a name. "Liquid Night, the new coolest place in Denver!"

"We should go for the subliminal, use loads of dry ice, crank the air-con all the way down, make it freezing in here. Blue tones, every drink comes with ice in frozen glasses. Force the people to dance to keep warm, it really will be the coolest place in Denver!"

Chapter Thirty-Nine

I left the team excited with their new tasks. I introduced them to the manager and set them up with a budget and a deadline of two months to get the club started. Giving them another month to establish it as a success, which would then get them a new contract. A little delicate and tight, but necessity is the mother of invention. These people thrive on coming up with interesting ways to do things, I'm looking forward to seeing what they accomplish.

They don't need me looking over their shoulders, so I'll leave them to it and come back when they are finished.

Meanwhile, I have business to take care of. I headed west from Colorado to California, a long trip, but I wanted some time to think, so I drove the whole way. Took me five days with a stop in Las Vegas along the way, which wasn't anywhere near as wild as it could have been. Our Vegas Myatt is as gaudy as can be expected. I'm not going to touch the perfectly oiled mechanism of money making they have with the burlesque theatre, casino and wedding business already doing extremely well. If I ever want to lose a huge amount of money and marry a stripper, all on the same night, I know precisely where to come.

· · ·

On reflection now, the thinking time didn't do me much good. The healing efforts of Bella therapy are worn away, the niggles of doubt and insecurity poking through my thoughts, especially with my appointment with the new StayAway owners tomorrow at their Silicon Valley headquarters. Quite different to Lottie's house in High Barnet where I last ventured to confront the StayAway people.

So far, I haven't noticed any change in the reviews, but I have a feeling it could flip anytime as the new owners decide how they will run the site. Better to get in there first and lay down some rules for our business with them. Sure, they send us significant custom, but in turn, we pay them handsomely for the privilege. I'm sure a mutually beneficial deal can be struck.

I downloaded their dating app, too, because I wanted to get a feel for their attitude. It's called 'Laid' which gives me a good idea immediately. Their catchline is 'Cut to the chase' which also leaves little to the imagination. I scroll their directory of women in the local area and find something quite different to the red-eyed, flash blown, dirty-mirrored festival of lust, thinly concealed with a lie about companionship, that the usual dating apps have. This is all immaculately groomed, perfectly tanned, professional headshots, teasing cleavage and slightly open mouths, lips glistening. Sections for every sexual orientation I can think of, with a few more I had no idea existed on top. Then bright as daylight, tick boxes for fetishes and perversions, as well as a length and girth question in the personal details. I choose to skip those, never having had any complaints. Some things can be left to experience on the night, as it were.

If I rewind my brain back a year or so, this app would have given me cause for celebration had I known about it. Like shooting fish in a barrel, it makes it ridiculously easy to seek immediate gratification, but now I have pause. Part of the experience is the hunt, the coy flirt, the delicate nuances and signals that let you know things are going well and a bed bounce is soon to follow. If you can just buy the experience with a 'Laid coin' and know you will get some, it detracts from the experience somewhat. The morning walk of shame will be far longer before one can stand tall again. 'Dating' has been reduced to a commodity. Available for purchase via an app. Formulaic, predictable and therefore worthless and boring. Nonetheless, I scroll the top shelf 'Laid maids' who require double credits to engage with, highly rated, five stars only. I can see how many dates they have been on, some of them even require a minimum star rating before they will accept a message. As a newbie to the scene, with zero stars, I'm locked away from those aristocratic royals.

Actually, they seem quite vapid and empty. They are disconnected from reality, Instagram stars, duck faced, and inch long Swarovski adorned fingernails. Perhaps this is just a slightly different version of hell?

I choose a girl who is available for a date this evening, accepts 'newbies' and is a little more to my taste. A glimmer of the 'girl-next-door' innocence to her, shining through the makeup and poses. Kym, black hair, twenty-seven years old, with fifty-seven five star ratings from her previous dates. She's been a member since a year ago. She's been busy! She lists her fetishes as mild bondage and sexual orientation as non-binary pansexual. From this I take it she'll go anyway the wind blows. Fair enough, whatever works, I guess. I purchase enough credits to engage her and send an 'icebreaker' message.

The San Jose Myatt is not special in anyway, a bog standard replica of any airport hotel, but positioned in the downtown area. There's nothing wrong with it, but nothing great about it either. This hotel would be on my list of places to jazz up, but I'm pausing any more hires for the moment, to let the Denver team do their thing for a while before I stir up any more reasons for

Rory to moan at me. I linger at the bar, not because I want alcohol, but because there's no room service here and I don't fancy a sit-down meal yet. Inevitably, a Belgian beer comes my way and I pull out my red phone to scroll the Laid app some more. Addictive in the way it makes a game of the mating ritual. My 'selfie' has already had thirty-three likes by women all over the California area. Hmm.

Kym has replied to me too, accepting my date for this evening, including a rather provocative photo of herself, totally nude, but covering the key points with censor stars, the message is 'peel off five stars for pleasure' and, somewhat unprecedented, she's requested I send a 'dick pic'. I don't quite know how to feel about that. I can't imagine why anyone would want to see a man's 'schlong', out of context, as it were, from the rest of him. I politely decline, saying I'm in a bar right now, so I can't really slap it out on the counter and snap a pic. I'm reminded of Ben and his arse-pic, pre-stored on his phone, and I wonder if guys here walk around with a pre-prepared photo of their erect genitalia already on the phone in their pockets? Gives a new meaning to the old boy-scouts motto of always being prepared...

Kym replies back within a minute that I should visit the bathroom and snap a pic for her. She's quite insistent, says she wants to know what she's working with. Good Lord, is this the norm? I decline again, saying she'll be adequately sated, not to worry. She's working with a professional.

She says she hopes I'm not shy later and that it's lucky I'm 'cute' or she'd cancel the date. Lucky, indeed.

I'm clearly not dealing with twin flame material here, not even a second date, but I'm partly doing this to gain an insight into the workings of the new StayAway owners business. This is already a shock and I haven't met the girl yet. Am I out of the loop here? I thought I was pretty trendy and with-it! I have the latest phone and I'm setting up Denver's coolest nightclub. I think back to our first computer that had internet access, when I was a child in the mid-nineties with a dial-up modem and bland slow websites, mostly text and information, photos that took three minutes to load, and I don't think anyone could have predicted a society of people walking around with powerful pocket computers that they use to instantly swap penis photos and organise scheduled sex dates.

How times have changed.

———

"Keith?" I turn around on my barstool to find Kym, perfectly photoshop presented, groomed and tan, an air of impatience about her as she sits down on the barstool. Her eyelashes flap like bat-wings. She's lost the innocence from her profile photo, she's harsh and to the point, seasoned, and a five-star date so everyone can just fuck right off. She's elite.

"First things first, I'm not eating. I buy my own drinks, and to get a five-star rating you have to make me cum at least three times. I have another date later, but I may cancel if things look good. But I gotta tell you, this place ain't getting you off to a good start. I had to, like, pay the Uber guy extra so he wouldn't tell anyone I came here. Oh, and I don't do anal, except on my period." She motions around the bar, with a look of distaste. I'm charmed, she may cancel her other date to stay with me for more than two hours, how flattering. What's wrong with this place?

"Er, pleased to meet you, Kym."

"I don't shake," she grimaces at my outstretched hand and shrinks back, but then a toothy smile flashes onto her face, "Now that's taken care of, Hi!"

Chapter Forty

W ell that was a fucking disaster. I woke to a notification
on my phone. A one star rating, a message that said
simply 'you suck' and a block on Kym's account.

After the harsh start, I thought things had warmed up a little,
she mellowed with the drinks she bought herself, decided to stay
and not ditch me for her second date of the evening. I'm sure he
was disappointed, on reflection I should have insisted she leave.
We didn't have much to talk about, so she told me stories of bad
dates she'd had. I listened in stunned silence at the things people
do. One guy apparently wanted her to dress his penis up in
Barbie clothes and play with it like a doll. Another declared his
scatology fetish as they sat down for a rare dinner date. A girl
she dated for a while spent more time in the bathroom, vomiting,
than with her in the bar. Her teeth lost their enamel, burnt away
from bile. Those stories aside, she kept telling me I was 'cute',
but she never asked about my history, so I didn't tell. I also
didn't use my full name as my Laid screen name, so she had no
reference to why I had chosen this 'dive' hotel for our meeting.

After the prerequisite number of cocktails, she suggested we
go to my room and I could try and earn that five-star rating, so
coveted among the Laid app users. Only five percent of men
ever get it, she said.

· · ·

It turns out that the pressure of performing in such a high stakes game got to me, and my usual rock solid act was ditched in favour of a flaccid display. I'm not going to sugar coat it, even if that would have meant she'd suck it like a lollipop, but as she lay there, expectantly and picture perfect, no tan lines, a neatly trimmed landing strip, delicately scented of crushed fruit, I simply couldn't muster any desire to jump on her and win my five-star review. She didn't want to kiss, no foreplay at all, unless you count the cocktail time. There was no lust, only a perfunctory brush against me as she elegantly stripped naked and lay on the bed, flicking the TV on and finding a music channel with her overly long fingernails. Something is probably wrong with me, because she was porn-star flawless, everything the shallow man desires, yet somehow not attractive at all. In the end I attended her needs with a flick of the tongue, but she tasted of bitter perfume, no scent of woman at all, washed away with a douche. I couldn't get into the spirit of things, so instead I poured a drink from the minibar and asked if she wanted to talk for a while.

This was not a good move. She didn't come to fucking talk, she said, she came to cum! She can talk with her roommates, no need for a date to open his mouth. She dressed, hurriedly, and left, and honestly, I was quite glad when she slammed the door shut.

This experiment has not done my ego any good though, and today I need to meet the people who run this terrible site. Basically pimps with millions of users all paying them to have meaningless sex. I'm trying not to be judgemental and accept that the world around me is changing, but I have a sneaky feeling that this app, and presumably any others like it, have possibly taken things a step too far. Then again, it isn't the fault of the software, people will behave as they wish regardless of the infrastructure. Laid is just an enabler.

★★☆☆☆ [2 out of 5 stars]

Kym Douchetoomuch. Perfectly presented, scented and tanned. But ironically, narcissism is a rather unattractive trait. Wouldn't try again. Can't anyway as I'm blocked from her profile.

Palo Alto, the birthplace of many a great technology company, not least Apple and Hewlett Packard. And also apparently, Laid. Digging around on their corporate website, there's an 'About Us' page that proudly states that they started in a garage as many other greats had. I think every Silicon Valley business is obliged to start in a garage now, by state law.

I'm meeting a lady by the name of Monika Loveless, a more fitting name I have never encountered. She's the CEO of Laid, worth a lot of money according to Wikipedia. Her photo shows a brilliant-white toothy smile, short cropped hair, a blurry bokeh of the Laid logo behind her. She's the image of corporate America. Efficient, energised, dedicated and above all, approachable and fun. I have my doubts about that, however. But I'll see soon enough.

My rental car, now quite filthy from the long drive through desert and city, looks rather dull against the other vehicles in the parking lot. None older than a year, all very expensive looking. Sex sells, apparently. The building is all glass and metal, a large plastic version of their logo outside on the grass, the door swings open as I approach into an air-conditioned reception. A screen on the wall shows the current statistics of the Laid users. Currently hundreds of thousands of users online, and almost as many out on dates right now, all across the world. They are absolutely raking in cash by the second.

The reception area has no desk, no staff, I look around and there are many cameras, so I assume someone will notice me shortly. Sure enough, another door opens and a slim young lad approaches, all smiles.

"Welcome, Keith, to the Laid headquarters! I'm Doug and

I'll be taking care of you while you're here." He blurts out his spiel before I can stutter, he's far too bouncy and energetic for my liking. All his clothes are tailored and new, hair slicked back, a phone in the hand that isn't shaking mine.

"Thanks, Doug, Keith Myatt, to see Monika Loveless."

"Oh, don't worry, we know who you are." He laughs, "I guess your date didn't go too well last night?" He subtly motions with his phone.

"What?"

"It's okay! A newbie can easily get caught off guard and make mistakes. Next time you'll do better."

Do they monitor every date and star rating? Shouldn't that be protected by some kind of information security law? I should have looked at the small print a bit closer before signing up for the app, I think.

I am ushered through into the building and along some corridors. There are various rooms of people working at clusters of screens, all the walls are glass. Another open area we pass through with bean bags dotted around, a few people staring at phones and tablets in their laps.

I'm deposited in a little lounge outside another glass office, I can see Monika inside, animatedly talking to a trifecta of monitors on her desk, looking from one to the other. She sees me and nods, taps her wrist and rolls her eyes, then goes back to the screens. I can't hear what she's saying, but it seems like she's wrapping up her video conference. There's another statistics display in front of me, showing the top ten dates of the day, male and female, with the most star ratings, some in the multiple hundreds, where do they find the time? Presumably my single one-star review is nowhere near.

The glass office door swings open, "Keith! So sorry to keep you, my meeting overran." She motions toward her computer. I stand up to greet her, a stunning woman, her photo is an accurate representation. She's probably early thirties, and definitely spends a lot of time maintaining her appearance, not a hair out of place, her makeup immaculate. I wouldn't be surprised if there's some kind of salon behind her office for frequent touchups.

"Monika, delighted to meet you."

She does the kiss and miss left and right cheek thing, which I find incredibly annoying, but I refrain from comment. She sits down on the couch and nods for me to sit next to her. The couch is heart-shaped, deep blood red, so I twist around to face her.

"I hear you tried our dating app last night?"

"Yes, I did. Look, I'm a bit concerned about that, isn't there a data protection thing around that information?"

"All our data is completely open, it's the safest way to be. There's nothing to steal, so no concerns about data hacking."

"What? Not even credit card information? Surely you must have some hidden info?"

"No, we don't touch that, you pay in the app, so Apple and Google hold that data for us. We are completely open, Keith. No one can blackmail us with data like some other dating sites, no one can steal nude photos or try and manipulate a client."

"Well, that sounds reasonable, I suppose. But it would be nice to know that up-front."

"You didn't check the terms and conditions?" She grins,

"No."

"It's all plain and clear to see, but no one reads it. Hey, it's the same with every other social platform, your data is absolutely not private. Facebook, Twitter, those are wide open, people post far more intimate information there than they do with Laid."

I suppose she has a point. Her spiel is well rehearsed, I'm sure she's given this speech many times and she knows what she's talking about. "Okay, I guess."

"So, you want to wipe that one-star?" she laughs.

"Ah, I'm probably going to delete my account, Monika. I think I may be too old for this."

"Nonsense, we have men much older than you doing very well. A newbie can buy a rating wipe up to three times, so you get three tries to get going. But since you are here, let me clean you up." She taps on her phone for a few seconds, and a moment later my phone buzzes in my pocket. I pull it out and I have indeed lost my poor one star rating. Back to being a clean zero.

"Thank you, it was quite embarrassing."

"Don't mention it. So, what did you want to talk about?"

"Well, your latest acquisition, StayAway..." I explain that our hotels had a rather symbiotic relationship with StayAway for a while, good reviews flowed our way, money for bookings flowed back to StayAway, I was happy with how that turned out, and we, at Myatt hotels, would like to keep up a good working relationship with the new management. I wanted to get to the front of the line of all the other hotel chains that might be knocking on her door anytime soon. We understand the changing horizon of social media, online advertising, reviews and ratings and we also understand luxury and have a long history of hospitality. Bad reviews are no good for anyone, and our policy is to deeply investigate the root cause of any genuine problem. I also add in a taster of my updates that I'm coordinating in Indiana and Colorado so far.

She nods and listens intently to my rant, her eyes occasionally straying to her phone, that buzzes continually.

"I'm sure we can come to some arrangement, Keith. Are you free for dinner? I just had a cancellation."

My phone receives a notification, a dinner date appointment from Monika. I tap on the accept button and smile across the couch at her.

"Don't you think the Laid app is a tad immoral?"

Monika picks up her glass of wine, carefully selected from the list. The restaurant she chose is wonderful, a Greek theme, which is something a little different. "How do you mean?" She rolls the glass around in her palm.

I can tell these signs. I'm on my own stomping ground now. "Well, it's almost like a prostitution service."

"Not at all, every transaction is one hundred percent mutually consensual. People like to have sex, Keith, I'm sure you know that?"

"Well, yes, but it's commoditised, available for purchase at the tap of a screen. It feels wrong, somehow."

"We just give people what they want, providing an infrastructure doesn't change the needs of people. In fact the entire reason we exist is because people demanded we do. If not us, then someone else."

"You are right, of course, but I suppose I'm a bit old-fashioned. The date I had last night was quite different to my normal experiences."

"Typical newbie, you jumped in and tried to bag a five star right out of the gate. You need to ease into it, learn the culture and format."

"Excuse me, I've had plenty of dates! I'm hardly a newbie."

"The world is changing, Keith." Her eyes grow wide and she nods around us to the couples on their phones and some with tablets and laptops out on their tables. "People play games on their phones. Laid is a phone game that has a physical presence. That's all. Games have rules, you need to learn them."

"Quite so." I pick up my wine glass, mirror her actions. "But people want actual relationships too, husbands, wives, security and safety."

"Yes, and there's other apps for that. Laid is not about that. I have a healthy stack of numbers that proves people want what we offer."

I can't fault her logic.

"So, can I ask, why did you buy StayAway?"

"We felt it was a market we could make an impact in, it has huge potential. The previous owner was on to something, but she wasn't exploiting it fully."

I raise an eyebrow, "Did you meet Charlotte?"

"You know her?"

"You could say that…"

"Yes, she came out to see us a while back. Lovely girl, a bit naive though. The brand could be worth triple what we paid, given some investment. We're looking to expand. There are some other services we're after too, these things all tie in with each other. Lovers need hotel rooms, after all." She smiles and sips her wine.

"Interesting."

"We're negotiating with some hotel chains about offering a shorter stay than a whole night for a discount. If you are interested?"

"What! No, certainly not. We're not going to turn Myatt into an hourly rate brothel hotel! If people want to fuck in a Myatt then they have to pay for the whole damn night."

"Suit yourself, speaking of which, you want to try and earn that five-star rating?"

Chapter Forty-One

I decided to linger in California for a little while, a couple of weeks jaunting around the state and exploring the wildly varied countryside. First up to San Francisco, then a few days at the Yosemite national park, which was a mind-blowing experience. Beautiful doesn't begin to describe it. Then a slow haul down to Los Angeles, which has a different feel completely with its Hollywood glitz and swagger. Finally tailing off in San Diego, which had wonderful eye candy everywhere I looked.

I fell back to my old tasks to keep me busy, arriving unannounced at our hotels, carrying out strict inspections, calling up the staff for any little niggles I found. The StayAway reviews will be different now, brutally honest perhaps. We need to live up to the name and no slacking.

What triggered this sudden flood of responsibility? Ben did. A call one lazy afternoon shocked me into reality. Lucy is pregnant.

Ben, the last person on earth who I would have expected to get his shit together, has done just that. He's going to be a father. A grown up, a real person who needs to be the adult in the room. I am a pathetic excuse of a man, flitting around the world, doing very little, shagging almost anything that moves, and I lost the woman who I thought was going to be my anchor to a better life.

Shit.

I took a good hard look through my life and decisions, counted up the women in my contacts list, deleted some of them, felt bad for most of them, and then stumbled on the entry for Bella. It crossed my mind to snap her up, take Bella and Daisy with me back to England, sell my shares, buy her anything she wants, give Daisy a good upbringing. All that sounded wonderful for a moment, I'd get an instant family and a loving young girl, but it wore off quickly. Bella is happy with Danny, he's far more appropriate for her. I can't just assume I can whip a girl away from her life just because I feel bad. Even if it would be a massive step up for her. It isn't fair. Instead, I messaged Bella I was going to be a real Uncle, as good as anyway.

I deleted my account on the Laid app too, after my date with Monika, where I did earn my five-star rating. I checked the messages frequently for a while, played the game and got some more favourable reviews, but the thrill faded quickly, the formulaic system bored me. I want some risk in my chase, to keep my skills honed and my charms up to scratch. Something more than my previous ratings and my face or dick pic to go on for a reason to jump into bed with me. There's no fun in a hunt where the beast is already lying placid, waiting to be speared.

★★★☆☆ [3 out of 5 stars]

Monika Loveless. Striking, well versed in the art of elaborate and kinky sex, but totally lacking in scruples. Probably best to avoid if possible.

. . .

Now I'm planning my route back east, incorporating a quick stop in Denver to make sure my team are progressing, then a few random zig zags ending up back in Boston, where I didn't actually get to stay last time I was there. After that, I've been invited to meet Mum and Dad who are somewhere in Europe, their retired life is a slower and more sedate version of mine, travelling the hotels and drinking the beer, probably not having as much sex, and preferring France, Germany and Netherlands rather than my usual USA. It's for my birthday next month, the first time in I don't know how long that they seemed to remember or care about it. Usually, I get nothing but an automated email from the hotel, the kind that any guest gets if they register their date of birth in our system. That and a gift from Aunty Joyce, which I won't be getting this year. Perhaps that's why the parental units are making an effort.

I open up the twin flame forums and look around, haven't done that in ages. I find some of the old messages and discussions I was having with a variety of women. I delete them all. Looking back at my words they were cheesy, cringeworthy even. What was I thinking?

There is one new message for me though, from a profile simply called Nellie. There's no photo, no other profile information, and the account was opened only a few weeks ago. The message has been pending for two weeks. I'm pondering deleting it and the entire forum account, but what the hell, I open the message.

'We have the same birthday :)'

Interesting. I filled in all the profile fields on the twin flame forum, not really thinking about it. Probably should have used a fake date in case anyone tried to hack my life or something. Not to worry, I suppose. I send a message back.

. . .

'Oh, well, then you'll be getting a year older soon, too. Hello Nellie, I'm Keith.'

<hr />

When I arrived in Phoenix, Arizona, Nellie had replied to me.

'I know your name, it's on your profile! A year older, yes, but maybe not a year wiser…'

Something about her drew me in and I replied. I told her I think I have saved up my last five years of wisdom and they all dropped at once on me recently. I asked where she was, but she wouldn't say. I asked if she had a photo, nope, apparently. Despite the secrecy, I played along, because what harm could it do? There were long gaps in her replies, there must be a time zone difference, but I can't deduce where she might be.

I stayed two nights in Phoenix, inspecting the hotel, talking to the staff, checking the kitchen and reception area, mostly fine, but there were scuff marks on the check-in desk. I'm being a total arsehole now, because that's how guests and people who leave bad reviews are. If you can't beat them…

In Albuquerque, Nellie told me where to get great Salvadoran food in a place I would never have ventured to, rough looking on the outside, but the salsa and guacamole must have been made by angels. She seems to be well travelled.

I moved on to Denver, my rental car looking increasingly filthy, but it didn't seem to be important. I was doing actual work, filing my detailed and accurate reports with Rory, avoiding the bar and women, getting good sleep. Something really has changed in me.

My team in Denver was progressing nicely. They showed me

a list of celebrities they have lined up to come to the opening night of their club, no one I have ever heard of, but that's unsurprising. The decor looks great, the marketing imagery is suitably elegant and elusive, creating an exclusivity that all the cool kids will want to get in on.

I moved on through Oklahoma, Omaha, Minneapolis, Milwaukee, clocking up thousands of miles, ticking off quality boxes, inspecting, correcting. All the while my text communications with Nellie turning into a habit, I'd tell her when I arrived, what I found when I got there, some amusing things I saw on the way. She told me she was travelling too but wouldn't say where.

By the time I hit Detroit, I found myself checking for messages from Nellie before I even checked into the hotel room. She says very little, but she listens to my rants, and there's something compelling about that. We started counting down the days to our shared birthday. I have a feeling that she's younger than I, but I can't tell for sure.

Finally, I arrived in Boston, the elegant new England architecture grounding me, making me feel more at home in this wild and massive country. The last few weeks have been a blur, thousands of miles, dozens of stops. I'm physically drained, my legs creak from the hours of driving. Even when I close my eyes each night, the endless road lingers in my mind's eye. I could never be a truck driver, doing this every day, relentless roads to nowhere and back again would probably kill me long-term.

Nellie replied quickly when I told her I arrived at my last stop on this tour, and I'll be back in Europe soon. A quick stop at home, before going over to meet the parents in Brussels. I asked Nellie what she's doing for her birthday, she told me she hadn't decided yet, but whatever it was would be relaxing. I've told her so much about myself, we've moved away from the forum posts now, using email instead. I spend an hour or two each evening just venting my thoughts to her, it's quite cathartic. But I know so little about her. If I ask something specific she avoids an answer, changing the subject back to me. I'm a little frustrated, because I'd like to get to know her better, I don't even have a photo. I may never meet her, right now she's just someone to talk to who doesn't judge me, and that's exactly what I need.

True to form, the Boston Myatt is as creaky as my legs. All the rooms are unique here, I'm staying in a blue room today. A large roll-top bath with cast iron feet in the shape of lions stands proud in the middle of the vast bathroom. I fill it with hot water, the plumbing complaining and knocking, drop in a small bouquet garni of herbs that claim to relieve aches and pains as well as stress, turn the lights off, play a new album that Nellie recommended from my phone, and climb in to the medicinal, life-restoring hot-tub.

Chapter Forty-Two

Whilst on my brief stop at home I went over to congratulate Ben and Lucy. She's looking fruitful, the pregnant glow is a real thing, apparently. Ben was a bit nervous, not sure what to do, he's trying to stop Lucy from doing the heavy gardening work, but she says she's fine for now. Pregnancy isn't a disease and she doesn't need mollycoddling.

I took him a case of Belgian, told him to enjoy the peace while it lasted. But their little basement may prove to be a problem soon. I wonder if Ben has thought about where the sprog will sleep and play?

Speaking of Belgian, here I am in the heart of the land, Brussels. Enjoying a lunchtime glass straight from the vat at a brewpub in the heart of Grand Place. Goes down smooth. These fellows certainly know their ale. A taxi driver once told me there was a pub somewhere that boasted over three hundred different beers, all proudly served in their own unique glasses. Sounds like a challenge!

However, not for today, as I'm due to meet the folks shortly, in the lobby of our historic Brussels Myatt, an old world charm that isn't exaggerated or fake, it actually charming and old. I woke to a 'Happy Birthday' message, not from Mum and Dad, certainly not from Rory, not even from Ben or Bella, but from Nellie, hard to forget if we share the same day.

I replied the same, but I added a single 'x' to the end of my message. A bold step!

"Keith!"

"Hello Mum, Hello Dad." I get up off the antique leather couch and into an awkward group hug and back slap situation.

"Happy birthday, son." Dad hands me a small parcel. "It's from both of us."

"Thanks, I'll smoke it later."

"Very funny, Keith, open it!"

They both look fit and healthy, the retirement is going well for them. I haven't seen them since the funeral, which wasn't exactly a happy time for anyone. I open the parcel.

"Oh, thank you, a wallet." It's nice leather, but nothing to really celebrate. I'm not sure what the fuss was about.

"Open the wallet, Keith!" Mum is flustering around, excited. I open the wallet and find the normal fake cardboard credit cards and stuffing for display, I look up at Mother and she nods. "Keep going!"

I open up the change pocket and there's a shiny thing inside, a ring. I pull it out and it's a delicately intricate Claddagh design, studded with a generous helping of diamonds in a heart shape.

"An engagement ring?" I'm a bit confused here.

"Yes, time you settled down and found yourself a woman to go with it." Mum finally looks satisfied she's delivered her message.

"Mum, I…"

"It was your Aunty Joyce's, well, almost."

"What?"

"You probably don't remember, you were only little, wasn't he, Mick?"

"Hmm?" Dad wakes up from his daydream, "Oh, yes, dear, very little."

"Joyce was almost engaged once, to a lovely man, wasn't he, Mick?"

"Yes, dear, lovely man."

"What was his name?"

Dad ponders for a moment. "I think it was Charlie?"

"Yes, that's it, Charlie."

"What happened to Charlie?" I'm incredulous, there's a whole backstory of family history that I have never heard before?

"Well it's a bit tragic really. He was knocked down by a bus on the way to propose to her."

"Seriously?"

"Yes, terrible really, number forty-two it was."

"Doesn't matter what number the bus was, Jerry!"

"No, well, I was just saying."

"My god, why did no one tell me about this?"

"Well, it was all so horrible, no one liked to talk about it. Joyce was devastated of course."

I look at the ring again, it's beautiful, must have cost a fortune. There's writing inside so I take a closer look.

"What the… It says Nellie inside?"

"That's what he called her, short for Eleanor."

"What?"

"I think he was Scottish,"

"No, Irish I thought?" Dad pipes up.

"Oh, well one of those."

"But why Nellie or Eleanor?"

"That was her middle name, didn't you know?"

"No. I didn't." Well, this has been quite a history lesson.

"Anyway, you can easily get that engraving removed, unless you find a girl called Nellie!" Mum chuckles.

"Quite so…"

"Joyce couldn't bear to part with it, but she told me once she had you in mind for it, one day, when you were ready. So, here it is. Happy birthday, son, no pressure! But we think it's time you got yourself a nice wife. Even your old friend Ben has one now."

"I know. But it isn't that easy, is it?"

I'm reminded of the expensive ring that's already at home on my nightstand, still there, I really should take that back now…

Over dinner, we discuss the tour I've just been on across the whole of America. I explain all the niggles I found and got fixed, the Denver and Indianapolis upgrades I'm doing and Mum and Dad seem impressed. They said they heard from Rory I was doing great things too, which is interesting. I wasn't aware he cared.

"We're going to Bruges next, why don't you come with us?" Mother announces, "Maybe you'll meet a nice Belgian girl, you always had a thing for Belgium."

"Mum! I like the beer, that's all. But yes, I'll come along." Bruges is a delightful city, a fairytale atmosphere to the place. Littered with tourists, but nevertheless. I haven't spent much time with the folks for years and they are being unnaturally friendly at the moment. They are also getting on in years, I should savour the moments we have left together.

"What about her?" Mum nudges me with her elbow, tipping her head sideways and winking towards a waitress. I look up from my soup, the woman she's indicating didn't seem to speak much English when she took our order.

"Mum, I don't think that would work."

"She's very pretty. You could do worse."

"Mum!"

"Well, I'm just saying."

"I can find my own wife, thanks."

Dad, sensible, stays in his own world, well away from this conversation. He's reading the paper. I can't believe people still read papers, even more so, the London papers here in Bruges.

"Well, get on with it then, Keith, you aren't getting any younger." Good grief. I'm never going to hear the end of this until I actually walk down the aisle with someone. "Dear," Mum waves the waitress over, "Can you get my son here another beer, he's single, you know."

"MUM!"

"Beer, another one." She picks up my glass and waves it at the poor girl.

I hope to fuck she didn't understand.

Dad looks up from his paper, looks at the waitress, then at Mum, chuckles and lifts his own glass, "Make that two." He shows her two fingers and a smile. I'm sure I caught him looking at her arse as she walked away, too.

"How about you and I go paint the town red tonight, Keith?" He gives me a wink, "We haven't done that in a while."

Going out drinking with Dad? That should be interesting.

"I don't think we've ever done that? But yes, should be a laugh. You buying?"

He scoffs, teasing, "Not likely!"

"Yes, that's a good idea, Mick. You two go see the sights, give me a chance to catch up with my shows." Mum seems delighted she'll have an evening alone with Dad out of the way.

I go to my room to shower before the night out with the old man, but I've been itching to check my emails too. I asked Nellie a question yesterday and I haven't had an answer yet. Sure enough, there's an email now from her.

I asked if her full name was Eleanor, if Nellie was a shortening.

She replied simply, 'Just Nellie'

Then to my other question - did she have a good birthday?

'Not as good as I'd hoped…'

It's like getting blood from a stone with this one. I get snippets of information sometimes, but mostly she's elusive. I have to read between the lines, extrapolate and guess. I don't really know why I even care, but there's something about the secrecy that makes me curious. Something in my subconscious that keeps me going back to her. I write her an email, telling her my Mother keeps trying to set me up with random women and repeatedly tells me I need to settle down and get married now I'm thirty-five.

I didn't tell her about the ring with her name in it, I'm allowed some secrets myself.

She's replied back by the time I finish my shower, 'Random women, huh? Be careful, we can be dangerous!'

Quite so.

There's something about the cobbled stone streets of Europe that make me feel at home. The clip of one's shoe against the stone makes that unique sound you simply don't get in America on neat asphalt sidewalks. Dad and I meander the short walk to a bar he's keen to show me. Seems to be down a narrow alley, you'd barely notice if you didn't know it was there. There's a small sign and a door that opens to a steep staircase down. Nothing more.

Inside however, is a different story. The high ceiling is made up of vaulted brick arches that give it an organic shape, as if the bar grew from the ground and we are inside the belly of some ancient beast. Lit by candelabras and multitudes of candles in bottles, the atmosphere is almost crypt-like, medieval. But the sounds and smells don't reflect that, there's good cheer, warmth and hearty beer perfume filling the air.

"This place is amazing!"

"Thought you'd like it, but wait till you taste the beer!"

A full-bearded bartender brings us both a long stick, five gaps cut out of it, each one with a different glass of beer resting on the wood. An efficient and elegant method of carrying booze. Apparently known as a 'Bierflug'. Dad asked for a selection of Trappist beers, all of them with generous alcohol percentages. Trappist monks are widely believed - incorrectly - to be a silent order, and you soon find out why after a couple of these wonderful ales. Aside from giggling, it is hard to make your face muscles function adequately to form coherent words. I look down at the five different coloured brews in front of me, a mirror version in front of Dad. I wonder where this will end up.

"Start on the left, working right, they are arranged in alcohol strength order. Well, cheers, son, bottoms up, etcetera!"

"Cheers, Dad."

Damn, that's good. The first beer hits the spot, a nutty blonde, head of foam, fresh aftertaste. Just how I like my women!

"Your mother means well, don't take it the wrong way. She just wants to see you happy."

"I know, but she is a little intense."

"Indeed. How are you doing anyway? With the ladies?"

"Dad!"

He holds his hands up, "Sorry, just asking. Man to man, as it were."

"All quiet on the western front, at the moment. But I have some works-in-progress."

Saying that out loud was a shock, the only work in progress I have is with Nellie, which is the vaguest of relationships I've ever had. Occasional emails and nothing more, not even a photo. But still, it's my only lead at the moment, if you don't count the Belgian waitress Mum was obsessed with.

After another Bierflug full of ever more interesting ales, we stumble up the stairs out into the world above, like moles, poking out into the night. Holding onto each other to stay upright, we wander seemingly aimless, laughing and joking as the clip of heel on cobble echoes into the evening. Dad seems to have a direction in mind, and I follow, without thinking, but when we end up outside a brothel, I'm shocked into sobriety, a little, at least.

"Fancy a go, son?" Dad nods towards the scantily clad young lady posing in the window.

"Dad!"

He chuckles. "Go on, you only live once. Does the old ticker good." Before I can object he's gone in and I have little choice, in my beer-soaked state, but to follow.

"But, Mum?"

"Son, if you only ever take one piece of advice from your old man, take this one. The key to a happy and long marriage is spice and variety. You don't get that by keeping it in your pants." He holds a finger up to his lips. "Mum's the word, eh!"

Chapter Forty-Three

S itting in the lounge of a brothel, waiting for your horny, drunk father, and trying desperately to resist the constant pestering of young, gorgeous, eastern European prostitutes, is harder than it sounds.

They plied me with drinks, free at first, but rather expensive once I declined the sex offers for the tenth time. There's only so much a hot-blooded man can take, before giving in to passions, and eventually, I had to wait outside despite the misty drizzle that had descended on the city. It was either that or get into something I'd rather not remember, in my dotage, when cradling a grandchild. A foursome with Dad and two hookers. I shudder at the thought even now.

I didn't have to wait too long though, and Dad was merry as Santa, big red nose to boot. We walked back to the hotel, me in stunned silence, him whistling a happy tune.

I learned quite a bit in those few days with the parents, family history, Mum's obsession to get me wed, and Dad's obsession, which I believe I strongly take after.

In any other circumstance I wouldn't have thought twice about the trip to the red light district, but there with the old man, it just didn't seem right. Not only that, but for some inexplicable reason, I have some kind of nagging guilt when I look at women now, a pang of doubt and uncertainty, then Nellie pops into my thoughts. Nellie who only exists in textual format, but metaphorically 'listens' to all my woes and jokes. We email frequently now, two or three times a day. But yet I still have no idea where she is or what she looks like. I'm getting a few threads of information, but tugging on them often results in a broken line or a dead end. I let her tell me things as she feels like it, rather than asking for details. She's more comfortable that way.

Back home now and I've been sleeping on the couch for the last couple of nights, rather uncomfortable, so I'm going to take a step I should have taken months ago, and clean out Aunty Joyce's room. It has been left as it was, barely touched at all, since she passed away. Even when Lottie was here, I told her I preferred no one went in there, that I'd get to it when I could. She understood, she said, and no more was mentioned on the matter. But now, I can't face the room I decorated with Lottie either. There's a lingering scent of her perfume still as I open the wardrobe, and echoes of morning cuddles together after long nights of rampant bunny-fucking. I thought I was over her, but those visceral memories flooded my brain, leaving dank and mouldy thoughts pervading.

I took the ring back to Covent Garden yesterday, whence it came. They politely complained, but I name-dropped the hotel and then they hastily refunded the money. Minus a 'service charge'. Miserable fuckers. Not my fault that my girlfriend fled the scene with barely a nod. Or maybe it is? But if it was my fault, I don't know what I did wrong. I told Nellie I had to return something important to a jeweller in London, something that brought up emotions I couldn't handle, something I would rather not discuss. She replied simply - 'sorry :('

.   .   .

Contrary to the perfume and sex memories of my room, Joyce's room has that old-lady funk to it. Not quite moth-balls, but support stockings, lavender, floral dresses and gaudy amber bracelets. I'm packing most of the clothes into big bin bags and intending to take them to a charity shop. They are mostly in perfect condition, either worn once or not at all. Some even with the tags still on. The wardrobe is more of a walk-in dressing room, so this could take a while. I'm also getting a new bed delivered and they are taking her old one away, because I can't stand the thought of sleeping with Aunty, even in spirit form. In fact, anything that isn't firmly fixed down, I'm clearing out and replacing. I need a fresh start.

There are boxes of paperwork, photos, accumulated junk of decades. Most of these I think I'll pass on to Mum and Dad to keep hold of, or maybe Rory and Jane would be interested. A lot of the photos are of the hotel, inside and out, from various events that have been held there. There's a few photo albums too, and some scrapbooks. I take a break from the dusty work of packing clothes and leaf through for a while. The hotel hasn't changed much in decades, perhaps a lick of paint here and there, but a time-traveller from fifty years in the past would be well at home if he landed in the hotel of today.

There are many people I don't recognise, over the years, photos of strangers in a book of forgotten memories. But there's one man who features quite regularly during a section in the book that, from the clothing and hairstyles at least, feels like must be mid-1980s.

Then there's a large photo, fixed in with tape. Joyce and the man together, happy, smiling, in the Myatt bar, his arm around her. Underneath is written 'Joyce and Charlie - November 1985'

The next page has a newspaper cutting, dated December 26th 1985, explaining how a man was mown down by a bus on Christmas Eve after leaving a jewellery shop. Oblivious to the world around him apparently, he stepped in front of the path of a number forty-two bus in Covent Garden. Mr Charles Webbe, aged fifty-seven, no children, no spouse. Survived only by a nephew, William Webbe, whom he acted as a father to, after William's own parents passed away in the 1960s.

Fuck me, he was going to propose for Christmas, with a ring he bought in Covent Garden? The ring I now have, still in my wallet, from the same place I took one back to yesterday? It can't be?

Charlie Webbe. Sounds a bit too much like Charlotte Webbe. I wonder, could they be related?

With the help of Ben and his Land Rover, I'm taking twenty-plus bags of clothes, assorted furniture and heaps of bracelets and necklaces to the local charity shop. I'm sure scores of old ladies will lap it all up. Ben reverses into the driveway and opens up the doors. After the usual back-slaps, we load up all the bags and a chest of drawers, a huge lamp, and a heavy mirror. It's a sad thing to have to do, but I think a healthy step. There's no point in avoiding parts of my own house forever.

"Good to get a fresh start, you'll feel better for it." Ben is chirpy. A bit happier since the last time I saw him.

"I think so. How's Lucy?"

"Oh very good, thanks. We had our first scan the other day. I couldn't see anything but squiggles, but apparently, there's a little critter in there, growing away like a bean."

"Excellent, did you get the sex?"

"Well, that's a bit personal! But obviously I did since she's pregnant!"

"No, you fool! The sex of the baby. The gender!"

"Oh, right. No, we didn't. Too soon, apparently."

"Ah, okay."

"I have been thinking though, my little basement isn't going to be big enough, really. It was fine for me, but now Lucy has taken over ninety percent of the place, I think the baby will take the other ten, leaving me to sleep outside!"

"Yes, I was wondering about that. What do you plan on doing about that?"

"Buy a house, I suppose. Isn't that the done thing?"

"Good plan, do you have the money?"

"Er, no, but I was thinking of getting a mortgage."

"Right, of course."

"We actually found a place that we liked the look of, close by to Mum, too."

"Ah, excellent! Get it sorted then, mate!"

"Need a deposit to get the mortgage, which is something I lack, by about twenty thousand pounds. Bit stuck without that."

Which, coincidentally, is the amount of money I swapped a small circle of metal and stone for, only the other day.

"I'll sort you out, Ben."

We arrive at the charity shop, somewhat abruptly, because Ben slammed on the brakes a bit sudden there.

"You'll, what? I can't possibly let you!"

"That ring I got for Lottie, I took it back, got my money refunded. Which gets you a deposit on a house. Swings and roundabouts, eh, mate?"

"But, oh my god. Thanks, Keith!"

"Don't mention it."

We unload all the bags and furniture into the charity shop to grateful staff, who'll probably buy most of the floral dresses themselves, by the looks of them. So that's that. Aunty Joyce mostly taken care of. Now to sort Ben out.

"Let's go back via the hotel, I have an idea."

We arrive at the elegant London Myatt, not really in London, but as we're on the tube, it still counts. But rather than go inside, we take a walk around the grounds, which Ben has kept so trim and neat for many years. He's a dab hand at topiary too, and Aunty Joyce did so love the gardens.

"I told you about the hotel modernisation efforts I was doing? The upgrades we're working on in America?"

"Yes, wonderful idea I think, good to keep things fresh and new."

"Indeed. But you know, one thing I have absolutely no idea about is the exterior of all those grand palatial hotels. I think I need a global artistic landscape designer."

"What?"

"Sounds like a full-time staff position, a bit of travel too, perhaps back and forth to Indiana if the need should arise." I'm pulling this job out of my arse here, but I think I can get the folks on my side now to approve it.

"Fuck me, mate, I don't know where I'd be without you!"

"Up the old brown creek, lacking a paddle. That's where!" I laugh and slap the old beardy fool on the back.

"Congratulations. A car, a wife, a baby, a house and a proper job. I'm jealous, Ben." I feel a twitch of emotion in my eyes, we can't have that. "I think a crate of Belgian at the offy is called for!"

Chapter Forty-Four

I f Lucy wasn't pregnant and married to my best mate, I think she would have knelt down and sucked my dick then and there when Ben told her the news. Apparently her original thoughts about the basement - that it was fine and actually quite charming - have rapidly swung south, having lived there for a short while. She's not a fan and can't wait to get out. Even the sound of the upstairs toilet flushing causes her unduly large amounts of stress. Probably emphasised by the hormonal complications of pregnancy, but still, I think it's best that they got it sorted very quickly. The house was already empty, which was a massive help, and we enlisted the help of our newly efficient Myatt solicitor for the paperwork. Then Rory, in an act of unprecedented generosity and kindness agreed to Ben's job upgrade and co-signed on the mortgage application, speeding it all through. He said Ben has always done solid work and he's happy to have him on board full time.

'Everything happens for a reason.'

. . .

That was the email I got from Nellie after I told her all the things I discovered about Aunty Joyce and the man she was almost engaged to. I wasn't planning to go into detail, but I found myself writing the email anyway. It's easy to discuss things with Nellie, she doesn't ask tricky questions. She just reads what I write and either says nothing, or something profound and thought-provoking. I feel safe and at home when I'm writing to her, irrational as that seems.

Then I added the similarities of my own life, buying an expensive ring on the same day, same location. Sure, I didn't get hit by a bus, but it felt that way when I got home that day.

But what is that reason?

Ben and Lucy are packed up, ready to go. I'm assisting with the move, of course. We're loading up everything into the back of the Land Rover. Lucy is rosy-cheeked and showing the baby-bump a bit now. There's a subconscious attractiveness to that. She's carrying small things, the bags and boxes that Ben allows her. She mostly ignores his fussing. I can see both sides of their argument and the love they have for each other. Damn, I'm a sad and lonely twat.

"Is this fucking couch filled with lead?"

"It is a tad heavy, isn't it?"

"There's nowhere to hold it either. Are you sure you need a couch?"

"Where else are we going to sit, Keith?"

"Thought you bohemians liked to sit cross-legged on the floor, or on a beanbag or something?"

"Well, okay, we need it for you to sleep on when you are too drunk to go home."

"Touché. Speaking of which, what does it take to get a bottle of water around here?"

. . .

I'm pouring in sweat when we finally lump the behemoth couch into the new house. I flop down onto it, needing a break. Ben goes to fetch a drink for us.

There's a buzz in my pocket, my black phone. I rarely even pick up the red one these days. A message from Nellie, unsolicited. Not an email, but a blue-bubble message.

'Had a feeling you'd need cheering up. All good things come to those who wait, Keith.'

There's a photo too. It's a pair of legs, in a bathtub, from the point of view of the owner of the legs. Nice shapely pair. Her toenails all painted different colours. Lottie used to do that, too. I wonder if that's a fashion? Anyway, that was a nice surprise and it has cheered me up. I reply back,

'Can I see more? :)'

'See above. All good things come to those who wait…'

I look again at those legs, the kind I'd like wrapped around me. The bath looks familiar, a roll top. I look at the photo closely, I'd swear that was the Boston Myatt bathtub. Could be wrong though, it's blurry at the edges of the photo, like the phone is in a waterproof case or something.

'Are you in Boston, by any chance?'

'Who's to say where we are, at any given moment.'

She's gone back to being vague and elusive. I'll let it go, or she'll clam up. But I know she's in Boston. Interesting.

"Right, break time is over! Back on your heads!" Ben gets up off the other side of the couch. I didn't even notice he was there.

"What are you smiling at?"

"Oh, nothing, just a pair of disembodied legs, you know."

"I worry about you, sometimes, Keith Myatt."

"I think I've been upgraded."

"Yes, to chief box lifter! Come on, there's a nice Belgian ale and a Chinese takeaway calling our names when this is done."

"Aye aye, captain! You sure know how to motivate a chap."

Glad of the couch now, the food and drink, and the friends I have. Lucy is pottering around, unpacking things and organising the nursery.

Despite me being soaked in sweat and probably stinking like a wrestler's posing pouch after we unloaded the last batch, she hugged me so hard I feared the baby might pop out early. I'd changed her life, she said, many times over. Just doing my job, I told her. She looked away with a tear in her eyes. Hormones!

I drew the line when Ben tried to hug me too. Lucy might have an olfactory disorder that prevents her smelling foul odours, but I have my nostrils to think of. We worked on connecting up the TV instead and now we're slumped in front of it, spewing out some contrived sitcom that I'm not even watching. Nellie is much more amusing. She's messaging me jokes and a photo of her dinner. I tried to figure out where she was based on the food and the plate, but it's hard to tell. I gave up the Kremlinology, because as she said, it doesn't really matter where we are, we can always be together in spirit.

"Who are you texting?" Ben turns the TV volume down and looks over at me.

"Hmm? Oh, just someone."

"Come on, you've got that look on your mug, who is she?"

"Nellie."

"The elephant?"

"Shut up, no, that's all she'll tell me."

I tell Ben what little information I have about the evasive Nellie, mostly what I know about her is that I don't know much about her at all, and that makes her all the more attractive. Nice legs, though.

"So, what are you going to do about this?"

"Just see how it goes, I suppose? Not really sure what else I can do."

"Not like you to have a relationship that isn't physical."

"I know, must be something wrong with me. Don't know if it's a relationship though?"

"She sent you a photo of her legs in a bath, that's a relationship."

"Really?"

"Oh yes. If it was just feet, then I could go either way, but legs, up to the thigh? Definitely a relationship."

"Interesting."

Ben cracks open another beer and passes it over to me.

"You should probably try and get to know her better."

"I've been trying! But she's hard to engage. Slippery customer."

"Well, clearly she likes you, for some reason. You said she messaged you first?"

"Yes, on the Twin Flame forum."

"What does that tell you?"

"She's insane? Looking for love? Trying to find her spiritual partner in life? I don't even know anymore."

"Maybe she's just lonely and reaching out? Maybe she doesn't even know what she wants herself."

"Could be."

"Or perhaps, she knows exactly what she wants, but she's trying to see if you are it. Or him."

"She has warmed a little, lately, I've been writing her long emails, spilling my heart to her. I don't even know why I did, it just felt right at the time."

Ben gives me a knowing nod, "That's what happened with me and Lucy... Now look where we are." He waves his arms around at the new house we're in, boxes of belongings all around us, a stack of beers and empty food containers on the coffee table in front of us. His blossoming wife nesting and organising a nursery room, probably deciding on paint colours and baby names as we sit here drinking. It's not so bad, where they are.

"I don't know what else to do, really."

"Just be yourself. That's always worked before with the ladies."

"It's worked plenty well for one night stands and casual sex, sure, but this is something totally different."

"Maybe you are totally different now, too?"

"Yes, I rather think I am."

Chapter Forty-Five

W ell, I wasn't expecting the message I woke to this morning. There must be some kind of epidemic around me and I'm the only one immune. Bella, my 'adopted niece', my MemphisBelle, is getting married. She asked me to walk her down the aisle, in place of a father. The reason for this sudden turn of events; she's pregnant. Thankfully not from me - I checked the dates. At least, I hope I'm right. But no, definitely not from me. From Danny. The little prick couldn't keep it wrapped, or perhaps it was a LARP night - in days of old, when knights were bold...

She's happy, I think. It isn't a bad thing. Daisy will get a sibling and a father figure. She says she does love Danny and he loves her back, and front. He's got good prospects, he isn't a drug dealing sack of shit. I'm happy too. But for fuck's sake, could my friends stop emphasising my empty and pathetic life?

The wedding, which will be held in a local registry office, is in a week. I'm flying out tomorrow. I've been enjoying the break from travel for a while, but I suppose I'm doomed to live a jet-set life.

.   .   .

Ben and Lucy, happily settled in their new house, agreed to take the cats from me. Now they have space and a garden, there's no sense in Ben driving back and forth to feed them here anymore. I'll miss the fluff balls. But I suppose they aren't going far and I'll see them frequently. Over the last few weeks they've been my only company most of the time. Them and Nellie, in non-corporeal form. Manifesting in my brain via the medium of text and occasional photos. She's a tease. Never shows me the top shelf stuff, always tells me to be patient and bide my time.

I've seen more bath-tub photos, amongst others, from various different locations. No face yet.

Seems she's on a perpetual holiday, much like myself. I've asked her what she's travelling for, she just said 'reasons' and nothing more.

I haven't had much to tell her lately, as I've mainly been lingering at home. There's only so many cat photos one can send before that becomes boring. She said they were cute, though. Said it's a shame they have to leave the house. She'd miss seeing them.

I have extrapolated some facts, I think, about her:

She's either incredibly rich or her job has her travelling a lot to expensive hotels - much like mine does. But if she has a job, I can't fathom what it is.

I estimate her age around mid to late twenties, based on my countless studies of her gams, attractively curvaceous as they are. Sometimes dripping wet, other times lying on a bed, pointed at a TV.

She occasionally drops off the radar, for longer than the time-zone difference would suggest. During those black-out periods, I have no idea what she is doing, but presumably her job, or maybe travelling?

She's no stranger to travel, knows the best places to eat in any city I ever mention.

And I have an inkling, that for some unexplained reason, she seems to like me, and all the things I tell her about my life. If I skip over some detail, she asks me to explain, genuinely

ADAM ECCLES

interested. Silly things, like what did I eat for lunch, did I remember to order cat food from the grocery store, and more pertinently, have I met any 'random women' lately. I haven't, but I am getting quite thirsty, here in this drought period. Especially with Nellie teasing me with photos and suggestive messages.

I told her I'm going back on the road too. After the wedding in Memphis, I'm heading back to Denver for the opening night of our fancy new nightclub. Literally ice-cool, attracting only the finest of Denver's modern youth for the utterly exclusive 'Liquid Night'. Will this really be a success and bring us business? Is it just a frivolous waste of time and money, will it upset the hotel staff and normal guests. I sincerely hope this isn't going to be a horrible disaster, but lately, I've had some niggling doubts. The team does keep me informed of progress and the hotel manager tells me he's happy with how things are going, for the most part, so I do try and keep up my confidence. It is hard though, when the fate of my three team members rests on a crazy idea we pulled from our collective arses. The crazy ideas are the best ones, I try and remind myself.

The tinkling of the fountain in the Memphis Myatt lobby will forever remind me of the first time I met Bella here, so sad, so tragic. So beautiful and innocent, yet so dangerous. I could have turned her away and left her to rot in a world of abusive convict boyfriends with a toss of a coin, but instead, I think I have changed the course of her life, hopefully for the better. 'Give me a chance', she said. So I did, and it was the right thing to do.

Now I'm to give her away to Danny, the up and coming LARPer who doesn't use condoms. Hope he understands the consequences of that. I might have to have a chat with him later. But for now, Bella and Daisy are coming to see me in my usual Memphis suite.

. . .

"Keith!"

I am greeted in the traditional way, a thousand kisses and hugs. I will never get tired of that. Then Daisy, awake and bubbling, I pick her up and give her a hug too. Cute little thing she is.

"Oh, I think I smell poop." I hand Daisy back to Bella to take care of. "I guess you'll have your hands full, with two of the little critters?"

"Are you mad at me, Mister Keith?" She deftly changes the soiled diaper.

"No, Bella! Why would you say that?"

"'Cos I done got knocked up again! And you wanted me to get my education and all…"

"Things happen, you are still young, you have time and you will get your education and make something of yourself. This isn't a setback." I pat her tummy, she smiles her tragic smile. Her eyes still sad. "Are you mad at yourself?"

"A little, but I love babies, so it'll be okay. I guess. Danny says we need a bigger apartment now, so he's looking."

"Let me know if you need some help with that. Financially."

"Oh, you shut up, you ain't giving me no more money."

"Can if I want." She laughs, the smile now reaching her eyes. "I only care about one thing, Bella."

"What's that?"

"Are you happy? With Danny, with your life?"

"I am, but it's all because of you." She rests her hand on my chest, then nestles in for a cuddle to hide her welling eyes. I wrap my arms around her once more, squeezing her tight.

"What about you, Mister Keith? Are you happy with your life?" She looks up at me.

"Um, well, I don't know, Bella. I don't have a measure to mark against."

"Is there someone in your life who makes you smile?"

"You do, Bella."

"Aside from me, dummy." She laughs and slaps me on the arse, still in my embrace.

Nellie springs to mind, her messages do fulfil that requirement. I just crave something more than a purely electronic relationship. "Yes, sort of. I think."

"Who is she?"

I tell Bella about the mysterious Nellie, how she messages me frequently now, and has for a while, but I don't even know her face, only her legs. How I don't know where she is or what she does. Yet somehow I'm drawn to her and I tell her about my life every day.

"That's kinda weird, don't you think?"

"I do, yes, but perhaps she has a good reason for her secrecy. She keeps telling me to be patient and all will be revealed."

"What's she waiting for?"

"I don't know."

"Be careful, Mister Keith. I don't want you to get hurt again."

"I'll be fine, Bella. Don't worry about me. Now, tell me about your wedding!"

"Ain't that much to tell, we go to the courthouse and get a license, then we go to the registry office and say the vows. I guess that's it!"

"No guests? No reception?"

"We can't afford all that fancy stuff, Mister. It don't matter anyway."

"I'm sure we can sort something out for you here, Bella. I'll take care of it. Don't you want your fairytale wedding?"

"Oh boy, I don't care about that stuff."

"Don't you want to invite some friends or family?"

"I don't have any."

"Your mother? Or grandma?"

"Mom is a drunk ass piece of shit. I don't want nothin' to do with her. Grandma, well, she don't really leave the house much these days, and it would complicate things. No, I got you, Uncle Keith, that's all I need." She smiles and picks up Daisy to feed her. "Can I stay with you. Until the wedding?"

"What? I… Well um…" I can't resist her puppy dog eyes, even though I know I should and everything about this is wrong. "Of course, Bella."

I hired a limousine to take us to the registry office. On reflection now it seems a bit ridiculous, all of us sat in the back. A million prom-night sweaty arses on these seats before us. Danny and I flank Bella, who holds Daisy on her lap. At least he didn't dress up in his LARP gear for the wedding, he's gone the traditional route and rented a suit, or a 'tux' as he insists. Bella and I went shopping for a dress, so she looks stunning in her simple white gown, tasteful cleavage, and her hair and makeup taken care of at the hotel salon this morning, while I held Daisy and tried to force back the emotions that suddenly flooded over me. I do love this girl, but in a strange way that I can't map to my previous experiences. When we make love, the fatherly feelings wash away and are replaced with lust, but then when I look at her sleeping, her baby lying next to her, a desperate desire to look after her and keep her safe rushes forward and I feel ashamed at our physical passions. But no more now, she's getting married, she's having another baby. She's off limits from now on. These thoughts most definitely won't make it into my messages with Nellie. Some things are best kept buried.

Oddly, Danny didn't want to invite any family or friends to the wedding either, said they might not approve, and he didn't want a fuss. I interpret that as he hasn't told anyone in his family yet that Bella is pregnant with his child, or perhaps that Bella even exists. Fair enough, he can take things at his own pace, as long as he looks after his new family I don't care who attends the wedding.

Ironically, or perhaps by design, the marriage license bureau is directly across the street from the divorce referee. I'm sure that makes the happy couples coming out, newlywed, flinch a little as they watch the happily divorced couples exiting opposite. Doesn't say much for the longevity of marriage. I did wonder, a little, why Danny and Bella are even bothering to go the official route, as it seems almost perfunctory in this age. Danny said he just wanted to make it right. So I guess the chivalry of his knight persona is a real thing. I don't have anything against the tradition, but it doesn't really make any difference in how they will live their lives.

Nevertheless, the marriage hall is a stately building worthy of Bella's beauty. The room is far too big for our party of four, including Daisy, who remains good as gold throughout. We did have to drum up another witness to sign the documents though. An old lady who was knitting, waiting in the corridor.

And that's it, five minutes later they exit, Mr and Mrs Danny and Bella Burgess and Daisy Hayes, along with 'bump' who is barely even a bump so far. Another family tied up and made whole with a few words and some official government paperwork. Fifty bucks and a stamp and she's a Mrs.

She's happy though, in the limousine back to the Myatt, there's joy in those usually sad eyes. A happy ever after, I hope.

I'm reminded of Ben and Lucy, of their impending baby too, and how everyone around me seems to be more of an adult, even eighteen-year-old Bella, than I seem to be. Then my thoughts return to Lottie and the ring, the similarities with Aunty Joyce and her engagement that never was. Then Nellie, her name already engraved inside the old ring. The only woman I have left available in my life and I don't even know what she looks like. Maybe it doesn't matter, she does make me smile regardless, there's something about her that I can't quite put my finger on, but even though I barely know her, I feel like I've always known her soul, deep down. Perhaps she actually is my twin flame?

I didn't think it was possible to have a smaller and more modest wedding day than Ben and Lucy had, but here we are, Bella, Danny and I. Daisy asleep in her buggy, in the Memphis Myatt dining room, at the back, out of the way, exactly where I sat with

Bella when we first met. I'm moving into a smaller room tonight, letting the happy couple take the suite for their honeymoon. Danny is only taking a few days off work, keen to get back and earn the money for them to get a better place to live before the baby is born. Fair dues to the lad, he's making an effort. I think I'll pay another visit to the ATM in the lobby before I see them off.

One last gift from Uncle Keith.

Chapter Forty-Six

There's a buzz in the air in the Denver Myatt, perhaps caused by the air-conditioning in the ballroom set to 'brass monkeys' on the dial. But the place looks amazing. Barely recognisable as the formal and elegant place it usually is. They've used twelve-foot high room dividers against the walls, draped with black velvet, for a deep darkness, contrasted with electric blue flashes. The DJ booth has a constant stream of cold mist washing over it like a waterfall, down onto the dance area. Dimly lit in the same electric blue. Projections, almost holographic against the fog, show a ghostly version of the Instagram account, which is brimming over with 'likes' and plenty of people tagging it with their intention to attend. The team have done wonders. I'm proud.

"It's fucking freezing in here!"

"It's meant to be, it's the coolest place in Denver!" India walks with me back to my room, pressing each floor button in the elevator as we go up.

"But is it safe? I mean, will people slip on ice?"

"It's not that cold, you have to dance to stay warm. That's the point. Besides, we've got a team of twenty 'hot chicks' who will be patrolling with free shots of a warming drink, to give to anyone who looks frozen."

"You've thought of everything."

"Yup, that's why you pay us, right?"

"Quite so."

"So how many people are coming?"

"Um, like twelve hundred. That's the maximum capacity anyway, for the fire regulations."

"Shit, that's a lot. And celebrities?"

"Oh yeah, we got a bunch." She lists through names I have never heard of and probably wouldn't recognise if I met them either, but I'm sure they mean something to the teens of Denver. I hope so at least. Apparently, they aren't traditional celebrities from TV or movies or even musicians, they are YouTube stars and Instagram girls. I have no idea what that means but I hope they bring kids with money to burn.

We have a few hours before the club opens. India gulps down a drink with me, then flits away back to the club floor to do last minute preparations. There's apparently three large industrial freezers full of 'glasses' made of ice that need to be wheeled into the bar area. Ironically, there's also a separate 'chill out' room that's actually a warm-up zone. One level up, a smaller space filled with soft couches and ambient music. You'll need an 'exclusive' ticket to get in there, double the price, limited to three hundred tickets. These guys certainly know what they are doing. I can't wait to see how this pans out.

I shower and get dressed in my new 'club gear' which is just new versions of the clothes I always wear and send a few photos I took of the ballroom to Nellie, then to Ben and Bella. Everyone says it looks great. I know I had little to do with this other than kicking it off, but it feels nice to have my work appreciated.

At the door of the ballroom, I'm issued my 'all-access pass' - I should fucking think so too, and a pair of thermal gloves, which is an odd thing, but I suppose it's so I don't get frostbite or hypothermia. I shan't be dancing, but if it gets too chilly I'll head up to the warm-up zone.

As I enter the room the music hits me in the face like a London bus, the bass thud so powerful my chest is reverberating. A pulsing, rhythmic beat, forcing me to take notice. Jude waves from the DJ booth, he's entirely dressed in white, glowing in the ultraviolet glare.

So far there are only a dozen or so people in the club, mostly congregating around the bar area, so I head over and find India and Sally serving drinks. I try to yell a hello, but the music is too loud, I can't make myself heard at all. I don't know how these kids will manage to chat each other up in here. Or perhaps that's the point, all you can do is dance and grope. I grab a glass of something that turns out to be fruity vodka and wander around.

It's even colder than it was earlier, there's a mist of dry ice a foot deep on the floor, a smell of ozone too. The lights are mostly deep purple and blue, occasionally red and white. On the ceiling a projection of aurora borealis in deep green, phasing to blue and back again. The whole effect is truly incredible. I gulp down my vodka and find somewhere to put the glass down. Even through the gloves, my fingers are going numb. I wave down one of the 'hot chicks' that passes by, hard to miss as they are wearing flame red jackets with 'Hot' emblazoned on the back. She smiles and passes me a little red shot glass of something, then moves on. Sure, she's got a jacket on, but her legs go all the way up and there must be a bit of a draught with only that tiny skirt... I gulp down the drink she gave me, but instantly regret it and almost spit it out. Fucking Southern Comfort!

The body count inside rises rapidly, from a few dozen to a few hundred in what seems like minutes, and there's a line of people at the door going back all through the corridors. I walk by unfettered with my golden wristband, but honestly, most of the staff probably know who I am anyway.

The chill out room is almost empty, I suppose not enough people need to defrost yet, but I spot a few bodies on a sprawling sofa next to the bar area. The music is desolate and quieter in here, so it is possible to talk. I think these must be the 'celebs' as they are also wearing golden wristbands and acting like arseholes. One of the girls is dangerously attractive though, she smiles as I walk by to the bar.

"Got any Belgian beer here? I'm not really interested in sugary vodka in chunks of ice." The barman laughs and nods, pulling me a glass of finest ale.

"Hey, do you know who they are?" I motion to the beautiful people lingering close by.

"Yeah, sure, everyone does."

"I don't."

"Oh, well, there's Skip, Finlay, Richmond…"

"No, never mind the dudes, who's that girl?" I nod towards the captivating one on the edge.

He sniggers, "That's Tamika Cove. She's a YouTube star. Millions of subscribers."

"Really? Thanks man." I leave the lad a healthy tip then pull out my phone and Google her name, sure enough, that's her, and she's indeed a YouTube star. I plug in headphones from my pocket and watch one of her videos, skipping through the initial eight minutes of pointless chit-chat, only to find that was the video. There's no actual substance or topic, unless you count a shopping bag of clothes she recently bought from some mall store and showed the camera. Is this entertainment?

I flick through some more of her videos and they all seem similar, sometimes she puts on makeup, other times she has a camera follow her through shops. I fail to see the reason for the millions of views, honestly - aside from her obvious asset, which is her undeniable beauty.

"Hello. Keith Myatt, just wanted to thank you all for coming to our little opening night." There are a few nods of acknowledgement from the group, but nothing more. I sit down next to Tamika, the vapid YouTube star.

"Myatt, like the hotel?" She turns to me, flashing her golden smile.

"That's right, Tamika? You have an interesting name."

"Thanks, it was a gift from my parents." I can't tell if she's being sincere or sarcastic.

"Likewise, my parents are big stones fans." I don't think she understood. "So what's your YouTube channel about?"

"Oh! Have you seen it? I just crossed fifty million views." The group around us give a little cheer at that.

"Wow, that's a lot!"

"Skip has over two hundred million." An annoying looking chap lying on the floor vaping gives a salute and the group cheer louder.

"Amazing, but what is your channel about?"

"I do hauls, tuts, fashion, you know?" I have no idea what those things are, so I just nod. I'm clearly far out of my depth here. It occurs to me that old Keith would have bullshitted his way into this girl's pants, one way or another, and I almost trod that line again, but something stopped me. So what if she's pretty? A lot of girls are pretty, this one is as banal as a tabloid headline. I have no interest in getting her knickers off, because there's nothing that interests me in her head.

What the fuck is wrong with me?

I'm saved from further embarrassment with the arrival of India and a photographer. She's excited, awed in the presence of these layabouts. The photographer snaps away as they all smile like toothpaste commercials and I move out of range.

"Guys! Oh my god! I can't believe you're here! The room is packed, we're at max capacity, there's twelve hundred kids freezing and desperate to mingle with the superstars! It's time for the entrance."

.   .   .

We slip out of the 'chill out' zone and down a back stairway, guarded by a hefty bouncer. Then we're ushered into a room I didn't know existed, and onto a circular platform in the middle of the room. The 'stars' seem to know what's going on, but I'm just blindly following, with India nudging me in excitement. We assemble on the platform and India mutters something into her headset. I can feel the boom of the bass through the floor, we must be directly above the ballroom. Abruptly, the sound ceases, and the platform we're on starts to move down, slowly at first, then speeding up a little. We're lowering down into the ballroom, a curtain of thick dry ice around the edge of the circle, pulses of lights flashing furiously all around us, lasers spinning brightly coloured symbols onto the mist. An epic beat starts to form as Jude turns up the volume, building into a crescendo of noise, a crashing boom as we hit the ground and the mist is blown away, leaving us standing in a bright white spotlight, a freezing wind blowing down. Then silence, a crowd of stunned faces all around us and the millennial superstars all lift up their arms and wave. The cue for the beat to rush back, and they all begin to dance, immediately surrounded by hordes of excited fans. Fuck me, what an entrance!

India takes my arm and leads me through the chaos to the DJ booth, a backdoor up into the nest where Jude is standing, fiddling with equipment. He nods at me, gives a peace sign and a huge smile.

"Fantastic work, Jude!" I scream as loud as I can, but he can't hear me. India takes off her headset and gives it to me, motioning towards my ear. I put it on and speak again, this time Jude can hear.

"Thanks, Keith, hope you liked the big entrance!"

"Amazing! I had no idea!"

"Took some convincing to get the permission, but we thought it would be cool."

"Definitely cool! This place is literally shaking. I couldn't be happier!"

There's a sea of people in front of us, dancing, drinking, enjoying themselves, a huge cluster around the celebrities, Tamika in particular. The room is packed, the bar is five people deep, desperate to get their gloves on a frozen squirt of sugary vodka.

I'm officially too old for this, I don't think my body can stand the pressure of sound for much longer, so I make my excuses, carry out some complicated handshakes and exit, sneaking back up to the chill out zone, which is a bit busier now. I head back to the bar and another Belgian, but I find Sally there, quietly drinking a glass of wine.

"Sally, congratulations, the place looks amazing."

"Thank you," she smiles, "I hear it's filling up."

"Jam-packed. A total success. This calls for a drink to celebrate!"

Stragglers left the club around four in the morning, I heard, after that a team of staff descended on the room and detangled all the cables, cleared up all the broken ice before it could melt, shuttered away all the decor and cleaned the place beyond recognition. The ballroom ready and waiting for a wedding reception the next day. I let the team get some sleep, then called them all to my suite for an afternoon meeting. The smiles are ear to ear, and so they should be. The night couldn't have gone any smoother.

"I've got some numbers from the manager I wanted to share with you." I open up my laptop and find the email. "We actually sold thirteen hundred tickets, and all the exclusives too. Estimates of the folks who didn't get in are around another two or three hundred. The bar was bled dry, both in the ballroom and the chill-out zone." Some laughs and gasps from the team. "We smashed through over two-hundred-and-twenty-thousand dollars gross revenue, which worked out to over one-hundred-and-fifty grand net, after we paid all the staff and whatnot. These are rough estimates, but guys, we did it! YOU did it!"

"We looked at the ballroom schedules and we think we can do one night every two weeks, more or less, so what's that, three point eight million dollars a year profit? Can we keep our jobs now?" India speaks for the team.

"Fuck, yes!"

Chapter Forty-Seven

B en is meeting me in Miami, Florida. The first trip in his new role as global grass coordinator, or lawnmower man, as I secretly call it. I'm doing my usual quality inspections in some hotels I haven't been to lately down the east coast, and Ben can assist with his weed inspection. Best do this now, before Lucy gets too pregnant for Ben to be away.

I leave Denver on a genuine high, the team signed up for twenty-five 'Liquid Nights' per year, free rein to come up with crazy new ideas for keeping the night interesting for the young folks. They were talking about getting some bands to play too. I fed all the details back to Rory and he seemed impressed. Hard to tell through his curt email replies.

I told Nellie all about it too, showed her some more photos and videos of the evening. She said it looked amazing and she wished she could have been there. I wish she had suggested that before, because I could have made it happen. When I asked where she was, I got the usual vague 'somewhere'. She's infuriating sometimes. Give me something to work with, woman!

. . .

I think I'm obsessed with her. The first thing I do when I wake up is check for messages from Nellie, the last thing I do at night is tell her 'good night', and in between, anything interesting that I see or do, I pop Nellie a message. She responds, sends me similar things, and lately, she's been adding a few 'xxx' to the end of her 'good nights'.

This is ridiculous. I'm acting like the teenagers who came to the Denver club, but there is a thrill in it, I enjoy this dance and slow baby steps towards something that may turn into a real relationship. This is new to me, usually the chase lasts a few hours, never before has it been months. If I do get to meet her finally, the build-up will be so massive that I may just explode in my pants when I hug her. Balls like two tins of condensed milk here...

Out of the ice-box, into the oven. Miami is a fiery hell of humid heat. I'm thankful for the air conditioning in the rental car, cranked down to the lowest setting. I had to wait at the airport for three tedious hours and Ben's flight to arrive, in a bar, not drinking.

Ben is in good cheer, and he made his first transatlantic flight, alone, with no disasters or panic attacks. He's wearing shorts, and the sight of his hairy legs is making me wish I didn't have breakfast on the flight. Men in shorts should be illegal, especially this particular man.

"Is that really necessary?" I motion to his 'squatch-legs.

"I knew you'd moan about the shorts, but Lucy said to tell you to shut the fuck up. It's hot."

"Does she fight all your fights for you?"

"Only the ones she'll win."

"Fair enough, but I don't have to like it. How's 'bump'?"

"Doing well! Can't believe this is all happening so fast."

"Indeed, before you know it the little critter will be in college, demanding money and a car."

. . .

265

We arrive at the hotel and dive straight in, walking around the perimeter. Ben mumbles some latin and makes some notes, presumably conjuring up a demon or something with his incantations. Seems a bit excessive, why not just use a spray of weedkiller?

"Well, what do you think?"

"Erm, well, nice?"

"It's shit, Ben. It's neat and tidy, trimmed, not a blade out of place, like a churchy MILF on a beach holiday. But it's boring."

"It is a bit, shame to waste this fertile land with plain old grass."

"Indeed. So your job is to sex it up."

"Right. Never heard the word sex in conjunction with gardens before, but whatever you say."

"Ah, well, you never met Emma Saunders, did you?"

"Doesn't ring a bell, no."

"Obsessed with shagging outside, she was. Up trees, in the park. We once did it in a graveyard at night. Edgy!"

"I'm sure that's what some poor ghostly spirit wanted to see, your naked arse bobbing up and down!"

"Do them good. Anyway, what are we doing about the grass?"

"I'll think about it. Draw up some sketches and ideas. Can we get a map of the grounds?"

"Should think so. Let's go check in and I'll have a poke around."

In my room, I open my laptop and the global Myatt system, I'm sure there's some maps around somewhere. But while I have it open, a thought occurs to me. I search our entire booking archive for the first name 'Nellie' and let it run. There aren't that many results, and even fewer this year. All the surnames are different though, and the dates and locations don't really add up. Worth a try I suppose.

I do find a map of the Miami Myatt though. Not very

good, but it will do. I email it to Ben, but realise the fool doesn't have a laptop. I'm not working with messy scraps of paper. I need to pull him, kicking and screaming, into the twenty-first century. I message him to meet me in the lobby ASAP.

"Ready?"

"For what? I was about to have a shower."

"Oh, well, perhaps I should have waited, but never mind. We're going out to get you sorted."

"Where to?"

"Apple store."

At the store I get Ben kitted out with an iPad and Pencil, MacBook Pro, and a new iPhone, while we're at it. His existing one looks like he's used it to dig holes with. He objects a little, but once the store training people show him the cool things he can do with these thin slabs of aluminium, he seems sold. Company policy, at least my policy: People I work with need to have proper equipment.

"Now that's sorted. Dinner?"

At the bar, Ben brings his new toys, excitedly showing me a drawing he's done overlaid on the map of the grounds.

"I found a garden design app, quite amazing!"

"Welcome to the modern age, Ben. You know all kinds of things are possible now? Space exploration, time-travel, drawing on screens, it's all quite wonderful here in the future."

"Indeed, well anyway, look at these ideas."

He's doodled over the map and there's some great plans in concept. Solar powered lights that blend into the flower borders by all the walkways, an organic herb garden for the kitchens. The Myatt logo depicted in shrubs that match the corporate colours. A kids garden with a little maze. This is the sort of thing we should have been doing for decades, but no one ever suggested it before.

"This is great, Ben! I love it."

"Thanks, it will add to the comfort feeling of the hotels, a subliminal thing. People may not notice, but they'll feel happier about being here. It will require significantly more maintenance, but the value will recoup, over time."

I took it easy for Ben with a slower jaunt than usual. He's not used to the travel, but also aware that he didn't want to be away from his ever more pregnant wife for too long, we made our way north, stopping briefly in Orlando, then over to Atlanta, through the Carolina's, which made me frown when we stayed in Charlotte, North Carolina. Ben said nothing, so neither did I. We moved on. A long stretch to Richmond, Virginia. Then Washington, up through Philadelphia and finishing up in Providence, Rhode Island. It's been a tough few weeks. I swore last time I travelled with Ben I'd never do it again, but it was mostly good fun. It was nice to have some company on the long drives.

When I tired of Ben, I had Nellie to keep me sane, tell me jokes, send me teases. She got to know Ben via my tales of his antics, she said he's good for me, keeps me grounded. Never thought I'd agree with something as unconscionable as that, but she could actually be right.

Ben ran the same critical eye over the grounds at each of the hotels we stopped at, some have very little land, others plenty. But there was always something to improve, and he developed a routine and style, a theme to be applied everywhere. Staying with local vegetation as much as possible, winding in a thread of similarity and recognition. I think he rather enjoyed it, despite the travel. He learned to use video chat and frequently checked in with Lucy. She showed me the cats, bounding around in their new garden, which she's already planning to gut and replant.

From the quaint splendour of Providence, where the old ones are known to roam and linger, we head back home to London. Ben said he enjoyed the trip, and he's still pouring over maps and landscape designs, but I think he'd prefer to do this work by proxy, for the next batch of hotels. We'll ask the local staff to send details and photos, then contract the legwork out, following plans created by the lawnmower man. His birth cry will be the sound of every mower on this planet revving in unison.

Chapter Forty-Eight

A t the Myatt, back home in the bar. I check the time and put my phone away, he's late. I glance up at the mirror, smooth down my hair. I've been summoned to meet with Rory. I know he meant to meet him upstairs in the lounge room, but I'm waiting in the bar, because it will annoy him to have to come and find me.

"Keith!"

Sure enough, he has. I turn around and he's beaming a smile at me, opening his arms for a brotherly hug. "There you are. Welcome back, I heard you had a great tour?"

"Not bad at all." I wonder where all the joy is coming from. Has Rory been kidnapped by aliens, and in his stead they left this happy replica?

"How are you doing?" He's awkward and fidgety, like we're kids again, and he's broken my favourite toy.

"Pretty good. Yourself?"

"Oh, yes, wonderful. Jane is insisting on a trip to the Maldives this year, but I really can't stomach it. Still, you have to keep the ladies happy, don't you?"

"Indeed. Did you ask me here to see how I am?"

"No. Well, that's a byproduct, of course, but I have an offer for you!"

"I already told you, Rory, I don't want to sell my shares now."

"No, not that one, a totally different type of offer."

"Oh?"

"What you've been doing is amazing! The nightclub idea, a total success. The improvements and clean-up all over the states, the reviews are massively recovered. Just unprecedented. It's like something has completely changed in you these last months. And the landscaping plans; to use the popular parlance of the day. Awesome!"

"Well, thanks. I'm glad you appreciate the effort. I have rather thrown myself into the work, of late."

"One might say, about time, too. But that would have negative connotations, so I won't."

"I think you may have let it slip."

"Quite so. Anyway, my offer, which came from a suggestion from Mother and Father, actually, is that we give you a new role within the company. As CMO."

"What's that?"

"Chief Marketing Officer! You'll be globally in charge of all the aspects of our Myatt presentation. You'll be able to set up interesting flourishes like the nightclub and the gardens wherever you please, and you can give up the endless tours, travel as you need to, stay home a bit more, work with our London office."

"That dreadful place? I think I'll start by upgrading that dive!"

"Yes, please do. Hate going to see Gavin out there. Mother and Father think it's important you feel grounded here."

What Rory is saying actually resonates with me. I'm getting the recognition I deserve, the freedom to hire cool people and set off firecrackers up the arse of boring and stale tradition. I do want to travel less, too. It is getting a bit old now. The novelty wore off a long time ago, but I was riding that never-ending wave of Belgian ale and casual sex. The wave broke though, and

I've been floundering on the beach, trying to find my feet. I think this is the break I need.

"I accept."

"Excellent! Would you like to come for supper?"

Fuck me, this is almost enough to make me suspicious. I haven't been to Rory's house in I don't know how long.

"Oh, yes. Why not? I don't have a car though, probably should get one."

"I'll give you a lift. Come on, Jane will be delighted."

Rory and Jane, with no kids, rattle around in a ridiculously large property, buried deep in the heart of all that is England. The driveway takes a full minute to traverse, tree-lined and suitably bumpy to keep the casual Jehova at bay. It's a lovely house. Georgian era, elegant and symmetrical. Surrounded by acres of woodland and a Koi pond feature at the front.

However, I've had to listen to a twenty-five-minute lecture on the various options of Mercedes or BMWs that Rory thinks I should be looking for on the way here. I was just going to get something efficient and simple. I'm not too fussed about a penis extension. I've tuned out and I'm messaging Nellie about my job upgrade. She's excited, says it sounds wonderful. Happy for me. I think I'm rather pleased myself.

Inside and I can hear voices, which means Jane has company. As we get to the kitchen, I see I've been set up.

"Keith!" Tanya and Jane are sipping deep glasses of red wine at the kitchen counter. "Long time no see."

"Quite so. Hello Tanya. Hello Jane." I give Rory an evil eye, but he isn't looking. He's busy at the drinks cabinet, pouring himself a large gin.

"Drink, Keith?" Rory waves me over.

"Ah, actually, I'm trying to stay off it, to be honest."

"But this is a special occasion! Have a snifter."

"Right, but just one. Have you got any Belgian?"

"Might be something in the fridge."

"So, you are looking well, Keith." Tanya beams a smile at me, patting the stool next to her for me to sit. Oh god.

"Same goes for you, Tanya. How have you been?"

"Very good, actually." I glance at her fingers. No rings.

"Tanya just unveiled an exhibition of her art, Keith. You should go take a look." Jane is as clear as one of Aunty Joyce's polished windows, she's trying to set me up with Tanya.

"Oh really? I didn't know you painted."

"Sculpture, erotic forms." It gets worse!

"Really. Sounds wonderful." Translation: sounds like hell, and wild horses wouldn't drag me to that exhibition. Rory has located a Belgian ale for me and pours a glass.

"Well, now we all have a drink. A toast to our new CMO! Hip hip!"

We all clink glasses and they shout 'Hooray', Tanya gets a womanly look in her eyes, the predator. A male of the species has an impressive job title and isn't married. I think I need to get out of here as soon as possible. But, I realise none of us can drive now. Getting a taxi out here is damn near impossible. I'm trapped!

Dinner is a lacklustre Sri Lankan fish curry that Jane read about in some magazine, edible, but probably not representative of the regional fare. Much hyperbole is thrown around about it, and I remain polite, because she did try, after all. I'm more worried about Tanya and the vast amounts of wine she's swallowed. The flirt quotient has exponentially increased as the evening progressed. She tells us how she modelled the erotic sculptures from her own body, studying detailed nude photos she had done for the purpose. Her vagina is now immortalised and on show in a gallery in Princes Risborough. I can't imagine a more fitting end! This isn't the dried up prune of a girl I remember, though. Tanya has grown horny as a pack of dogs. Now in her early thirties, she isn't unattractive, so it's odd that she's still single.

. . .

"Keith, I'd love to add some male themed sculptures to my collection."

"Seems only right, to add some balance."

"Would be wonderful if you'd pose for me?"

I almost spit a mouthful of curry over the table. "What?"

"Or I could do it from memory." She smiles and tilts her head. So drunk that the 'subtle flirt' motion is more like 'drowsy wasp' as her elbows slip off the table into her lap.

"Er, you know, it's getting late. I should probably get going, I have a lot of work to do tomorrow in my new role. I want to get started right away."

"Nonsense, Keith, you can stay in the spare bedroom. Jane has it all ready, you'll never get a taxi now." Rory is either in on the set-up or totally oblivious. He's been necking gin all evening.

"Right."

"I'll show you up, if you like?" Tanya moves to stand up, but doesn't quite make it, falling back to her seat with a bump.

"No, I'll be fine thanks."

"Sure? I can tuck you in, get you all comfy." She slurs her words, giving me what she probably thinks are 'fuck me' eyes. But instead, they come across as a tad manic. I don't really know what's wrong with me. Normally I'd jump at the chance to jump on her bones, as long as she didn't expect me to stick around tomorrow and wax lyrical about her plaster pussy, but I have zero desire to go near her, drunk and desperate. She's just vulgar, and undoubtedly she'll regret this in the morning, either way.

"I have a girlfriend!" I blurt it out, probably shouldn't have, but it just sort of happened.

"Oh." There's a cold silence.

"Really? You didn't say. Who is she?" Rory looks up, keen to hear.

"Erm, her name's Nellie."

"The elephant?"

"No! Just Nellie."

"That rings a bell, actually. That's what Aunty Joyce used to be called for some reason, isn't it?"

"Indeed. So I hear."

"What a coincidence. When do we get to meet this Nellie?"

"Well, sometime shortly after I do, I suppose…"

Chapter Forty-Nine

Tanya and I did sleep together, but sleep is the keyword. She was comatose from the wine, I had to carry her up the stairs and dump her in the bed. Clothed. The set-up was such that only one spare room had been prepared, so unless I fancied sleeping on the couch, there was no choice. I felt sorry for her, and this morning I tried to sneak away as quietly as possible so as not to wake her, but it didn't work. She woke in a hazy fug of wine hangover, embarrassed and regretful, as predicted. So I had to console her for a while with a long cuddle, and a pep talk on how she is a beautiful and talented woman and she'll find someone meaningful for her very soon, I'm sure. I stopped short of telling her about the twin flame phenomenon. She's the type to get obsessed with it and start posting rabid long-winded rants to the forums about all the men who wronged her. No one wants to see that.

I left her with a kiss on the cheek and then she went to cry in the shower, she said.

Women!

. . .

It was certainly a mistake to mention Nellie at dinner. I was bombarded with questions after that; how can she be my girlfriend if we've never met, what do I know about her, when will I meet her, what does she do? I had no answers. All I could do was say it was a feeling I had, and she will tell me the rest when she decides to. Tanya said that it didn't seem like much of a relationship, and I can't really argue with that. Still, I'm fairly sure that it is an affair of the heart, and not just an excuse why I didn't want to hook up with Tanya.

I arrive home, courtesy of a taxi driver who complained profusely about having to 'come all the fackin' way out 'ere' until I tipped him a fifty and told him where he can see female body parts on display for free.

I told Nellie I was home and made some breakfast while I pondered the reality of my new status. She replied quickly, so I asked if she was on my time zone. She said yes. She just got back.

Back to where though? I asked if she was in the UK, she said yes. Interesting. She wouldn't say anymore though. I changed the subject, told her I didn't really know where to start with the new job. It sounds wonderful, having power and influence, but what do you do with it? I really should start by upgrading the marketing department to a new location and hiring some new talent.

Nellie told me to follow my nose and wag my tail, whatever that means.

Perhaps I should get myself an office too, a secretary? Nope, I'm getting ahead of myself. I can work from anywhere and I don't need a distraction. Just a plan.

I haven't told Ben yet, so I send him a message asking if they want to come over for dinner and a surprise. They do, apparently, so I make a shopping list of food to cook, then realise the last time I did that was with Lottie and she ended up cooking. So, instead, I find a takeaway restaurant that will deliver.

"I hope you like Indian, Lucy?"

"I hadn't tried it until I came here, but yes, I love it!"

"Good stuff. No one else wanted to deliver to me, said it was too far."

"We could have brought Chinese?" Ben brings a modest bag full of beer and sparkling water for Lucy.

"This calls for something different."

"What does?"

"All in good time, Ben."

I tell them about dinner at Rory's last night, how Tanya was there. That it seemed like a setup to get us re-acquainted, and how there's some kind of family conspiracy to see me settled and married. Then about the erotic forms exhibition, making Tanya, quite literally, an exhibitionist. An odd turn of events for sure. Ben couldn't believe it, said he remembers her from the old days and thought she was a prude. Times have changed, apparently.

"Is that what you called us over for? Your ex-girlfriend has her tits cast in clay?"

"Yes, I thought that merited curry and poppadoms, Ben. No, you fool, I have real news!"

"Do tell!"

"Fetch more ale, and I shall!"

Lucy is driving them home later, since she can't drink anyway. She's gradually bumping out. Ben said their nursery is lovely, and they are starting some odd yoga class together soon. Real adult stuff.

"Your ale, Sir Myatt!" Ben bows with a flourish and passes me a beer.

"You could have opened it!"

"Fuck's sake, can't think of everything!" He throws a bottle opener at me. "Are you going to tell us or not!"

"Alright! Keep your hemp knickers on! I'm building up to it."

"I'll have you know these underpants are finest cotton!"

"Information I definitely needed as the new CMO of Myatt Global!"

"What?"

"That's why Rory came over, told me he loved all the work I did, and you too. Mum and Dad probably pushed him, but I'm now the Chief Marketing Officer! I get to make decisions and set things up, I don't have to travel the world anymore, inspecting the back of every toilet in America. I can choose when I go somewhere, hire cool people, come up with new policies. I get to kick arses!"

"Nice one!"

"Congratulations, Keith. You certainly deserve it." Lucy smiles and raises a glass of water. "To the kindest CMO any company has ever known!"

I blush a little, but I'm putting that down to the booze. Good food, good company, good beer.

I feel a buzz in my pocket. Probably a message from Nellie.

'Say hi to Ben and Lucy for me!'

"Oh, Nellie says hi."

"Hi!" they chime in unison. Feels a bit odd having an electronic girlfriend like this, but Ben and Lucy don't judge me. I reply back to Nellie, sending a photo of our table full of pots of curry and colourful poppadom dips. She replies back promptly.

'Wouldn't mind a good curry myself.'

. . .

I tell her she's welcome to join us, there's plenty spare.

'Keep it warm, see you tomorrow.'

WHAT? Is she joking? Is she really coming over? Am I dreaming? I feel a crash of adrenaline in my chest, I'm actually nervous. Scared to ask what she means, but I tap a message. I look up and Ben and Lucy are probably wondering what's happening.

"Er, Nellie said she'll see me tomorrow!"

"Oh, wonderful! Finally you get to meet her?"

"I think so, but this is quite sudden. I'm not sure what to think."

"Sudden? I thought you'd been talking with her for months now?"

"Yes, but, I had no idea when I'd actually get to meet her. I mean, I don't even know what she looks like. Never heard her voice even."

"Should be an interesting blind date!"

I send the message to Nellie. Just a question mark.

'Was there something unclear about that last message? I'll see you tomorrow, at your hotel. Don't be late. 3 pm.'

I ask, how will I know her?

'You just will.'

I have so many questions, but she'll probably clam up if I ask them. I want to know why she suddenly had a change of heart, why all the secrecy, if I will meet her tomorrow, can't I see her face now? But I don't ask anything, I reply - See you tomorrow then! Can't wait. xXx

I look back up at Ben and Lucy, quietly munching their dinners. I can't focus now, I'm suddenly agitated and fidgety, a thousand thoughts rage in my brain, what should I wear? Do I need a haircut?

Then a massive iceberg sized idea hits me square in the bow. The ring with her name in it. Should I take it? Should I ask her to marry me, having never met her? Is that utterly ridiculous?

I think about all the women I've been with, the rampant nights of passion and lust, how I've had none of those with Nellie, but I still have a deeper feeling for her, just from messages. Surely, she's the one?

"Lucy, can I ask a question?"

"Of course."

"Would it be absolutely insane to propose to someone on the first date?"

"Oh, my!"

"Ah, okay. Crazy, I shouldn't have said it."

"No! I mean, I think that would be amazing, if you feel that way. How does she feel?"

"I have no idea."

"She loves him, Lucy. I know she does." Ben motions towards my phone with a fork full of lamb tikka masala.

"How do you know?"

He taps the side of his head. "I just do. In America, you were never off that damn phone, messaging her at every rest stop and constantly when we were having dinner. Every time you got a message there was a big Baboon sized grin on your face. She knows what she's doing."

"But that was me, you don't know how she felt."

"Same as you, as plain as the nose on your face. She got the same thrills and laughs, otherwise, she wouldn't have messaged so often. You two are meant to be together, trust me."

"Should I propose, then?"

"Take the ring. You'll know if you want to. If it feels right."

"Yeah, thanks, mate. Good advice."

Chapter Fifty

I couldn't rest, much less sleep. Going from pleasantly tipsy, into clear crisp sobriety, then to disbelief that I'm not already asleep and dreaming, and Nellie isn't actually coming to meet me tomorrow. Then to stark realisation; this is happening.

Wild racing thoughts flit between pedantic pointless details of what I should say, how I should react when I finally meet her, should I shower just before I leave or in the morning? Then the ring. I took it out and put it back in the nightstand drawer probably a hundred times, before moving it to my wallet for the last time. Conflicting angels and demons fought for hours in my brain, leaving me utterly exhausted, finally falling asleep sometime after four in the morning. Twists of daylight already snaking into view through my window as I wondered why this was such a traumatic event for me. I've met plenty of women before, but never has there been this mess of anticipation and stress.

I woke then at midday, startled and leaping from the bed as I realised the time and the impending meeting. Don't be late, she said. I put the shower and the kettle on at the same time, drank my tea while on the throne. Shaved, combed, picked out clothes, put them back again. Picked out different clothes, realised they were almost identical to the first set. I should probably go shopping at some point.

All that took me to one o'clock, sitting on the couch, gnawing at my fingernails, wondering what to do for the next two hours.

I check my phone, there's an email from Nellie.

Keith,

I'll see you soon, but read this before we meet. I know you, you know me. We have a connection. For a long time now I've been confused about what it all meant, the emotions strong, the time wrong, and I'm sorry if I have been vague and confusing. I just needed to understand it all myself.

I do now. You will soon.

I didn't believe in all that soul mate, twin flame rubbish. Thought it was ridiculous. But after some time, I didn't know how else to explain it all. So I did some research, took a break from life, tried to see things in a different way. Perhaps from your perspective.

I'm not proud of how I behaved in my past, but now I believe it was necessary to get to where I am now. A journey from a selfish history to a better future. You have to understand I have gone through heaven and hell to get here, but the trip was educational, and, I think in the end, worth it. There was a moment of clarity, a sudden flood of total understanding. For a minute I looked around at where I was, and I knew absolutely nothing in the world mattered, everything made sense. I had to find you.

This sounds ridiculous, but I swear it happened. I've never been a spiritual person, but. Fuck...

Mostly, thank you for being so patient with me.

I can't wait to see you.
   xXx

Wow. I don't quite know what to make of all that. This isn't the typical first date I was expecting, even if I knew it would be a little odd. She sent that two hours ago. I don't know if I should reply or just wait until I see her. Sending a short text now seems like it would be trite, given the emotion and depth of her words. But I'm saved the stress of wondering how to react as a text message pops in from her.

'Did you get my email?'

I reply that I did, and sorry I didn't reply to it earlier. I overslept.

'You don't have to say anything. Just wait and see.'

I take the ring out of my wallet once again, roll it around in my fingers, reading the engraving, and polishing the diamonds. It feels right.

ADAM ECCLES

I got to the hotel ridiculously early, but I couldn't wait any longer. I think I need a drink to loosen the nerves a bit. The bartender gives me a nod and smile. Pours me a Belgian, slides a bowl of nuts over to me and goes to serve another customer. In the mirror behind the bar there's a man who has changed a lot over the last year. He's gone from playboy waster to, well, something a little better, I hope. Someone settled and ready for real life to hit and wash over him. Solid, dependable, a little wiser, perhaps?

I pull out my phone and scroll back through the email again, then the entire history of our relationship, documented in text, from initial cautious steps, to provocative teases, with photos interspersed. There are a lot of messages, a diary of my life since this started. I find the first indications of affection, those subtle 'x's denoting a virtual kiss. It's strange how text can be so passionate, so deep and direct, a telepathic link to the brain. Those words gave me thrills and endorphins, some more than casual sex ever could.

'Almost there, just do me one favour? Don't be angry.'

Why would I be angry? Now there's a whole new set of ridiculous thoughts to calm. Have I said something wrong? Has she done something wrong? Does she have an offensive face tattoo of Nazi propaganda? I reply that I won't be angry, despite not knowing why.

I wave the barman over for another beer, following with a whiskey. The anticipation is flooding my veins with toxins, stress and worry, panic and fear. I want this moment over with. My possible future, in female form.

I check my phone, but there's nothing more. Then a buzz, I quickly look again, but the message is from Ben.

. . .

'Good luck! Let me know how it goes.'

I can't even reply, I can't pull together a coherent message for him. My brain so muddled and discombobulated as it is.

There's a prickle of hairs on my neck, a cold draft from nowhere, then an explosion of heat in my chest. Beads of sweat form on my brow. I probably should have eaten something before I started drinking today...

"Keith!"

Another slam of adrenaline floods my veins as I hear my name. I turn around on my barstool and my jaw drops open, dumbfounded.

"Close your mouth, you'll catch a fly!"

I try to say something but my mouth is somehow disconnected from my brain, it takes several seconds before I can pull myself together.

"Lottie!"

"Yes, or Charlotte, or Nellie, or Winona, Maybe Cristina, sometimes Meryl or Angelina. Whatever you like, really. But yes, it's me. Hello Keith. Sorry it took me so long."

Chapter Fifty-One

ONE YEAR LATER

C harles Webbe, *1928 - 1985*, didn't quite make it to propose marriage to Joyce Eleanor Myatt, *1931 - 2018*. They were soul mates who drifted alone for more than fifty years before they found each other. A long search. One flame snuffed out before it could be merged with its twin.

He had a brother, Wilbur Webbe *1926 - 1960*, who had a son, William Webbe, who spent a good deal of his childhood with his Uncle Charlie due to an unfortunate accident with a tram on holiday. William had a daughter, Charlotte Eleanor Webbe, who he named in honour of Charlie. She's a tricky one.

But Keith Myatt, great-grandson of Charles Myatt, the founder of the first Myatt Hotel, did make it to the proposal of marriage to Charlotte Eleanor Webbe, in the bar of the London Myatt hotel, and the marriage ceremony soon after in the local registry office, much to the amazement, joy and chagrin of his immediate family. Not in a church? How very modern. Benedick Hogg was best man, of course, and they had a sedate stag do in the quaint old town of Prague, studying the ancient architecture and interesting beers.

Benedick Hogg and Lucy Bonham-Hogg had a beautiful baby boy, who they named Richard Keith Bonham-Hogg. Bit of a mouthful, but Keith was ecstatic at the honour.

Bella Burgess, or MemphisBelle, and her daughter Daisy Hayes, added little Keith Burgess to their family. Keith Myatt was emotional by this stage. How many little Keith's will be running around the planet?

Myatt global, the luxurious hotels dotted in four hundred major cities of the world, changed their brand image from stuffy, posh and dignified, to quirky, exclusive and fun. Also boasting elegantly landscaped gardens in most of their locations. 'Like staying at your Mums, but cooler' is their new motto.

"What are we celebrating this time?" Ben lugs in a crate of finest Belgian ale, Lucy follows with little Richard fast asleep in a buggy.

"All in good time, Ben."

"Smells good, anyway!"

"Lottie's making her special spag bol."

"Excellent!"

"Getting much sleep yet?" I motion to the sleeping baby.

"Ah, a little, here and there." They look tired. We probably won't make it through that crate of ale tonight.

Ben sets up a complicated baby monitoring device on the buggy and we move into the kitchen.

"Hi, guys!" Lottie and Lucy embrace, then she gives Ben a peck on the cheek.

When I told Ben a year ago that Lottie and Nellie were the

same person, he was stunned, so was I to be honest. I had no idea. Perhaps I should have twigged, but signs are easy to miss. She said she ran away because she was scared by the intensity of it all. She'd never had feelings like that before. She needed some time to come to terms with it.

She spent that time travelling in my footsteps, across America and Europe, staying in our hotels, observing silently the changes and improvements I made in our hotels, and indeed myself. Trying to see the world through my eyes. Sometimes overlapping with me, other times in totally different parts of the world. She said my nightclub in Denver was ridiculously cool. I had no idea she was there, of course.

Then, a fuse tripped in her brain, that's what it felt like, she said. Something just changed, no longer sceptical, she burned with a sensation that we should be together. But Lottie is a tricky one, she wasn't just going to tell me straight what was going on. Where would the sport be in that?

Now my wife, standing in our kitchen with my dear friends, and she's the same fallen angel that I first saw through the closing lift doors in Austin, Texas. Her first word to me forever etched in my memory - 'Arsehole!'.

The food is delicious as usual, and as predicted, we barely make a dent in the booze crate. Never mind, it will last. Ben tells me about his trip to Atlanta he just got back from. The landscaping just completed, and he said it looked lovely. He went on his own. Become quite assertive and authoritative, now he's a Dad. A real adult, reliable, sensible. It suits him well.

"We have some news, don't we, Lottie?" I can see she can't hold it in any longer. She smiles.

"Yes, we do!"

"Do tell!"

"We're packing it all in, moving to Bulgaria and becoming goatherds."

"What?"

"Yeah, had enough of this rat race! We're going to be hippies like you. But without the beard."

"Shut up! No, we aren't!" Lottie digs me in the ribs. "We're pregnant!"

"Well, Lottie is, anyway. I'm just full of spaghetti." I pat my tummy.

"Congratulations!"

"Wonderful news! Richard will get a little buddy!"

"Two little buddies, actually. It's twins!"

"Oh wow!" Lucy is wide-eyed, "Stretch mark lotion, Lottie. Bathe in it daily!"

"Noted."

"Yes, we can join the ranks of the sleep-deprived, knee deep in soiled nappies. Tripping over Lego and scraping dried up Play Doh out of the carpets."

"You'll love it."

Aunty Joyce would be delighted and proud that her house will finally echo with the patter of tiny feet. Mum and Dad are over the moon of course, finally I'm settled down and they can retire in peace and dote on their grandchildren. Rory seemed quite indifferent, but I'm sure he's a little jealous too. He's loosening up, slowly. We actually went out for a drink together recently and it wasn't awkward or strange. Jane told me Tanya was pregnant too, by a taxi driver she met at her erotic forms exhibition. An art critic in his spare time, apparently. Quite taken by the mouldings, he was. Good for her!

Lottie has that pregnant glow about her. It's especially noticeable when she runs to the toilet in the morning to puke her guts out, and then complains about not being able to drink her morning coffee. Then she blames me for all the twin flame talk somehow triggering the twin babies. I'm not sure of the science in that, but I'll let her have it.

I don't know if I am ready for parenthood, but I don't

suppose one gets a choice in the matter. Nature will have its way and we must adapt. One day at a time.

I'm still quietly relieved every morning when I wake and find Lottie next to me. There's still a niggle of paranoia that she'll be gone one day. But those times are over, she says. Then she kisses me, and her hair gets caught in my beard stubble and I know all is right with the world.

She's got this idea for a website that lets people leave honest ratings and reviews for nappies and baby products. There's so much bullshit, lies and misdirection about the baby industry, she wants to make it transparent and true. RateMum.com. I told her I think that name might be a little misleading and be misconstrued by some. She told me to shut the fuck up and massage her feet.

★★★★★ [5 out of 5 stars]

Charlotte Eleanor Myatt, angelic features, dangerous, talented and smart. Slippery though, hard to keep a hold of. But once you do, she's a keeper. Overall, I'm glad I played the twin flame game.

The End

But, keep reading for free sample chapters of my other works...

Do me a favour?

I genuinely hope you enjoyed this story and I'd love to hear about it. So would other readers. I would be eternally grateful if you would leave a review on Amazon for me.

I don't have a big-name publisher or agent, or any marketing help. I rely on the kind words of readers to spread the word and help others find my books.

In a world of constant rating requests from everything you buy, I know it's a pain, but it does make a huge difference and it encourages me to keep writing.

Thanks!
Adam.

www.AdamEcclesBooks.com

Keep in touch

Be the first to hear about future books!

Website: www.AdamEcclesBooks.com

Connect with me on social media:

facebook.com/AdamEcclesWrites

twitter.com/AdamEcclesBooks

Also by Adam Eccles

- **Time, For A Change**
- **Who Needs Love, Anyway?**

Time, For a Change

A feel-good tale about life changes, romance, and hope - even in the midst of an IT department.

Terry's dead-end IT job is about as much fun as an internal cavity search. Chances of promotion? None. Chances of a raise? Not happening. Chances of romance? Nada.

It's time for a change, but that's easier said than done when your prospects are as dismal as the Irish weather in January. Enter stage left a gorgeous young girl who inexplicably finds him interesting. Toss in a mysterious wooden box hidden in his late father's workshop and the dull monotony of Terry's life is broken.

But will it stay that way? What is in the wooden box? Can love conquer all - even the terrible tedium of a dead end job?

This is for all the office workers, all the cynics, all the souls who look into their future with nothing but dread.

Get it now from Amazon

Time, For A Change (Sample)

CHAPTER ONE

Friday 24th August

A warm, wafting stench of body odour assaults my senses as someone walks behind me. A squawking, exaggerated laugh in my periphery. A dull constant throb of distant air conditioning, mingled in with a dozen phone calls, all competing for attention.

The random but frequent slam of a toilet door, followed by the artificially floral air-freshener scent, drifting over, heavy and mixed in with cheap bleach.

A middle-aged man struts past my line of sight, his hair cut like a twelve-year-old-boy, his shirt tucked into trousers, pulled up high, gesticulating as he argues with his Bluetooth headset. His face slug-like, his neck and chin blend into his body, his eyes mobile, poking out on stalks.

Welcome to work. Gainful employment and regular pay, in exchange for only your eternal soul and mental stability. A sensory circus in a dull and meaningless existence.

4:30 pm on a Friday and someone has scheduled a conference call, probably to satisfy their inflated ego. Fifty-seven people have dialled in. The call subject: lost to the mists of time, some kind of all-hands meeting. Absolutely no one cares what the point is anyway. They merely want their chance to raise their 'personal brand', or something equally vulgar. I can see the comments in the meeting chat: "Awesome deal!", "Nice work!", "Go, team!". None of them are sincere, none of them are congratulating, they only scream 'look at me, look how great I am'.

I'm at my desk, headset on, dialled into this pointless waste of my life, checking emails, filling in a tech-sheet, browsing the web, and logged into the local instant message system. I also have my phone in my hand, scrolling Twitter. I multi-task, therefore I am.

[16:35] Ward, Terry B:
> This call is intensely boring.
> Pissing with rain outside. Hope it clears up for the weekend.

[16:36] O'Brien, Ted:
> Meant to be nice.

I open up my weather app. It duly insults me, and then presents a weekend outlook of pleasant weather, not too hot, not too cold. No rain, minimal wind. That's perfect for my needs.

[16:38] Ward, Terry B:
> I still always find it amazing that tons and tons of water, and snow and stuff, can be just floating around up there in the sky.

[16:39] O'Brien, Ted:
> Magic elves do it.

Ted is a programmer. He keeps me sane. They keep him shuttered away in some distant office. I haven't seen him for years. Doesn't matter, instant message is a direct link to someone's brain. You can tell an awful lot from a short string of text.

Someone on the conference call is talking about gold awards given to team members who did a fantastic job; I didn't get one.

[16:42] Ward, Terry B:

I thought so.
The same lads who do the rainbows?

[16:44] O'Brien, Ted:
Ya, different group within that group though.

Someone on the conference call is now reading out a list of silver awards given to team members who did a great job; I didn't get one of those either.

[16:46] Ward, Terry B:
Ah.
They know each other though?
Say 'Hi' as they walk the halls?

[16:51] O'Brien, Ted:
They know each other to see each other, but they wouldn't be very close.
More like acquaintances.

Someone on the call is now presenting a long list of bronze awards given to team members who did an okay job. Basically, they showed up to work every day and didn't murder anyone. Oddly, I didn't get one of those either. Last time I checked, no one died due to my project management skills. I've worked here for ten years, a decade of my life doing the same thankless tasks, nothing ever changes or improves, despite the constant meetings to discuss what went wrong and what we can do better next time.

It was exciting at the start, meeting new customers, coming up with innovative IT solutions for their specific needs, travelling around Europe, America, and even Asia, staying in expensive hotels, eating expensive food, shitting expensive shits, all on the company credit card. But now I am tired, bored, beaten down to a bitter core, forgotten by management and drifting slowly into obscurity. It could be time for a change. #YaThink?

I randomly post a tweet as an idea pops into my head.

Just came up with an invention for a device that would totally eliminate fart noises.
#MillionEuroIdea

I send the tweet off into the world, not really sure why because rarely does anyone read them. I don't know how, but I have over a thousand 'followers'. I think most of them are bots or spam accounts or something. But still, I feel an idea written down is an idea saved. This type of random thought sometimes just appears in my head, I've learnt to mostly ignore them. Still worth saving sometimes because you never know what will happen.

Some days at work I'm busier than a one-armed man trying to masturbate in a shed full of angry bees. But today has dragged, the hours passing glacially, probably because I'm distracted with my weekend plans. I just want to get out of here and get this weekend over with.

[16:54] Ward, Terry B:
That's the problem in these big teams.
If they worked together more - we might have more snow-bows.
Which would be nice.

[16:54] O'Brien, Ted:
Ya, it would brighten up the day.

[16:54] Ward, Terry B:
Bring a bit of colour to the winter.

The call takes an ugly turn, handed over to the sales manager for Europe, explaining in a friendly tone, how each and every one of us must contribute to the whole team, by filling in new time management reports every week. Documenting every piss and shit-break we take and how long it takes to do it.

[16:55] Ward, Terry B:
> You don't see many rainbows at night either.
> The night elves are a different team I'd say.

[16:56] O'Brien, Ted:
> They repair shoes.

[16:56] Ward, Terry B:
> Nice sideline.

[16:56] O'Brien, Ted:
> Totally different group.

[16:56] Ward, Terry B:
> Different cost centre?

[16:57] O'Brien, Ted:
> Yep, they get night-shift allowance though, extra pay.

I must have forgotten to set my chat status to 'Away', because another chat window pops open on my screen.

[16:59] Greene, Judith:
> Hi Terry, have you got a second? Just wanted to ask about the procurement on those cards for DeltaWave.

Seriously? 4:59 on a Friday? No, I don't have a fucking second. I quickly close the chat window and change my status to 'Appear Offline'. I'd rather drown in a bucket of rat piss than talk to her now.

We at C.S.Tech are happy to take care of your custom IT installations, from scoping to lights on, we have you covered!

'Terrence B. Ward, Custom Project Manager'
That's what it says on my business cards. Cards that I never give to anyone.

Terry Brian Ward. My parents, Monty Python fans and a tiny bit cruel.

T.B. Ward - if I hear another joke about being consumed...

[16:59] Ward, Terry B:

> That's at least something for them.
> I don't though! So I'm outta here.
> Smell you later Ted.

[17:00] O'Brien, Ted:

> Smell you later Terry.

The call wraps up on time thankfully, and I've already prepared to leave on the dot of five. My laptop is in my bag, and I'm up and heading for the door quicker than a silent fart fills a meeting room after a canteen curry lunch. But I leave a small packet of salt on my chair to keep the slug-people away.

I've got things to organise after work, walking into town rather than driving home, I need to pick up a rental van for the weekend.

After a wet walk to the van rental place, I grab a takeaway pizza and drive home, wondering all the way if this weekend plan is going to be a pointless waste of time.

Get it now from Amazon

Who Needs Love, Anyway?

Twice divorced single dad, Danny Watts, is having a midlife crisis.
Well, technically more of a midriff crisis, if he's honest. Still, the Dad-
bod is *'in'* these days, isn't it?

He needs a girlfriend. But even though he's constantly surrounded by
women, he can't seem to escape from the friend-zone slammer.

Keeping the kids alive and entertained, working all hours, and then
spending half your income on shopping, aren't easy things to deal with.

Trying to find love and happiness is even harder. Those dreams of
'happy ever after' seem like an unreachable utopia. But that hasn't
stopped him trying.

Will Danny ever find his special someone? Or will he live out his
remaining decades in dismal celibacy?

What if he's been looking in all the wrong places? What if love is
right around the corner and he doesn't even realise?

Dad lit at its cynical best - hilariously relatable.

Get it now from Amazon

Who Needs Love, Anyway? (Sample)

"Winona, are you sure you want to do this?"

"Yes, Danny, I've never been so sure of anything in my life." Winona looks up at me with those big, brown eyes. My heart melts.

"But, we just met. Aren't you married to Scott, or is it Keanu?"

"They mean nothing to me, now, Danny."

She seems quite insistent, and I am, after all, but a human male.

"Well, if you're sure…"

Winona lies back on the bed and spreads open her legs, inviting me down with a 'come hither' motion. "Danny, come get me."

What can I do? I bury my head in her bosom and navigate in my heat-seeking missile. Slipping easily into the moist, warm, happy cave.

"Oh, Danny, Danny, Danny."

"Oh, Winona. Oh, yes."

"Danny, Danny, Danny." Her tone changes as I thrust, deeper, harder, faster. Her hands on my shoulders, shaking me. "Danny, Daddy! DADDY!"

"Ugh. What?"

My eyes creak slowly open, the harsh light blinding me.

Wetness at my groin.

"Daddy, I need a pee."

"Ethan... Ugh. What time is it?" Winona has left the building, replaced with my eight-year-old son, standing next to my bed in his Spiderman pyjamas.

"Six-thirty-eight."

"Jesus Christ."

"I need a pee!"

"Well, go to the toilet?"

"There's a big poo in there. I'm scared."

"Flush it?"

"It's scary."

"Ethan, it's poo. It isn't scary. Just flush it away."

"No! Can you do it for me?"

I can barely speak, let alone get up, and there's the mess in my underpants to take care of.

"You know there's another toilet downstairs, don't you?"

"Oh, yeah. Thanks, Daddy." His face lights up and he runs off down the stairs.

I check my watch on the nightstand. He's right. It's the wrong side of seven in the morning on a Saturday. I was hoping for a lie-in. Some chance of that. Maybe if I just stay here, Winona will come back?

Now, where was I?

Winona, lying in my bed, the glisten of sweat on her lips from our heated passions, her hair flowing over my pillows, "Do you want another go, Danny?"

Do I ever? I roll over onto my side, my hand caressing her milk-white breast.

"AGHHH."

A scream comes from downstairs.

I roll back over. "NOW WHAT?"

"I stepped in cat puke."

Wonderful. Game over, I suppose. Save it for later, Danny, you never know, tonight could be your lucky night.

I pull on a threadbare dressing gown. Must have shrunk in the wash, because it used to fit me fine.

The toilet, as mentioned by Ethan, is indeed harbouring a

floater that would put a sizeable dent in the Titanic. One flush alone is not enough. I throw my pants in the bin, wipe away the excess love juice and aim, bleary-eyed. Perhaps the force of my piss-stream will break the shit-berg in two?

"ROSIE! Please flush the damn toilet after you go."

From her room, a distant, matter-of-fact, "I did."

"Well, you didn't get rid of it. You know Ethan is scared of poo."

I move to the sink and wash away the eye crust and sleep sweat. Gradually, feeling and sensation come dribbling back to me. I didn't drink last night, but it was around one in the morning before I lay down. I check my sleep tracker app, which confirms; Five hours and fifteen minutes. A sleep debt of thirty percent. Try to get to bed earlier tonight, the cheery message pops up.

Bugger off.

I turn to exit the bathroom and jump, startled. Rosie is standing in the doorway, arms folded.

"Sorry, Daddy. I did flush."

"Okay, sweetheart. Just make sure it does the trick next time, eh?"

"Yes, Daddy. Would you like a cup of coffee?"

"Fu... I mean. Yes, please, Rosie. That would be wonderful."

Almost a teenager, she will be the death of me someday. Cute as a button, smart, dangerously innocent and spoiled rotten. I'm dreading when the boyfriends start to appear.

"Can you see what Ethan stepped in, please?"

"It's not cat puke. I dropped a tea bag earlier."

Well, that's something, I suppose.

"Why are we up this early on a Saturday?" My little family and I are assembled around the dining table, enjoying a healthy breakfast of oatmeal, sprinkled with fresh fruit and seeds. Okay, that's not strictly accurate. I am sat at the table with sweet black coffee, Rosie is on the couch, Ethan on a beanbag. They both have iPads and toast. The TV is blaring some inane shit into the void. Ethan opted for jam on his toast, Rosie for brown-sauce.

"We're going to the park today." Ethan pipes up.

"But that's in about four hours?"

"Got to get ready." Rosie looks up. "We need clean clothes, or Mum will call the police again."

Oh, yes. Meeting Mummy at the park, won't that be a riot?

"Right. Is the laundry done?"

"Nope."

"Can you do it?"

"Nope."

"Thanks."

"We've got homework, Daddy." They both flash me a saccharine-sweet grin and return their attention to YouTube.

Shit.

As always, leaving the house is as close to impossible as it gets. After three failed starts, we manage to leave the driveway, only to go straight back because Ethan forgot his iPod headphones. After four failed starts, we trundle along through Saturday traffic in the direction of the park.

Their mother, Elise, my second wife no more, is a vindictive bitch. Only, there's nothing for her to get revenge for. She shagged some guy called Brian. She decided to leave us. She got a load of my money. She took the decent car. What more could she want? Blood, apparently.

We meet on neutral ground, not according to any schedule, but whenever she decides she wants to see the kids. She butters them up with toys and sweets, then flits off back to her love cave with Brian, and we don't hear from her until the next guilt trip.

Not that I'm bitter or anything.

We arrive three minutes late, my beautiful prior BMW already waiting for us. Elise taps her wrist at me through the window as we bundle out into the car park. I ignore it. I bet she only just got here herself.

Through clenched teeth, I smile back at her, and under my breath mutter 'go fuck yourself, Elise.'

"Hi! How are you guys?"

"Have you got any presents for us, Mummy?" Ethan is

straight to the point at least.

"Wait and see, darling." She looks up at me with a look that translates as 'Why do you teach them to ask for gifts? You selfish bastard.'

I look away.

"I'll come back in two hours, then?"

"If you can trouble yourself to be on time, Danny, that would be great."

I kiss and hug the little ones and offer a wave towards Elise, but she's already turned away and walking off into the park. Her black hair blowing in the wind. It was her thirty-ninth birthday last week. I suppose I should have got the kids to make her a card or something. Oh well. She looks younger, like she did when we got married. Bright and made-up like a dog's dinner. An aura of patchouli perfume surrounds her perpetually.

Things were simpler back then. We loved each other, genuinely. We cared, made plans, and we had amazing sex. Did things that would make Winona in my dreams blush. But now, I feel the gaping black void of hate when I look at her. Funny how things change so drastically.

Love? Don't make me laugh. Love is an ideal sold by the media to keep people in check. I don't believe in love anymore. The spark of romance in me died when Elise told me the same lies and bullshit that my first wife did. That one lasted eighteen months, before Steve, or was it Simon? I can't remember now, came along and stuck his dick in my first love.

I shudder away the dark thoughts. I've got a date tonight. Can't all be bad, can it?

Back at home, I have time for a shower and some breakfast before I go back and get the kids again. Don't want to be late for Her Majesty. Then I need to get some shopping done, before the babysitter arrives.

The steamy hot water massages my back, finally breathing some life into my tired old bones.

In retrospect, I probably shouldn't have stayed up as late texting with Maria; whom I'm meeting for the first time tonight.

A blind date, because she doesn't have a photo on her dating profile. I'm usually wary of those, but she assures me she's real, and a 'genuine, kind, bubbly girl at heart' and more poignantly, she says I'm a handsome catch.

I'm a forty-two-year-old single Dad, who works to pay the bills, dreams about a movie-star no one even knows these days, and hasn't had 'the sex' for many a cold year. I take what I can get. Maria may be a cave-troll, hiding behind a claim she doesn't want to be stalked by weirdos, hence no photos. But at least she's a female cave-troll, who wants to spend time with me.

I shrug and let the shower rain run down my back. Turning around and washing any remnants of dried cum from my crotch with a scrubby pad and some minty shower-gel. Ooh, that smarts. But in a good way.

Freshly clean, eggs on toast scarfed down, twenty minutes of PornHub surfing to find something worthy to edge to, and I'm back in the car again to the park.

Thinking about it, I probably should have given the kids some lunch before they went to see Mummy. They must be starving by now. Never mind, we'll stop at McDs on the way home. It's a treat day, after all.

I swore, in my youth, that my children would never see fast food as a treat. Instead, I joked it should be a punishment to eat the clown-food. But here we are. Convenience outweighs ideals every time. At least they eat it and I don't have to wash plates.

"Hi, guys. Did you have a nice time?" Elise and the kids are waiting in the car park as I pull up.

"They are starving, Danny. Did you feed them, at all?"

"We're going for a special treat, aren't we?"

"Fast food, again?"

"No, not 'again'. Just fast food. It's a rare treat."

"Well, thankfully I had a couple of protein bars in the car, or they'd have passed out."

I look at the kids. Ethan plugged into a game on his iPod,

Rosie listening to music. They seem fine to me.

"Come on then, let's get you home…" Via McDs and Tesco's. Oh, what a joyous Saturday afternoon.

Elise makes a show of hugging the kids and then ignoring me as she gets into MY car. Winding down the window as she turns around. "Ethan trod in dog-poo, and Rosie has a big hole in her leggings. Please try to take care of my children, Danny."

Bugger off.

The dog-poo proved too ingrained to be scraped off with a patch of grass.

I'm now forty quid down on the day, and Ethan has new shoes. Rosie new leggings, courtesy of Tesco finest. He rode in the trolley until he got the shoes, much to the disgust of various old biddies who stuck their noses into our business. "He's too old to be in the trolley."

I ignored them, but these stabs in my back all add up. There's only so much bullshit a man can take before he explodes and 'accidentally' slams the trolley into someone's fat arse as he goes by.

Back at home, I pack away the shopping into the cupboards and fridge. Tumbleweeds roll by in the empty silence. Weird, because only a few seconds ago there was a multitude of children, strong and able to help put the food away. I trust they are busy somewhere, doing their much-celebrated homework.

The sitter should arrive around six, which gives me time to relax for a while and then make some dinner for the kids. Fish-fingers and beans, they asked for, which means they'll eat hot dogs and popcorn, or similar. Always have a backup plan for dinner. I learned that the long, expensive, hard way.

Jessica, the babysitter, is a young lass from a few streets away. She's been a godsend the last year or two. She wanted to make a few quid, and I wanted to have the odd evening off. I know the kids love her, and she's trustworthy. Wins all around. Quiet girl, studying for med-school or something. I usually leave her some food in the fridge and she gets the kids to bed, then watches some tripe on Netflix until I get back.

I pop a text to Maria. A nervous, paranoid, final check that she wants to meet me this evening. Because another stand-up is not what I need right now.

The last time I tried to lure a woman out for the evening, I ended up sitting for an hour on my own in the Chinese, then finally getting a text that she had an "unexpected family situation" and couldn't make it. I never heard from her again. I have my suspicions that the 'unexpected situation' was more to do with a younger and less off-sprung man that had suddenly contacted her. The arrangement had been sketchy in the first place. She told me, "Yeah, sure, I don't know what I'm doing yet." when I asked if we could get dinner, maybe?

Maria replies that of course we are still on for later and she's very excited to meet me.

I wish I could drum up the same level of enthusiasm, but my expectations are set very low, after so many failed attempts. There's no point in getting my hopes up, only to have them dashed against the rocks again, breaking every optimistic bone in my body, once more. They say a broken bone grows back stronger, but I feel as fragile as a teenager asking a crush to go to a school dance. I'm rapidly exiting the first half of my life and screeching to a dreadful halt in my midlife crisis.

Dating sites, miserable cans of beer with Netflix, alone. Oven pizza that tastes like cardboard, and the churn of work, school-runs, and masturbation. This is the life I have carefully carved out for myself. My parents must be deeply proud.

I don't know what Maria expects. I've been honest, told her my situation, my loneliness.

My dating profile says, 'Just see what happens.' as my goal. I don't think I know what I want either. I mean, a casual shag would be nice, but ultimately, do I think anyone will wake up next to me, year in, year out, until one of us, probably me, dies in the arms of a loving spouse? Those dreams of 'happy ever after' seem like an unreachable utopia. Does anyone actually

ADAM ECCLES

have a happy relationship? I struggle to believe it. At least if they are sentient and intelligent. I don't think men and women are designed to live together, long term.

Maria has told me barely anything about herself. All I know is: She's female, aged thirty-two, never married, no kids, speaks English.

Ah well, I suppose I'll 'Just see what happens.'

The doorbell rings bang on time, and I open the door to Jessica. But it's been a few months, maybe six, since I saw her last. She's grown a bit, upfront. Her homely look is replaced with downright sexy. Made-up, hair styled, and dyed black and blue, a nose piercing and an outfit that would make a prostitute blush. She smiles, and waltzes in like nothing has changed.

"Hi, Jessica."

"Hey, Danny."

"You look... Good..." I'm hesitant to say pretty, in case she takes it the wrong way and I'm arrested for sexual harassment or something. I think she's nineteen now, but until five seconds ago, I saw her as an older child. Now she's definitely a woman. A bloody hot one, too.

"Thanks. You aren't so bad yourself." She smiles and goes through to the kitchen. "Normal plan, is it?"

"Yeah. Food in the fridge. Kids on their iPads. Help yourself to Netflix, and whatever drinks you want." I know it's safe to say that as she won't touch my "nasty beer." She told me before.

"Where are you going?"

"Got a date. Going to the Kings Head, then the Italian."

"Nice." She gives me a 'look' that I can't interpret and then dives into the fridge, pulling out a beer.

"Jessie!" Ethan and Rosie appear in the kitchen like a couple of Tasmanian devils, laughing and roaring. Jessica gives them both a hug and spins them around, giggling. The kids haven't noticed her recent puberty changes.

"I'll leave you to it, then?"

Jessica nods and they vanish off into the living room with bags of crisps.

316

. . .

I elected to walk into town rather than drive or get a taxi. It's a nice evening, I rarely get to take a few minutes to myself, and I could certainly use the exercise.

The Kings Head is where I used to go with Elise when we were young and excited about our marriage, but as that excitement turned to hatred, and she found other outlets for her entertainment, I haven't been in a long while. It could be a mistake to meet a date in the same place, but Maria suggested it, and I know where it is, so I agreed.

Doesn't matter, I suppose. I don't have the energy to be sentimental about a pub I don't go to anymore.

I look around as I go in, but as I don't have a clue what Maria looks like, the task seems pointless. There aren't any obviously single women floating around.

I drop down at the same barstool I sat in all those years ago, when we first found out Elise was pregnant with Rosie. She asked for a Guinness. Said it was good for the baby. Iron and all that.

I flag down the barman and get myself a pint with a whisky chaser. I need something to calm my nerves as I'm suddenly freaked out. Maybe a blind date was a bad idea. What if she's totally not my type, will it be awkward? What is my type, anyway?

Female, with a pulse, at this stage.

I'm spared from too much self-indulgent pondering by a tap on my shoulder. I spin around to a small woman, shoulder-length brown hair, a simple blouse and skirt, suede jacket and matching boots. She's... Okay looking. Her nose is a bit bigger than I'd normally be happy with, but who am I to judge? No, she's nice.

"Maria?"

"Yes. Hi, Danny."

Get it now from Amazon